*Come Hither to Go Yonder*

MUSIC IN AMERICAN LIFE

*A list of books in the series
appears at the end of this book.*

# COME HITHER
# TO GO YONDER

*Playing Bluegrass
with Bill Monroe*

Bob Black

Foreword by Neil V. Rosenberg

UNIVERSITY OF ILLINOIS PRESS

URBANA AND CHICAGO

Library of Congress Cataloging-in-Publication Data

Black, Bob, banjoist.
Come hither to go yonder : playing bluegrass with
Bill Monroe / Bob Black; foreword by Neil V. Rosenberg.
p.   cm. — (Music in American life)
Includes bibliographical references and index.
ISBN 0-252-03002-8 (cloth : alk. paper)
ISBN 0-252-07243-X (pbk. : alk. paper)
1. Black, Bob, banjoist.
2. Monroe, Bill, 1911– .
3. Banjoists—United States—Biography.
4. Bluegrass musicians—United States—Biography.
I. Title. II. Series.
ML419.B53    2004
787.8'81642'092—dc22    2004030071

This book is dedicated to those
who "wore the hat."

*Pickin' on the strings, tapping of your feet,*
*Well, these are age-old things, but who can say how sweet.*
*When there's a ring around the moon; long, long time 'til day,*
*Play me one more tune; please don't go away.*

—Greg Brown ("Ring around the Moon")

# Contents

# Foreword

## Neil V. Rosenberg

In 1988 Bill Monroe said: "I believe Bob Black is the best playing fiddle tunes of any banjo player."[1] His statement came in an interview by Tony Trischka and Peter Wernick for their book *Masters of the Five-String Banjo*. They asked him about banjo players who'd made a big contribution to his music and Monroe, whose music drew deeply from the fiddle-dominated old-time rural southern music of his youth, shaped the answer to reflect his perspective: a good banjo player knows how to play the fiddle pieces.

The sound of the five-string banjo is familiar today from soundtracks such as *The Beverly Hillbillies* and *O Brother, Where Art Thou?* That "silvery, pinging sound," as Alan Lomax described it, was introduced by Earl Scruggs in Bill Monroe's Blue Grass Boys on the Grand Ole Opry in 1945. It helped spark a movement that grew into "bluegrass," the musical genre that took the name of Monroe's band. The Blue Grass Boys became a training ground and showcase for banjoists. The rough-and-tumble world of life on the road with an Opry star guaranteed that plenty of five-string pickers had a chance to test their mettle with Bill Monroe. Bob Black was one of the most memorable of the many fine banjo pickers who worked with him.

Getting the news about Bill's latest banjo picker was part of keeping track of the state of the art in bluegrass. Thus, when Monroe hired fourteen-year-old Sonny Osborne in 1952, it was only a matter of months before 78s featuring the teen prodigy were being sold over the air from WCKY in Cincinnati. And in 1963 when Bill Keith, the Massachusetts college graduate, who emerged from the folk music world of Cambridge's Club 47 with a unique new style, joined the Blue Grass Boys as Brad Keith, he drew a whole new audience to Monroe.

In November 1974, I received such bluegrass news in a letter from my old friend Jim Peva of Plainfield, Indiana. Jim and I had known each other since 1961 when we met at Monroe's Brown County Jamboree in Bean Blossom, Indiana. We soon became Bean Blossom regulars, and often brought our tape recorders to Monroe shows. Jim wrote about Bill's new banjo picker and his rapport with Monroe's fiddler, the legendary Kenny Baker:

> Bill is supposed to be at Bean Blossom on Sunday to close out the season and I plan to go and tape the show. I haven't done much taping in the last few years but the band has an exciting new banjo picker who I think is the best since Bill Keith. His name is Bob Black and he is from Iowa City. I have listened to him "jam" with Kenny Baker from midnight to sunup for the past two Bean Blossom festivals on several occasions. He knows all the old fiddle tunes and I have never seen Baker stump him. They complement each other's artistry very well and because Bill has always favored the old fiddle tunes, I am looking forward to some excellent bluegrass from the combination of Baker, Black, and Monroe.

Bob Black's performances and recordings have given me, and countless other fans of his banjo picking, hours of listening pleasure. I'd often wondered what his experience with Monroe was like. This fascinating book not only tells of Bob's two years with Bill Monroe—which came at a pivotal time in Monroe's career—but also gives a fine portrait of a musician whose modesty, talent, and spirit led him on a difficult but rewarding path.

# *Acknowledgments*

I couldn't have written about these experiences at the time they were happening. I had to wait and see how the story ended. Time and distance have sharpened my focus, and larger truths have now become apparent. I feel vulnerable because many of the naïve and misguided notions of my younger days are herein exposed to the world. Fundamental feelings don't change with time, however. I'm still motivated by the same beliefs and values I had back then, and I continue to try and live by them. I've met a number of people down through the years who weren't afraid to live by their principles. The most remarkable of them all was a man named William Smith Monroe. I'm glad to have had a chance to meet him, work with him, and get to know him.

I want to thank the following people for their help in writing this book: Judy McCulloh, Tom Ewing, Robert and Ruth Black, Forrest Rose, Kenny Baker, Ralph Lewis, Erma Spray, Doug Hutchens, Rolf Sieker, Matthias Malcher, Tony Trischka, Wayne Shrubsall, Carl Fleischhauer, Jim Peva, Saburo 'Watanabe' Inoue, Aleta Murphy, Alan Murphy, Frank Greathouse, Wayne Lewis, Dave Lynch, Randy Escobedo, Tut Taylor, Takeshi Sonoda, Scott Zimmerman, Tom Adler, Peter McLaughlin, Lois Marchant, Roger Anderson, Alan O'Bryant, Julia LaBella, and all the people with whom I've played Bill Monroe songs, traded Bill Monroe stories, and quoted Bill Monroe sayings.

Thanks most of all to my wife, Kristie, for her invaluable assistance in writing this book, and for her unwavering support, encouragement, and love and for helping me to understand what Bill Monroe was really all about—believing in yourself.

*Come Hither to Go Yonder*

# Introduction

There'll be fiddles and guitars and banjo
   pickin' too,
Bill Monroe singin' out them old Kentucky blues,
Ernest Tubb's number, "Two Wrongs Don't Make
   a Right"
On the Grand Ole Opry every Saturday night.
   —Chorus of the "Grand Ole Opry Song"
      by Hylo Brown

## Nashville, Tennessee

*"And now ladies and gentlemen, let's make welcome a member of the Country Music Hall of Fame—here he is with his Blue Grass Boys—the great Bill Monroe!"*

That was how announcer Grant Turner introduced Bill on stage at the Grand Ole Opry, and as we took our places at the microphones, Mr. Turner continued in his well-practiced yet sincere tone of voice: *"Give him a great big hand—Bill's coming out to center stage to play for you right now."* A crescendo of applause rose up from an adoring audience.

"Howdy, folks, howdy—we're glad to be with you here tonight," Bill said in his Kentucky-accented voice. His tone was honest and down-to-earth as he greeted his fans. "Kenny Baker's on the fiddle, on the guitar we have Ralph Lewis, on the bass fiddle is Randy Davis, and with the five-string banjo we have Bob Black. We've picked out a number that we get more requests for than any other—it's called 'Uncle Pen.'"

Bill stood proudly at the microphone, his white hat gleaming as the spotlight centered on him. I felt that pride radiating into me as well. I wondered if my folks were listening back home in Iowa. Ralph played the introductory guitar notes before Kenny launched into the familiar melody on his fiddle. Bass, mandolin, and banjo added their distinctive sounds to the musical mixture, and Bill Monroe's voice charged in above it all. He was singing once again for the people who loved him. The song ended with Kenny playing part of an old-time tune that Bill's uncle Pen used to play, called "Jenny Lynn." Bill danced a few steps. The audience roared its approval. Bill Monroe was comfortable at the Grand Ole Opry—like a traveler returning home to his family.

Those nights at the Opry were probably the most exciting moments for me during my stay with the Blue Grass Boys. Playing on the Grand Ole Opry was a euphoric experience for anyone, but performing there with Bill Monroe was special: he had been a member of the show since 1939. The Solemn Old Judge himself, George D. Hay (who gave the Grand Ole Opry its name), had told Bill when he was hired: "If you ever leave here, you'll have to fire yourself." Also present at Bill Monroe's 1939 audition for the Grand Ole Opry were Harry Stone, the Opry's manager, and David Stone, an announcer for the show. Bill performed there with his first band of Blue Grass Boys the very next Saturday night after the audition, starting with the song "Mule Skinner Blues"—for which he received three encores (according to Bill). In one interview, he said it was the first time any artist had ever received an encore on the Opry.

For me, Bill Monroe *was* the Opry, and playing on that show with him was a tangible link with history. I think about those moments often, and I treasure them in my memory. But Bill was also a tangible link with the future—by playing for him I joined a proud musical family that had dreams for what was to come, as well as roots deep in the past. The style of music called "bluegrass" was still evolving. Its antecedents went back for literally hundreds of years, and it possessed a timelessness that was personified in Bill Monroe; at the same time one could observe changes taking place in the music every day. The 1970s were a time when bluegrass underwent many transformations. The baby-boom generation had discovered it, due in no small part to the release of an enormously popular and successful album, *Will the Circle Be Unbroken,* which showcased many now-famous bluegrass artists. Released in 1972 by the Nitty Gritty Dirt Band, the album featured performances by such greats as singer and guitarist Doc Watson, Jimmy Martin (known as the King of Bluegrass), Merle Travis (inventor of the finger style known as Travis picking), and Maybelle Carter (of the famous Carter Family of Virginia, which had a more far-reaching influence on country music than any other group in history). *Will the Circle Be Unbroken* sold over a million copies and spawned a popular interest in bluegrass that lasted for many years. Bill Monroe, not wishing to alienate his conservative bluegrass fans by associating himself with the long-haired members of the Nitty Gritty Dirt Band, refused to take part in the project.

Baby boomers had begun to alter bluegrass music to suit their own needs. I am a member of that generation, and I was very excited about the new musical territory being carved out by bluegrass groups who were presenting music rooted in styles other than bluegrass—especially rock and country-rock. One of these groups was the Bluegrass Alliance, which over the years featured many innovative and now-famous musicians including Sam Bush (mandolin), Dan Crary (guitar), Courtney Johnson (banjo), and Tony Rice (guitar). Another band also got my attention: the New Grass Revival. That group was made up of former members of the Bluegrass Alliance—Sam Bush (mandolin), Courtney Johnson (banjo), Ebo Walker (bass), and Curtis Burch (guitar). Another progressive-style band that caught my ear was the Earl Scruggs Revue, founded by Scruggs after the dissolution of his partnership with Lester Flatt in 1969; spotlighted in that band were Scruggs's sons Randy, Gary, and Steve.

At the same time, I still loved the music of more traditional performers. Lester Flatt and Earl Scruggs were probably the most well-known to me. Powered by Scruggs's driving, syncopated banjo style, their band, the Foggy Mountain Boys, had received a great deal of media attention before Flatt and Scruggs parted ways. The music of the Stanley Brothers and their band, the Clinch Mountain Boys, also occupied an important niche in my growing bluegrass consciousness. They played a mountain/folk style of bluegrass showcasing the lonesome voice of Carter Stanley and punctuated by the rhythmic, old-time bluegrass banjo style of Ralph Stanley. (Stanley later had a prominent vocal role in the soundtrack to the 2000 movie, O Brother, Where Art Thou?) Another traditional bluegrass group I liked very much consisted of Don Reno and Red Smiley, who recorded a large amount of material now considered to be classic bluegrass. (Don Reno worked for Bill Monroe in 1948, and cowrote the tune "Feuding Banjos," later known as "Dueling Banjos" and featured in the 1972 movie Deliverance.)

No one was more conscious of the new directions bluegrass was taking than its founder, Bill Monroe. He had links to the past that forever tied him to bygone days. He had been surrounded by music as a child in Rosine, Kentucky. Gospel music was performed in church. His father danced. His mother sang and played the fiddle during breaks from her housework. His brother Birch (1901–1982) played the fiddle. Another brother, Charlie (1903–1975) played the guitar. His sister Bertha (1908–1997) also played the guitar. At the age of twelve, Bill was playing guitar accompaniment for country dances around Rosine with his uncle, Pendleton Vandiver

(1869–1932). Bill's song "Uncle Pen" was written in honor of the old-time fiddler, and some of his favorite tunes were ones that he learned from his uncle: numbers such as "Sally Goodin," "Goin' Across the Sea," "The Old Gray Mare Came Tearin' Out of the Wilderness," and the one he always closed the song "Uncle Pen" with—"Jenny Lynn."

Time-honored tradition thus occupied an important part of Bill's essential nature. But he was also the person who had taken the old-time music he had known and loved since childhood and energized it to create a new form. Innovation lies at the very soul of bluegrass music—change comes to it as naturally as a tree growing and spreading its branches in all different directions. Though his music was alive, vigorous, and spontaneous, just as Bill was himself, he also felt there was no need to change bluegrass music at lightning speed. I personally heard him say, many times and about many groups, "That ain't no part of bluegrass." He believed that care had to be exercised in making changes to the music. Bill was once heard to comment, "Let's advance bluegrass music just one year at a time."

I was ready to be a part of that advancement, and when Bill hired me, he let me do just that. It was going to be a rough ride in some respects, but I didn't know it at the time. My youthful enthusiasm was my survival kit. I was at the dawn of a new stage in life, young and idealistic, looking forward to a career that seemed to have few limitations, and I was intoxicated by thoughts of performing in the public arena with some of the world's greatest musicians. Eager to take part in the new music scene that was blossoming all around me, I wasn't going to let anything hold me back.

The morning after I arrived in Music City (a common nickname for Nashville, Tennessee), I auditioned for Bill Monroe and was lucky enough to get hired solely for my musical abilities, even though I was just a newcomer from the state of Iowa. With a reference from the Bill Monroe Talent Agency, I was able to rent my first apartment in Nashville (on Ferguson Avenue). I probably would have had a much harder time finding a place in Music City without that reference. Landlords were often reluctant to rent to musicians, who frequently drifted into town and stayed for only a short while.

I was quite willing to work for Bill Monroe by his rules, but unfortunately I didn't have any rulebook to help me negotiate the hazards of living as a musician in Nashville. I was lucky to have steady employment—competition was fierce for jobs and exposure. Talented songwriters and performers were everywhere, working at any jobs they could find. Drug and alcohol abuse were common. Vagrants filled the streets, especially in the downtown area, where down-and-out panhandlers accosted every pedestrian who wandered by. It was easy to feel swallowed up by the big city. Periodic trips back home to Iowa became necessary in order for me to keep my sanity; in fact, in December 1975, I went back to Des Moines to visit my folks for Christmas even though a blizzard was predicted. The storm held off until I was on my way back to Nashville, and I plowed through blowing and drifting snow all night and all the next day in order to make it to the Grand Ole Opry in time to perform with Bill Monroe and the Blue Grass Boys.

I'd been singing all my life, but I wasn't prepared for the type of harmony singing required in Bill's band. I was expected to sing baritone on the gospel-quartet numbers, and I hadn't really learned those baritone vocal parts yet. For a while I had to do some vocal "searching around"during performances, and I'm sure Bill wasn't extremely pleased about that. Songs like "Wicked Path of Sin" (written by Bill and recorded in 1946) were a scary challenge for me. Many singers agree that baritone is one of the hardest parts to learn in harmony singing. I had to learn quickly about "mush-mouthing": if I didn't know the lyrics to a particular song, I would just sing the vowels and let Bill do the enunciation of the important consonants. There was nothing wrong with that—lots of bands sing harmony that way, because it's very difficult for all the singers to get in perfect synchronization with consonants such as "t," "p," and "s." One thing made all of the harmony singing much easier: when we sang quartet numbers we would all gang around one microphone—an arrangement which helped each person hear all the others more clearly. This made the harmony much tighter, and it helped me immensely in hearing my own vocal part. One other thing helped too: Bill's powerful tenor singing dominated all the harmonies, and if the rest of the parts weren't quite right the listeners couldn't always tell because they were concentrating mostly on Bill's voice anyway.

There was much more to Bill Monroe's music than just the singing however, and I was primarily an instrumentalist in those days. I would never have joined the band if it had been an all-vocal group. I was a banjo player with a style of my own—that's how I preferred to think of myself. (I'll talk a little later about how I developed that style.) I wasn't cocky about it, but I had studied Bill Monroe's instrumental music a lot before joining the band, and I felt I could do it some real justice. After Bill hired me I found out I had a lot to learn. I couldn't incorporate my own style, as it existed then, into the music we were playing. I had to develop a new style based on musical interaction with Bill as it took place within his own strict guidelines. In other words, I had to learn to crawl before I could walk.

## Come Hither to Go Yonder

In spite of all the apparent stylistic restraints that went along with the job of being a Blue Grass Boy, I got the feeling that Bill understood my need for self-expression instrumentally, and he was willing to give me that chance. "Come Hither to Go Yonder" is the name of one of Bill's compositions, and I think that title reflects an attitude or belief about his role as a teacher. His band was a training ground for inexperienced musicians like me; playing for him prepared us for successful careers elsewhere.

One of Bill Monroe's many special qualities was that he was a real person with genuine feelings—he empathized with other people and took an interest in helping them. He wasn't merely a one-dimensional stage personality, thinking only of personal career advancement. That's what set him apart from the galaxy of other county-music performers in Nashville. It's also one of the reasons I'm writing this book.

Bill Monroe was held in very high esteem among all the musicians I knew. He was practically worshipped by many. There was a popular joke going around Nashville during the time I was there. One variation of it goes like this: A bluegrass musician dies and goes to bluegrass heaven. There he sees all of the greatest bluegrass performers who have ever lived. Before too long, he notices an individual who very much resembles Bill Monroe, standing high up on a hill, wearing a white hat and playing a mandolin. "Wait a minute," says the musician to himself, "Bill Monroe's not dead yet." He asks one of his fellow paradise residents: "Is that Bill Monroe standing over there?" The other person replies, "No, that's God. He just thinks He's Bill Monroe."

It's been said that living in Nashville during the 1970s was like living in Paris during the 1930s. Both times were marked by a musical renaissance. In the 1930s, Paris witnessed the coming-of-age of "hot" swing with such legendary musicians as Django Reinhart and Stephan Grappelli and their Quintet of the Hot Club of France, which exposed a generation of musicians to vast new possibilities in the field of jazz expression. In Nashville, the 1970s were the coming-of-age period for modern acoustic string music. Styles of music that were rooted in old-time country, traditional blues, and mountain singing were being transformed by the sounds and influences of swing, jazz, and rock and roll. "Newgrass" was in its early and most exciting formative years. (Newgrass is an all-inclusive label that refers to music played by contemporary bluegrass bands drawing their material from sources outside the bluegrass idiom: blues, jazz, and rock and roll.) Clubs like Randy Wood's Pickin' Parlor, Earl Snead's Bluegrass Inn, and the Station Inn (started in 1974 and still in operation today) were providing venues for all musicians—both established and upcoming—to present their art to fellow pickers as well as to fans. Nashville was a musical melting pot unlike any other city in the world.

All of this formed a backdrop for my experience of working for Bill Monroe. The heady atmosphere of Music City in the 1970s was an exciting counterbalance to the more serious and demanding work of traveling and performing with the Father of Bluegrass Music. Bill Monroe was my anchor in a sea of musical change.

Bill's influence remains with me very much today. The music I play is still governed by the rules laid down by him. Bill's example is the reason I continue to feel a strong need to stick to the melody as defined by the writer of any particular song that I'm doing. When I play a song on the banjo, I try my best to play the same melody the singer is singing—I don't change that melody to fit my musical style without serious consideration. One of the most significant concepts I learned from Bill is this: the music is more important than the player. The mark of true virtuosity is the ability to make the listener notice how pretty the music is, not how gifted the musician happens to be.

This memoir recounts the two years I spent as a Blue Grass Boy, as well as the effect of those two years on my life afterward. For over twenty years, my career was deeply enriched by frequent musical encounters with the Father of Bluegrass. Each occasion holds a place of honor in my memory.

Today, I find it difficult to believe how many experiences were crammed into the short time I played with Bill Monroe. Recollections of that two-year span pass through my mind with astonishing frequency. It's time now to write them down. I'm pleased and proud to share these memories, in the hope that at least a rough sketch will emerge of Bill Monroe and his potent effect on me, as well as on everyone else who knew him.

My experiences with Bill Monroe form the basis of many of my most strongly held beliefs about music. They make up the electrical charge that powers my performing and songwriting today. I hope this book will convey some idea of the impact that Bill Monroe had on me—because in my mind he's still just as much alive today as when he actually walked the earth.

# I. REMEMBERING THE OLD DAYS

---

"Let's never forget the old days." Bill's voice was soft and sincere. He always spoke from his heart. My wife, Kristie Black, and I were visiting my old boss on his farm just outside of Nashville one day in early November 1992. We were on our way to Cedars of Lebanon State Park where I had been invited to supervise some banjo workshops at the Tennessee Banjo Institute. At the last minute, we had decided to drive out to Bill's place just to see if he was there. It was a beautiful afternoon, and the sun was shining on the tree-lined bluff to our right as we drove up the lane. When we pulled in, there was Bill, hulling a pile of walnuts he had spread out on the ground. He was stepping on them to mash the hulls off. We noticed the walnut stains on his trousers as he walked over to greet us with a friendly smile, as though he had been expecting us. About five minutes after we arrived, he went into the house to get his mandolin, saying he had some tunes he wanted to show me. We sat down together on some benches he had placed outdoors, enjoying the warm autumn sunshine as it streamed down through branches still thinly covered with leaves. He tuned up his mandolin with great care, bowing his head close to the strings while I waited in anticipation. Then he began to play. As I listened, I was transported back in time, realizing that once again I was the student and Bill Monroe was the teacher. It was just like the old days.

I was struck by the amount of energy and passion still present in the older man. At the age of eighty-one, the Father of Bluegrass Music hadn't lost his touch. His music was still a part of him—strong, vital, and filled with the spirit of tradition. Old-time melodies were resurrected in his

Bill Monroe and Bob Black at Bill's farm just outside of Nashville, November 1992. Photo by Kristie Black. (Used by permission.)

hands. The past lived on in Bill Monroe—he had never forgotten the old days.

Nearly twenty years had gone by since I first met Bill. In 1974 he hired me to play in his band, the Blue Grass Boys, and I was given the chance of a lifetime to learn from a musical master. Now, as I listened to the melodies that sprang from his fingers, my mind went back to those exciting times. Some of the tunes were familiar; he had taught them to me while we were on the road. These songs made me think of the thousands of miles we had traveled together and the scores of shows we had played. As though from a scrapbook of old photos, pages from the past were opening up. The images were only slightly faded.

How could I forget the old days? My years as a Blue Grass Boy would always be a part of me. Playing with Bill Monroe was much more than an opportunity to increase my knowledge of songwriting and performing. It was also a rare chance to glimpse the personality of a man who had a profound effect not only on the lives of musicians, entertainers, and fans, but also on the entire course of American music itself.

His playing took me back to the old days. I was listening to the source. When it came time to leave I had to tear myself away, but I knew I would be back. I would always be back because Bill Monroe and his music would always be there. He was impossible to ignore and, like the choruses of his many songs, he was impossible to forget.

## The Lore of Bluegrass

We Blue Grass Boys called him the Chief—partly out of respect for his skill, drive, and dedication, but mostly because we just plain admired him. For most of us, this admiration was born long before we got to know him personally. Listening to Bill Monroe's recordings and watching his live performances, we came to recognize the true significance of this man and his music. Our special regard for him never diminished even after our active days as Blue Grass Boys. His remarkable personality continued to affect our attitudes about music, performing, and life in general. He was a role model for us all. Approximately 175 musicians passed through the ranks of Bill's band down through the years, and there wasn't one not deeply affected by the experience.

Long known as the Father of Bluegrass Music, Bill Monroe created the style of that music and wrote many of the songs still performed by bluegrass bands today. Born in rural Kentucky, near Rosine, Monroe absorbed a number of musical influences while growing up: old-time fiddle tunes; country music; southern blues; and Methodist, Baptist, and Holiness gospel singing. These, along with jazz and Scottish bagpipe music, are the principal elements he later combined to create one of the few musical art forms truly indigenous to America: bluegrass.

Bill often described his music as having "a good drive and a high pitch," and many times I heard him use the expression "singin' from my heart to yours" when discussing his expressive vocal style. Bill admired the Carter family, and he liked the singing of Jimmie Rodgers (1897–1933), the famous Mississippi singer and songwriter who originated many stylistic elements common to country music today, including yodeling and use of the blues as a defining component.

Bill loved the distinctive old-time fiddling of Clayton McMichen (1900–1970), a Georgia musician whose playing incorporated elements of many different musical genres including country, jazz, and swing. He also respected the music of Fiddling Arthur Smith (1898–1971), a Tennessee native who developed an innovative style of fiddle playing still copied by bluegrass players today.

In addition to his regard for these musicians, Bill frequently talked about how much he admired the guitar playing of Riley Puckett (1894–

1946), a Georgia musician who created his own style that featured bass note runs between the chord changes. Modern bluegrass rhythm guitar styles can be traced back in part to Puckett.

After the death of his father, Bill, at age sixteen, moved in with his fiddle-playing uncle Pen Vandiver. Pen used crutches and needed help carrying water and wood. According to Bill, his uncle had broken his hip when his mule slipped in the mud, pinning him and his fiddle underneath. Uncle Pen's fiddling influenced Bill's music in a fundamental way, especially with respect to rhythm and timing. Bill frequently talked about what a wonderful sense of timing Uncle Pen had; that same important element of his uncle's playing later found its way into Bill's music.

Another musical influence from Bill's childhood was a black railroad employee and farm worker named Arnold Schulz, who played blues on the guitar. Whenever Schultz came to Rosine, Bill would listen to him perform. Growing to love the blues, Bill later incorporated elements of that musical genre into his music.

Inducted into the Country Music Hall of Fame in 1970, Bill left a lasting impression on the landscape of American music, and his influence can be heard and felt in many diverse musical styles today. In 1982 he received recognition from the National Endowment for the Arts as a master folk artist in the first National Heritage Fellowships. Bill Monroe is now acknowledged as the founder of an original musical art form.

I first heard of Bill when I was a high school student in Des Moines, Iowa, in the 1960s. Folk music was enjoying a renaissance back then, and that's what opened the door to bluegrass for me. I was instantly attracted to it as a good alternative to the mass-produced, commercial, "Top 40" sounds saturating the radio waves. I found bluegrass music to be exciting and driving, full of creative expression in the interpretations of individual musicians. It was an acoustic music—that is, none of the instruments were amplified electronically. In addition, the singing regularly featured two-, three-, and four-part harmonies, which made an impression on me. I realized the performers had to be expert singers as well as skillful musicians. Bluegrass instruments included a fiddle, banjo, guitar, mandolin, bass, and sometimes Dobro (a commercial brand name often used to describe any type of resonator guitar. In bluegrass, the instrument is generally played with a metal bar).

The banjo was the instrument that really turned me on. The first bluegrass record I ever heard featured a good banjo player by the name of Kenny Wertz. He was part of a group called the Scottsville Squirrel Barkers. A friend of mine named Steve Herbert had purchased their album,

*Bluegrass Favorites,* at the Hinky Dinky grocery store on Ingersoll Avenue in Des Moines. Steve and I listened eagerly to their spirited renditions of such great bluegrass songs as "Shady Grove," "Cripple Creek," "Reuben," and "Hand Me Down My Walking Cane." (Later, I learned the group was also known as the Kentucky Travelers—different editions of that same album listed this name for the band. I liked the name the Scottsville Squirrel Barkers better!)

Additional bluegrass albums purchased by Steve at the Hinky Dinky store included *Bluegrass Banjos on Fire* by the group Homer and the Barnstormers, and *Ten Shades of Bluegrass* by the Lonesome Travelers, featuring the banjo talent of Bob Johnson. Also featured on that album, on mandolin, was Norman Blake, an artist who later achieved fame as a guitarist. None of the musicians were given credit on the editions marketed in Hinky Dinky stores, but these inexpensively produced projects, and others similar to them, helped to fire up an interest in bluegrass music among shoppers who might never have gone into actual record shops.

Steve and I made a deal: he would learn the guitar if I learned the banjo. My father rented an instrument for me from a downtown Des Moines music store. It was a cheaply made Kay brand. I took it to the basement as soon as I got home and spent nearly eight hours sitting on the cellar steps practicing and learning from an instruction book I had obtained. Quickly, I became hooked. I was going to learn the banjo come hell or high water! Steve—though he tried—never really got the hang of playing the guitar. As a result, I found myself embarking on my musical odyssey as a solo act. I had no idea where the trip would take me.

I soon discovered that the greatest banjo player of that time, or any other for that matter, was Earl Scruggs, part of the famous group of Lester Flatt, Earl Scruggs, and the Foggy Mountain Boys. He had a finger-style approach to banjo that was a more sophisticated offshoot of earlier playing techniques such as those practiced by North Carolina banjo greats Charlie Poole and Snuffy Jenkins. Performing all over the United States, especially on college campuses, Earl Scruggs introduced myriads of young people to bluegrass and banjo playing. Many of those same people eventually became leading exponents of the music as we know it today. Scruggs's banjo style was what I was trying to emulate, and I worked hard to duplicate the subtle nuances of tone and timing he had so masterfully achieved.

I combed through record stores in the Des Moines area during the late 1960s looking for bluegrass music, purchasing mostly Flatt and Scruggs albums. These two musicians had achieved a great deal of fame after their music was featured on the popular television comedy series *The Beverly*

*Hillbillies.* A further boost for their career came in 1967 with the release of the movie *Bonnie and Clyde,* featuring a soundtrack spotlighting Earl Scruggs's banjo composition "Foggy Mountain Breakdown." (Flatt and Scruggs won a Grammy for "Foggy Mountain Breakdown" at the eleventh annual Grammy awards ceremony in 1968. Earl Scruggs won a second Grammy for his more recent recording of "Foggy Mountain Breakdown" at the forty-fourth annual Grammy awards ceremony in 2002.)

Somewhat in the background, at least as far as I was concerned, stood Bill Monroe, the man who had first brought Flatt and Scruggs together by hiring them in 1945 to play in his band, the Blue Grass Boys. According to an interview with Bill in *Masters of the Five-String Banjo* by Tony Trischka and Peter Wernick, Scruggs wrote "Foggy Mountain Breakdown" after performing a very similar Bill Monroe tune called "Blue Grass Breakdown."[1] It must be said, however, that Scruggs disputes Bill's claim of authorship of "Blue Grass Breakdown," asserting that *he* actually wrote that tune as well as "Foggy Mountain Breakdown."[2] One thing is clear: both "Blue Grass Breakdown" and "Foggy Mountain Breakdown" are wonderful vehicles for "Scruggs-style" banjo picking.

Authorship disagreements aside, Flatt and Scruggs owed a great deal of their popularity to the Father of Bluegrass. He had given them valuable performance experience, as well as important popular exposure on the Grand Ole Opry, a radio show he had been a member of since 1939. Bill's band was the perfect training school for Flatt and Scruggs—and when they felt it was time to "graduate," they struck out successfully together, making their own mark on the music world.

During my early searches for bluegrass LPs, I also discovered recordings by many other pioneering groups, including Jimmy Martin, Jim and Jesse, the Country Gentlemen, and the Osborne Brothers. Younger bands that had generational appeal, such as the Dillards and the Greenbriar Boys, were also high on my list of personal favorites.

My awareness of the true extent of Bill Monroe's influence grew as I continued to study bluegrass. In the liner notes of many of the albums I purchased, I read that Bill was credited with creating bluegrass music. He had been the driving force behind the entire musical genre, bringing together all the elements to create the sound that I was now becoming fascinated with. I soon realized that all the bluegrass groups I was listening to owed their inspiration to Bill. The more knowledge I acquired, the greater my respect grew for the man who had breathed life into this musical art form.

When I looked at the pictures of Bill Monroe on the covers of his albums, I was reminded of my grandfather, Ersie Wilson, who was a farmer and lay preacher with rigid, old-fashioned principles. Although he was very kind, he was a bit stern and at times had a stubborn streak. Those same qualities seemed to be reflected in the face of Bill Monroe. I had the feeling he would be hard to work for and difficult to be around. In the pictures he stood erect, with a distant gaze in his eyes that never seemed to center on the camera. He appeared austere and forbidding. The cover of *Bluegrass Instrumentals* (Decca74601, 1965) is a particularly illustrative example. In that photo, Bill is standing stiffly sideways, face turned toward the camera, with a look that could almost be described as belligerent. I never imagined myself working for him!

I learned with interest that Bill and his brother Charlie had performed as the Monroe Brothers in the mid-1930s on radio station KFNF in Shenandoah, Iowa (my boyhood hometown). Owned and operated by the Henry Field Seed Company, KFNF had an interesting and colorful history as a performance venue for gospel groups, old-time fiddlers, and early string bands. Sometimes called the "Friendly Farmer Station," it was one of the earliest and most powerful radio stations in the Midwest.

Bill and Charlie made twenty-five dollars a week at KFNF (according to an article in the *Nashville Tennessean*, June 25, 1972). Sponsored by Texas Crystals (a laxative), their show was an important first for Bill in two respects: It was the beginning of his full-time professional music career (prior to moving to Shenandoah, Bill and Charlie—along with their brother Birch—had made their living in the Chicago area as refinery workers and played music only part time). It was also where he first started playing lead solos on the mandolin. Bill stated this himself in an interview at the 1963 Chicago Folk Festival. In a lead solo, one musician presents his instrumental interpretation of the melody while the other instrumentalists—in this case Charlie, on guitar—play a secondary or supporting role in providing musical background or accompaniment. Birch Monroe, who was the fiddler for the trio, stayed in the Chicago area after Bill and Charlie left for Shenandoah. In the absence of the fiddle, Bill had to learn to play lead solos on the mandolin. Before that, he had just been playing background chords and rhythm while the fiddle played all the lead solos.

Having spent my childhood in Shenandoah, I felt a slight connection to the Father of Bluegrass. Much later, I learned that this little town on the banks of the Nishnabotna River was the place where Bill had met his first wife, Carolyn. Her full name was Carolyn Minnie Brown. Born in Marshalltown, Carolyn was living in Red Oak, near Shenandoah, when Bill first met her—Bill told me this himself one day while we were talking about Shenandoah. He liked Iowa a lot, and often expressed to me a fondness for the Tall Corn State.

## The Lure of Bluegrass

Music was the furthest thing from my mind while I was growing up in Shenandoah. I do remember my mother playing an upright piano—mostly on hymns such as "In the Garden," and "The Old Rugged Cross." There was a family band on my mother's side many years before I was born. The Pinckney Band, which included five brothers—Joseph, Leo, George, Charlie, and Reuben Pinckney—was formed near Macksburg, Iowa, around 1910. They performed mainly in parades, on an open-topped horse-drawn wagon with the band name painted on the side. I've always enjoyed parades, and I can easily imagine the Pinckney Band wagon rolling down Main Street in all its glory.

My father was a journalist working for the *Shenandoah Evening Sentinel* during the 1950s. I remember riding my bike down to the newspaper office on occasion, where Dad would buy me a Coke and let me watch the linotype operators at work. (The Coke helped counter the heat radiating from the molten metal used to cast lines of type.) I marveled at the enormous rolls of newsprint that were fed into the old rotary letterpress, and I recall the metallic clatter of the lead type as the day's edition rolled off.

The *Shenandoah Evening Sentinel* had a couple of young newspaper carriers who later became singing sensations: the Everly Brothers. Don and Phil, who grew up in Shenandoah, came to the *Sentinel* every Saturday to deliver the weekly proceeds from their paper routes. My dad was sometimes the one who collected their nickels, dimes, and quarters. Ike Everly, father of the future singing duo, was an entertainer who performed regularly in the late 1940s and early 1950s on one of Shenandoah's radio stations, KMA. Dad used to drop by the KMA studios to gather news in the early afternoon while Ike Everly was on the air. Everly, along with other performers, played in a place called the Mayfair Auditorium, which contained a studio and stage partitioned by a sheet of glass from a large auditorium that seated several hundred people. On Saturday afternoons the glass partition was raised and a live country music jamboree was broadcast. Folks came from all over southwest Iowa and parts of Missouri and Nebraska to attend. Some brought basket lunches. One of Ike Everly's most popular numbers during those shows was "The Crawdad Song." He later went over to KFNF, where the Monroe Brothers had performed, and took part in an early morning family program. His sons Don and Phil, along with their mother, Margaret Everly, also participated. They were a hit! Early morning listeners especially liked one of their songs, a tune called "Molasses."

In 1958 my family moved to Des Moines, Iowa. Music classes were part of the curriculum at our school, Greenwood Elementary. Mrs. Neal was the music teacher. The students didn't like her because she was a strict disciplinarian. She had a habit of rubbing her chin all the time, as though she had a beard, and we often made fun of her behind her back because of that. She was actually a very good teacher. She taught us to sing together in harmony, and we put on Christmas concerts in the school auditorium. (In those days, religious carols such as "Silent Night," "The First Noel," and "We Three Kings" were sung in public schools.)

Shenandoah, Iowa, mid-1950s. *Left to right:* Neil Black, Phil Everly, Jim Black, and Bob Black, posing next to the upright piano played by the author's mother, Ruth Black. The Everly Brothers were performing in Omaha, and Phil had come to visit his old hometown of Shenandoah. After interviewing Everly for the *Shenandoah Evening Sentinel,* Robert Black Sr. invited the singer to his family home, where he took this photo. Ruth Black remembers Phil Everly as being very polite. When addressing her, he always used the word "ma'am." Photo by Robert Black Sr. (Used by permission.)

I also took violin lessons at Greenwood. (My older brother, Neil, took French horn lessons.) My violin teacher was a kindly old man named Mr. Shaw. He had white hair and a little white moustache with pointed ends. He played for the Des Moines Symphony Orchestra. I was impressed by the beautiful tone he got from his violin with his bow. Mr. Shaw taught me to play melodies such as "Annie Laurie" and "The Volga Boatmen."

There was a school orchestra at Greenwood, and Neil and I became part of it almost as soon as we started taking lessons. I was last chair in the violin section. There were several girls ahead of me. I didn't know how to read the sheet music we used—I just faked it, playing mostly by ear.

The violin lessons ended after two years, and apart from singing in church, I didn't return to music seriously until 1965, when I discovered bluegrass. That was about the time I began writing songs. The very first song I ever wrote was a gospel song called "Christians and Sinners." Today, I can only remember the chorus:

Christians and sinners, both eat the same dinners.
You'll never know the difference till
You go to heaven or to hell,
And then it won't be hard to tell the Christians from the sinners.

I also wrote my first banjo instrumental around 1965. I made it up while fishing from the banks of the Raccoon River one night. I was using crawdads for bait, so I called my tune "Crawdad Pincer Blues." I often used to take my banjo along when I went fishing. I carried it over my shoulder in an old white canvas mail sack. "US MAIL" was printed in black letters on the side. (I got the mail sack from a lady my mother worked for. My mom was hired as a typist, addressing junk-mail brochures to be placed in mail sacks and taken to the post office.) One dark night I was walking home from a fishing trip, carrying my fishing pole and my banjo in its mail sack. A nondescript-looking car pulled up to the curb next to me. The window was rolled down and a voice asked, "What's in the sack?" I thought the stranger was going to steal my banjo, so I told him, "Er, uh, just some old clothes." He turned on the dome light in his car, and I saw he was wearing a policeman's uniform. The vehicle was an unmarked patrol car. Seeing "US MAIL" on the sack, he thought I'd been stealing mail from a postal box. I explained myself and showed him the banjo. Then I offered to play him a tune, but I guess he wasn't a banjo music fan because he declined and quickly drove off.

My friends gave me the nickname Catfish. (Many folks still call me by that name today.) I always wanted to catch a flathead catfish big enough to

Bob Black at age sixteen, with the rented banjo that he learned to play on.
Photo by Robert Black Sr. (Used by permission.)

make a banjo head out of its skin. Banjo heads come in two types: archtop
and flathead. Since mine took a flathead, I figured a flathead catfish skin
was just what I needed. Unfortunately, I never hooked one big enough to
do the job.

I played the banjo all through high school and college. While still un-
derage, I entered and won many local talent contests. I sometimes used a

phony ID to get into the country-music taverns where the contests were held. The ID I used had been originally issued to a person named Jim Strenkowski. I used that name when entering the contests, and when the leader of the house band would announce the winner he would say, "Tonight's first-place winner is Jim Strenkowski." "Foggy Mountain Breakdown" was the tune that most often won me first prize—generally around twenty-five dollars. Luckily, the prize money was always paid in cash instead of check. I always hoped the real Jim Strenkowski would not be present in the audience.

I had a record player with several different speeds: 78, 45, 33⅓, and 16 RPM. I found that by slowing LPs down to 16 RPM, I could figure out banjo phrases that went by too quickly to hear at the normal 33⅓ speed. Unfortunately, I ruined lots of albums by raising and lowering the needle repeatedly in order to comprehend the most elusive banjo parts. The records got so scratched up that they wouldn't play any more. Many of those albums were classics, no longer available today.

I went through several banjos during those first few years, and I performed some grossly nonprofessional modifications on them that make me cringe with embarrassment when I think about them today. I ordered another Kay brand banjo from Sears and Roebuck, and I made some crude "Scruggs tuners" for it, using screw eyes, carriage bolts, and faucet washers. Invented by Earl Scruggs, Scruggs tuners are special adjustable cam-type tuning units that are installed on the banjo by drilling holes in the peghead between the other tuning pegs. The cams are then mounted in such a way that they can be used to push the strings sideways, thereby raising or lowering the pitch of the strings at will. They can be used to change the tuning in the middle of a song, much like the pedals of a pedal steel guitar. I would have bought some ready-made Scruggs tuners if I had known where to get them, but music stores in Des Moines carried very few banjo accessories in those days. I sold the banjo in 1970 to a fellow musician named Mike Condon, and recently he returned it to me—tuners and all. It had been sitting in his closet for over thirty years. I guess he was embarrassed about the stove bolts in the peghead too. Those Scruggs tuners still work, though, and Kristie has convinced me to leave them on the banjo.

Next, I purchased a Vega long-necked banjo from a music store. It was a folk-music instrument, not intended for bluegrass (which I didn't know at the time). It differed from a bluegrass banjo in two important respects: it had an open back (bluegrass banjos have a resonator fastened to the back of the banjo's body that deflects the sound outward toward the front), and

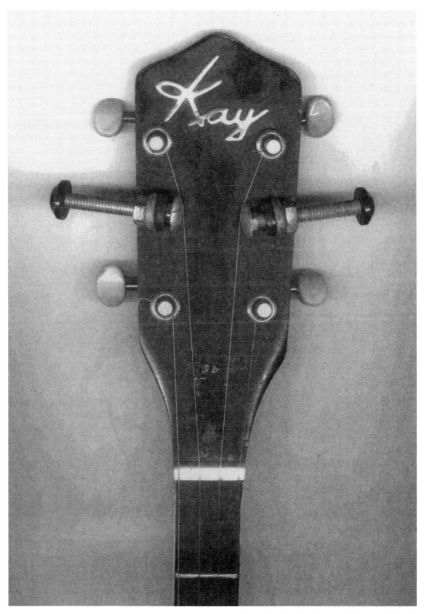

The homemade "Scruggs tuners" Bob Black fashioned from carriage bolts, screw eyes, and faucet washers. When a bolt is turned perpendicular to a string, it pushes on the string, resulting in a higher note. For a lower note, the bolt is turned parallel to the string. Photo by Bob Black.

it had a 25-fret neck instead of a standard 22-fret neck. The longer neck design is credited to folksinger Pete Seeger, and it enables the banjoist to play easily in more keys. I became dissatisfied with the extra neck length as soon as I learned it wasn't considered proper equipment for bluegrass, so I cut out a section and glued the neck back together with Elmer's Glue-All to make it a standard length. Unfortunately, the glue joint didn't hold, so I clamped it together with an automobile radiator hose clamp! Shortly after that, I sold it and purchased another Vega banjo—this time a Pro II model with a standard neck and resonator included.

I couldn't leave that banjo alone either—I decided to make a different neck for it because the original neck had pearl inlays (position markers) in the fingerboard that didn't look fancy enough to suit me. So I ordered a neck kit from the Stewart-McDonald company in Athens, Ohio, and I made a mahogany neck with pearl hearts-and-flowers inlays. The inlay job wasn't too bad, but the peghead—which I tried to cut into a fancy shape—was a bit asymmetrical in form. I was happy with this banjo, though, and it's the one I had when I joined Bill Monroe's Blue Grass Boys. It sounded good, and I even used it to record several albums, including one with Bill (*The Weary Traveler* [MCA2173, 1976]).

I joined my first group in 1970 while attending Drake University in Des Moines. It was a variety assemblage called Captain Mel's Touring Revival Show, and it featured mostly folk-oriented music. We performed in coffeehouses and folk clubs around the Des Moines area, including the Catacomb on the campus of Grandview College, Know Where in West Des Moines, and the Cellar near Drake University.

Later, I became part of a more serious bluegrass band called the Willow Creek Boys. In that group, which featured guitarist Mike (Red) Conner and fiddler/mandolinist Steve Day, we performed bluegrass material by Jim and Jesse, Jimmy Martin, Bill Monroe, the Dillards, the Greenbriar Boys, and many others.

In June 1971, three years prior to joining the Blue Grass Boys, I attended Bill Monroe's largest and most well-known bluegrass festival in Bean Blossom, Indiana. The existing music site was originally the home of the Brown County Jamboree; Bill purchased the site in 1951 and founded the Bean Blossom Bluegrass Festival in 1967. (Many people wonder how the tiny town of Bean Blossom got its name. The story I heard was this: one time a truck overturned at a nearby creek, spilling a load of beans. The beans sprouted and blossomed, and thereafter the place was known as "Bean Blossom.")

Bean Blossom was the first festival I had ever been to, and it gave me a lifelong case of bluegrass fever. The number of amateur musicians was astounding, and their excitement was intense and contagious. Bill Monroe's presence had everyone so fired up that they played their music nonstop, day and night, as if possessed by demons. I noticed Bill walking around the grounds too, and I must admit he had the same effect on me. He projected a regal presence with his white hat, suit and tie, and courtly bearing. He was the centerpiece of the festival, like a rooster who ruled the barnyard.

At Bean Blossom I first heard many of the musicians who were later to make important and lasting contributions to bluegrass and acoustic music. It was there I met Jimmy Arnold, a nineteen-year-old musician from Fries, Virginia, who was incredibly good on banjo and guitar. He showed me some great licks on the banjo that I still use today. Arnold later became a legend among followers of bluegrass. During his tragically brief lifetime he performed with many groups, including a short-lived band (1972–73) with Keith Whitley called New Tradition (or Country Store—the band went by both names). Jimmy Arnold passed away in 1992.

I was lucky enough to get the chance to listen to Dobro player Tut Taylor jamming with guitarist Norman Blake at Bean Blossom. Taylor, not well known outside of bluegrass circles at that time, is today highly respected among his peers. Norman Blake was a regular performer on the *Johnny Cash Show* (1969–71, ABC-TV), and had been featured on Bob Dylan's famous 1969 album *Nashville Skyline*. He later appeared on the Nitty Gritty Dirt Band's landmark recording *Will the Circle Be Unbroken*, as well as on the soundtrack for the 2000 movie *O Brother, Where Art Thou?* At Bean Blossom, Taylor and Blake displayed their incredible musical talents for people like me to listen to and learn from. (I was privileged to have Norman Blake and his talented wife Nancy Blake as fellow musicians on my 1979 banjo album *Ladies on the Steamboat* [Ridgerunner0018]. The two still perform and record today.)

At Bean Blossom I was also greatly impressed by the New Deal String Band, a group of hippies who played "newgrass" as well as traditional-style bluegrass. Based in Raleigh, North Carolina, the band arrived at the festival in a limousine that looked kind of like a hearse. (It had once belonged to the governor of North Carolina.) I had never heard of newgrass before, and the New Deal String Band really opened up my mind to it. The group was one of the original newgrass bands, contemporaneous with other such groundbreaking groups as the Bluegrass Alliance and the Newgrass Revival. The New Deal String Band had made a record the previous year containing a mixture of traditional bluegrass (including several Bill Monroe songs) as well as songs by the Beatles, the Rolling Stones, and Bob Dylan. Bill called them the "hair boys" when he shared the stage with them in 1970 at Carlton Haney's bluegrass festival in Camp Springs, North Carolina. He liked performing with them though. I stood in the crowd of eager listeners as they jammed at Bean Blossom. Although I enjoyed each of their newgrass arrangements, I remember being surprised to find that my favorite song by the New Deal String Band was a haunting Bill Monroe classic, "Memories of Mother and Dad" (recorded by Bill in 1952), the chorus of which goes like this:

> There's a little lonesome graveyard—
> On these tombstones there, they say:
> On Mother's, "Gone But Not Forgotten,"
> On Dad's, "We Will Meet Again Someday."

Years later, I learned that those inscriptions can be found in the Rosine cemetery, on the gravestones of Bill's parents, James and Malissa.

The 1971 Bean Blossom festival was where I first heard melodic-style banjo playing—a technique reminiscent of classical guitar in which many more melody notes are played than in traditional Scruggs-style banjo. Old-time fiddler and banjo player Tommy Jarrell, who had been jamming with Jimmy Arnold, listened to my playing and told me I should study fiddle playing if I wanted to learn the melodic banjo style. He suggested I get an album by Kenny Baker called *Portrait of a Bluegrass Fiddler*[3] and try to learn the tunes note for note as closely as I could.

I witnessed a strange scene one evening at Bean Blossom that year. A group of folks were gathered underneath the eerie glow of a mercury vapor light, listening to a jam session. For no apparent reason, a little dog ran up to an old man and bit him on the leg, tearing his trousers and drawing blood. The man was intoxicated and flew into a rage, reaching into his pocket and saying, "Where's my damn pocketknife? I'm gonna slit that damn dog's throat!" The young couple who owned the dog pleaded with the man not to hurt their pet. Opening his knife blade, he stumbled around, trying to chase down the dog. The animal kept dodging him, barking its head off. The man was never able to get his hands on it. Finally the dog's owners were able to pick the animal up and carry it away.

Bean Blossom was a memorable and (for the most part) beautiful experience, but the 1971 festival was a carefree vacation for me—much different than in 1975 when I worked there for Bill Monroe. That year, musician friends from Iowa City stirred my envy as they partied and sang, while I labored under the watchful eye of my boss. To me, it was like being stuck on a chain gang in the middle of Mardi Gras.

My first exposure to bluegrass at Bean Blossom had cast an irreversible spell on me. I was anxious to become a full-time musician. I was still in school, close to graduation, and I earned a bachelor's degree in graphics in the fall of 1971. Then I got my first "for real" music job: working with a traditional country music show that was being organized by recording artist and local TV personality Larry Heaberlin. A good singer, Heaberlin had made several recordings on the K-ARK label. (One song, "Honda," had been getting lots of airplay—at least on Des Moines–area radio stations.) Heaberlin's country show was to take place in Cutty's Campground just outside of Des Moines.

I discovered during rehearsals that very little bluegrass was to be included in the show, so I quit after only a couple of weeks when I was invited to join a band in Iowa City called the Bluegrass Union. I had become acquainted with the band members earlier that summer when Red Conner and I traveled to Iowa City to participate in an onstage jam session at Bart's Place, a tavern where the Bluegrass Union regularly performed.

After becoming a member of the band I was exposed to the traditionalist views held by fellow Bluegrass Union members Alan Murphy, from Iowa City (fiddle); Carl Hoppe, from Cedar Rapids (guitar); and Billy Britton, from Tennessee (bass). This exposure led to my increased appreciation of Bill Monroe, the man who started it all. Some of the membership of the Bluegrass Union changed while I was in the band. Billy Britton decided to leave and was replaced on bass by Celia Wyckoff, from New Jersey. John Purk, from Toledo, Iowa, joined the group on mandolin. Dave Teeter, who hailed from Peoria, Illinois, became our guitarist. Then we changed the name of our band to Grassfire. Two brothers from the St. Louis area, Dennis Wadlow (mandolin) and Phil Wadlow (guitar), came into the group. Despite all the personnel changes, the focus of the band always remained our devotion to traditional, Monroe-style bluegrass.

Bluegrass music was enjoying a tremendous upswing in popularity partly due to the success of the album *Will the Circle Be Unbroken.* Iowa City is a college town, and the students were enthusiastic about the newly discovered sounds of bluegrass. We provided it for them three nights a week at Bart's Place, which was our primary performance venue. (Before Jack and Betty Bartholomew opened their business, the building had housed a club called Kennedy's, which featured exotic dancers, female impersonators, and comedy acts.) The clientele at Bart's Place included many blue-collar workers as well as college students. Fights often broke out while we played there, but Betty Bartholomew, who was a tough, no-nonsense type of person, always rushed in fearlessly to break up the combatants.

Our band also performed one night a week in an Iowa City establishment called the Mill Restaurant, a restaurant and bar owned and operated by Keith Dempster: bluegrass fan, motorcycle enthusiast, and harmonica player extraordinaire. Keith opened the Mill Restaurant in 1962, and it was (and still is) the best venue for bluegrass and acoustic music in the state of Iowa. Its cozy stage has hosted such great performers as John Hartford, Bela Fleck, Greg Brown, Keith Whitley, Eddie and Martha Adcock, and Norman and Nancy Blake. In addition, it has always been a place for young singers, songwriters, and musicians from all over the Midwest to gain experience and self-assurance in the art of performing in public. Keith encouraged me a lot in my early musical career, and the Mill provided me with a place to hone my stage skills. (The Mill Restaurant is still actively in business today. Pam and Keith Dempster retired from the business in 2003, and the restaurant is now owned by Dan Ouverson and Marty Cristensen.)

We made many friends among the people who attended our performances in Iowa City. Nearly every Friday and Saturday night was spent jamming at someone's house after the show. "Jamming" means getting together informally, and often spontaneously, with other musicians to play for the pure enjoyment of it. Often an exchange of musical ideas takes place. Different musicians have different ideas about jamming. For some, a jam session is a competition in which one musician tries to outdo the others by playing tunes that are challenging, fast, or difficult to follow. I believe that type of musician should be called a jam buster. Often, jam busters are excellent musicians who can't figure out why no one ever wants to jam with them. In my view, jam sessions are about playing music *together*, with communication between musicians being the most important keynote. Sometimes the quest for musical interaction requires playing tunes that are less technically challenging and therefore more open to creative interpretation.

Frequent jam sessions occurred at a "party residence" on Iowa Avenue, where bashes were held almost every weekend. We were always invited to come and play music while sharing in the festivities. One night I brought along one of my favorite records: *Aereo-Plain*. The 1971 album was recorded by John Hartford—instrumentalist, singer, songwriter, author, and riverboat pilot. Hartford (1937–2001) is perhaps best known in bluegrass circles for having brought rock and roll esthetics into bluegrass, creating what has been called "hippiegrass." (Hartford's song "Gentle On My Mind" became a Top 40 hit in 1967 when Glen Campbell recorded it. After that it became one of the most recorded songs in music history, with well over three hundred versions produced over the years.) Our student hosts loved Hartford's album *Aereo-Plain,* and they played it at almost every party. Hartford surprised the members of Grassfire one night by showing up at a local tavern where we were performing. He had just finished playing a show in Iowa City. We asked him to join us, and he got on stage and sat in the rest of the evening. I remember being impressed that he didn't take over the show. He stayed at the back of the stage, playing backup and stepping forward only to play lead solos on his fiddle. He wasn't John Hartford, the star, he was just plain John Hartford, the bluegrass picker. After that night, every time John performed in Iowa City we got together with him at jam sessions, trading musical ideas and telling stories. We developed a friendship that lasted until his life was tragically cut short by cancer in June 2001. John expressed his philosophy of music and life to me once when he said, "I always follow my heart."

Grassfire often served as the warm-up act for shows featuring well-known bluegrass groups touring in the area. For example, we opened the show for Jimmy Martin and the Sunny Mountain Boys at the All-Iowa Fair in Cedar Rapids. One of the most memorable warm-up shows Grassfire performed took place inside the newly built Hancher Auditorium at the University of Iowa in Iowa City on February 23, 1974. An "Evening of Bluegrass" was how the program had been advertised, and the featured acts were Doc and Merle Watson, and Bill Monroe and the Blue Grass Boys. Thrilled and honored to be sharing the stage with such famous entertainers, the band had practiced a set of some of our best material. Smokey McKinnis, a fiddle-playing friend of ours from St. Louis—and one of the most loyal Bill Monroe followers I'd ever met—had just taught us a tune that Bill had recently written: "Jerusalem Ridge." Bill had named the tune after a place near his hometown of Rosine, Kentucky, where he used to run foxhounds when he was a young man. Smokey had learned "Jerusalem Ridge" from listening to Bill play it on a radio broadcast of the Grand Ole Opry. It had a distinctively different original melody in the key of A minor, and it was full of dramatic-sounding chord changes. We were planning to play the tune during our portion of the program. I was secretly hoping to impress Bill with our version. But as we rehearsed it, Kenny Baker, who had been Bill's fiddler for quite some time, entered the dressing room, saying to us: "I wouldn't do that number if I was you, boys. Bill hasn't recorded it yet." So we deleted it from our set list—which was a good thing, because we weren't playing it quite right anyway! (Little did I know that I would be recording "Jerusalem Ridge" with Bill just a few months after that.)

The Blue Grass Boys were scheduled to come on right after our show, and I remember them standing in the wings and listening to part of our program. Kenny Baker told us he liked the tune we finished our set with. (The song was "Southern Filibuster," composed by Dobro player Tut Taylor, who recorded it on his 1972 album, *Friar Tut*. Taylor was one of the band members featured on John Hartford's *Aereo-Plain*.) After the show was over at Hancher Auditorium, I went into Bill's dressing room and shook hands with him. It was the first time I had ever met him personally. We didn't talk much.

I performed with Grassfire until the fall of 1974, when I resigned from the band in order to explore my potential on a wider musical front. (In other words, I got mad and quit.) Celia Wyckoff, the bass player, left the band at the same time I did, and together we paid a visit to Smokey McKinnis at his home in the St. Louis area. When we got there he urged me to try to get a job working for the Old Man (his nickname for Bill Monroe). To help me, he called Bill up on the phone. As I stood by trying to listen to the conversation, I could figure out what was being said. Bill's banjo player had just turned in his resignation. Smokey told him about me, saying I was ready to go to work any time. Bill asked him to send me down to Nashville for an audition. I had been waiting to spread my wings, and now it looked as though I was going to get my chance. Somehow, I knew my life was about to undergo a drastic change.

## My Audition

I drove to Nashville with Celia and she dropped me off for the audition, which took place on the morning of Thursday, September 19, 1974. Bill's business office was located at 726 Sixteenth Avenue South. The street was lined with many houses that had been converted to office buildings containing music-related businesses.

I wanted to make a good impression. I had cut my hair before making the trip; it had been nearly shoulder length. I was dressed in a polyester shirt and slacks, a drastic change from my customary garb of blue jeans and work shirt. I wasn't a bit nervous—I was too young and dumb and cocky to be nervous. I had utmost confidence in my own musical abilities. Indeed, I felt as though I was meant to play music. I naively figured my talent alone was enough to take me to the top.

As I walked into his office, the first thing I noticed was how well dressed Bill looked in his business suit and tie. The second thing I noticed was the large, expensive-looking ring on his finger. It was shaped like a mandolin and studded with diamonds. The gems gleamed brightly in the sunlight shining through one window. A cassette player was squawking on the cluttered shelf behind his desk, playing a tape of a bluegrass band I had never heard before—a cheap recording made at a live show. Bill left it running all during the audition, presumably to see if it would rattle my nerves.

Confidently, I uncased my banjo and played him an old-time tune, "Shelby Rock." I had learned it from a Kenny Baker record, one of many tunes I had studied on Kenny's recordings. Though originally a fiddle tune, the piece had nice possibilities for melodic phrasing on the banjo. Bill registered no reaction, other than an unintelligible grunt, so I decided to play him what I thought was one of his own tunes: "Blue Grass Breakdown." After a minute or two I stopped, waiting for a comment.

"That's fine," he said in his soft tenor. "Of course you've got to be able to play numbers like 'Bill Monroe's Kentucky Mandolin' and the 'Watson Blues.'"

I retuned my banjo to G minor, trying to be quick about it because I knew speed counts when you're playing on stage. Then I played him "Kentucky Mandolin." He said nothing, so I took that for an indication of approval. "The Watson Blues," which I later had the honor of recording with Bill, was a tune I had just learned from a tape loaned to me by Smokey. He had made it from an Opry radio broadcast, and I was now able to play it for Bill, who had cowritten it with guitar legend Doc Watson.

"Okay," said Bill. "We're leaving tonight at 3 A.M. to play a festival in Black Mountain, North Carolina. You got your clothes?"

He was telling me that I was already a Blue Grass Boy. I couldn't believe how quickly he had made up his mind. I concealed my surprise. Not wishing to drop the rhythm of our verbal exchange, I quickly told him I didn't have any stage clothes yet, but I could pick up what I needed later that day. Bill gave me directions to meet him at VanAtta's (located on Dickerson Road, north of Nashville), a small service station whose owner dabbled some in local politics. Bill and his band parked their cars there while on the road. I cased up my banjo and walked back out onto Sixteenth Avenue.

That brief audition was destined to have a lifelong impact on my career. I had just passed my entrance exam, and I had become a full-fledged enrollee in the Bill Monroe School of Music. I felt elated, eager, anxious, and proud—all at the same time. I was looking at the world through different eyes. This was the real thing: I was into it and there was no turning back.

## 2. MY FIRST DAYS AS A BLUE GRASS BOY

When I got to VanAtta's, I found that we wouldn't be taking Bill's tour bus, the Blue Grass Special, because it was having mechanical problems. Instead we would be riding in Bill's station wagon, a brand new shiny red Pontiac Safari with matching red interior. (Later on we occasionally used bass player Randy Davis's Buick station wagon.) Two of the Blue Grass Boys were not present—Randy Davis and Ralph Lewis (who was the guitar player). They both lived in Asheville, North Carolina, which was near Black Mountain, so they were meeting us at the festival.

I felt very aware of my status as a newcomer to the band. There I was: a brand new transplant from the North getting ready to travel three hundred miles across Tennessee and into North Carolina to perform for a southern audience. After being in the Nashville area for only two days, I could already sense the cultural differences between the North and the South. These differences went far beyond the dissimilar speech patterns and vocal inflections characteristic of my fellow band members, as well as of the general population. A distinctively southern way of thinking was rapidly making itself known to me as well. There seemed to be an indifference to the exciting and adventurous aspects of traveling on the road to play music. Practical knowledge—how to work on engines, choose the quickest routes, or find the best truck stops—seemed to carry more importance. Performing music was just part of the job. It was something you didn't talk about very much—you just did it. (Later, I realized my first impression wasn't accurate. The passion for the unusual and creative lifestyle of the traveling musician was definitely there in the other band members—it just didn't show on the surface.)

Dwight Dillman, Bill's then-current banjo player, was behind the wheel of the station wagon. He was still working during his two-week notice before leaving the band. I sat in the back seat with Kenny Baker while Bill rode in the passenger seat up front. We drove in near silence, and Bill fell asleep practically before we were out of Nashville. Both he and Kenny had brought pillows. It had occurred to me to do the same, but I didn't want to appear soft or weak—so I left my pillow at home.

I didn't know it yet, but we would be traveling all over the country in this station wagon because the Blue Grass Special was seldom running. We would be crowded together, all five of us, with our instruments (including a large upright bass), suit bags, suitcases, boxes of records, and hats. When three men sat on the rear bench seat, their combined weight pressed it downward so much that they could noticeably feel the metal framework inside, especially on rough roads. Try sitting on an apple for about three to four hours, and you will understand the sensation. We didn't care though—things like that never dampen the enthusiasm of musicians who are truly dedicated to their art!

We never fastened our seat belts. Compulsory seat-belt laws hadn't been enacted yet, and Bill was opposed to using the belts, often stating his belief that they could trap passengers inside the car if a wreck occurred.

Nobody talked much during the long nighttime hours on the highway. We didn't want to disturb Bill, who frequently slept while we traveled. Often we would drive all night. More than once Bill said, "I like to drive of a night." He never got behind the wheel during tours while I was in the band, but he recalled driving back in the early days, before interstate highways had been constructed. They seldom saw any other vehicles late at night, he said, and the roads were very curvy. He told us he would "straighten the curves" by weaving across the centerline, saving "ten miles out of every hundred." He also said he could drive to any town in the country without looking at a map. In spite of that claim, however, he always kept a road atlas in his station wagon. He bought a new one every year and protected it with a leather holder that he'd purchased at a truck stop.

There was no radio in the vehicle—it had been torn out, leaving an empty square opening in the dashboard. The thought occurred to me more than once that Bill had taken the radio out on purpose, so that we Blue Grass Boys wouldn't have our musical tastes contaminated by hearing any of the commercial music being broadcast over the airwaves. Of course, that's pure speculation on my part. Probably a more realistic explanation was that a radio distracted Bill from the music he listened to in his mind. Many of his songs were written while traveling down the highway. I also think he "played possum," only pretending to be asleep, quite often, just so he could concentrate on the music he was composing mentally.

Three out of the five of us smoked cigarettes, so the air in the station wagon was frequently hazy with smoke. Bill, who was a nonsmoker, never seemed to be bothered by it. Chain-smoking would help keep me awake when I was behind the wheel. (Thankfully, I kicked the smoking habit many years ago.) When I drove I usually had no trouble staying awake during the dark hours, but when dawn arrived I would get sleepy. Once, while driving at night, I swerved to avoid what I thought was a huge hole in the road. It was only a section of blacktop patch, and its darker color fooled me in my sleepy state. We changed drivers shortly after that. Kenny Baker once said, "When you start seeing mules standing in the road, it's time to switch drivers."

We drove all night for my first job with the Blue Grass Boys. In the morning we arrived at the festival. It was held at Monte Vista Park, a facility that was also used as a horse ranch. In those days, bluegrass festivals were not always held in choice spots. Often small farm fields served as festival sites, with showers and flush toilets the exception rather than the rule. This didn't usually matter to bluegrass fans, however, because their passionate devotion to the music transcended all physical discomforts. In this respect the fans were like the musicians. Indeed, many of the fans *were* musicians, and they came to festivals as much to meet and play with other musicians as to see the stage performances. This is still generally true even today. My first bluegrass festival with Bill Monroe, at Monte Vista, was a little better than many of the later ones I worked at, as far as the site itself was concerned. It had a reasonably well-constructed stage with a better-than-average sound system.

I got to meet and visit briefly with my fellow Blue Grass Boys, Ralph Lewis and Randy Davis, before going on stage with them. Ralph and Randy had known each other for a number of years. They had auditioned for Bill at the same time—in July 1974 (shortly before I entered the group). Kenny Baker had called Ralph when Bill was looking for new band members, and Ralph suggested that Randy come along as well to try out for the position of bass player.

Randy, who had just graduated from college with a degree in accounting, had previously performed in a local rock and roll band, a church choir, and his school band. He seemed very confident in his knowledge of

Bill's music, as well as in his own playing ability. He was calm and poised both on and off stage. I felt comfortable around him. He always seemed to know what was going on: when and where we were playing next, what the concert promoters' names were, where to set up the record table, how to communicate with the sound people, and countless other details involving the band. He was very focused. Such was the air of professionalism he projected that I didn't know at the time that Randy had been playing bluegrass for a much shorter time than I had.

In contrast, Ralph Lewis was fun-loving and relaxed—a country-type person who sang and played all the old songs with easy-going skill, knowledge, and soul. He spoke with an accent that reminded me of Andy Griffith. I felt I had known him all my life. Ralph started playing mountain music at the age of six, and had performed with many people, including Tennessean Carl Sauceman (who had been playing and recording this style of music long before it was called "bluegrass") and the Morris Brothers, from North Carolina. (Zeke and Wiley Morris are famous for a 1930s song they wrote that became a standard still played by virtually every bluegrass band today: "Salty Dog Blues.")

Among the other entertainers featured at the festival were Ralph Stanley and his band, the Clinch Mountain Boys. Stanley was a banjo player and singer who, along with his brother Carter, had pioneered bluegrass music from its earliest days. I was a huge fan of Stanley's music, and it was a special thrill to get to play on the same show with him for the first time. His keen, hard-edged banjo style was a major influence on me in my early years of learning to play the instrument. Ralph had developed the style early in his career. His playing differed from that of Earl Scruggs in a number of ways. He often used his index finger to play melody notes, while Scruggs relied more heavily on his thumb for playing melody, and Stanley played closer to the bridge (the thin piece of wood that raises the strings above the circular top of the banjo head), which resulted in a sharp, staccato sound. Stanley also seemed to experiment less than Scruggs did—he didn't branch out into other genres of music besides traditional mountain-style bluegrass.

Dwight Dillman and I both played our banjos on the Monte Vista show. (Bill called every performance a show. He hated the word "gig.") We took turns at the instrumental banjo solos. Our performances went well, and I was grateful for the chance to ease into the job. The audience was very good, and they made me feel welcome, which meant a great deal, since I was only twenty-five, a stranger, a greenhorn, and dog-tired from lack of sleep. I began to feel like a real Blue Grass Boy.

The following day we returned to the Nashville area and performed an outdoor show at Middle Tennessee State University in Murfreesboro. The audience was a mix of age groups, and I recall that their response to our performance was one of cordial acceptance, though not marked by wild enthusiasm.

The next day—Sunday, September 22—we headed to Parker's Lake, Kentucky to perform at a western-style theme park called Tombstone Junction. The park, constructed in the 1950s, was a popular tourist site during the 1970s. (It burned down in 1989; nothing was left but the park's train ride.) While we were waiting backstage before our show, Bill composed a tune on his mandolin and began playing it with us. I improvised a banjo solo, trying my best to do justice to the melody. The first part had a sort of yodeling sound, and the second part flowed smoothly, using sustained notes. Bill named the tune "Tombstone Junction." I was impressed—it was the first of many songs I witnessed the birth of during my tenure with the Father of Bluegrass.

Those first three days with the band had been challenging and scary for me. My original cockiness was transformed into a mixture of self-consciousness, and uncertainty about whether I truly wanted to be a Blue Grass Boy. I began to realize that the job carried with it several difficult requirements. I would have to make some tough sacrifices, not the least of which would be giving up my own musical style in order to blend in with Bill's sound.

Bill had seemed to me quite intimidating with his formal bearing and business-like attitude, and I had been looking anxiously for something to soften that impression. The creation of the song "Tombstone Junction" opened my eyes. When Bill crafted that tune and played it with us, I saw his true personality. He wasn't strictly business after all. He loved making music. Everything else he did was simply a means to that end. My faith in Bill and in his music remained firm.

When we returned to VanAtta's after my first three days of shows, Bill asked me, "How much do I owe you?" I had never asked Bill how much he paid his sidemen—I was so excited about just getting the job that I hadn't even thought about the salary. Fortunately the other Blue Grass Boys had told me how much money I would be making: starting pay was musician's union scale, fifty dollars per day, on days that shows were actually played. We weren't paid for travel days when no performances took place. Bill always asked how much he owed me when we got home from a road trip. I would figure it out ahead of time so I could tell him. Looking back, I now realize that Bill would probably have been willing to negotiate on the payment—but I was too green and scared to even think about haggling with him.

Bill invariably paid in cash, and he seemed to have rolls of bills in every pocket. It was fascinating to watch him pull bills out of various pockets as he was paying someone he had hired. I heard him once say that he didn't think flashing lots of money around was a very good idea: "That's what got Stringbeans killed." "Stringbeans" was David Akeman's stage name, which was later shortened to "Stringbean." The first banjo player ever to be a member of the Blue Grass Boys, Stringbean often kept thousands of dollars in the pockets of his overalls, showing it to many people. In 1973 he and his wife were both killed by burglars in their home. Many people, including Bill, believed Stringbean's death was the result of his lack of discretion in flashing large sums of money around in public. Bill's actions didn't seem to agree with his words, however. I often observed him showing off large denomination bills in public. In addition, I saw paper sacks full of money sitting around after shows in Bill's motel room, in the station wagon, or on the bus. Bill would leave thousands of dollars completely unattended. No money was ever stolen, though, as far as I know.

## The Grand Ole Opry

I'll never forget my first night at the Grand Ole Opry with the Blue Grass Boys. The country music radio show, already close to fifty years old, had been in its new location for only six months when I first performed there. (On opening night at the new Opry House—March 16, 1974—President Richard M. Nixon made an appearance. He played a few songs on the piano and took an onstage yo-yo lesson from Roy Acuff. A visit from Alabama governor George Wallace also highlighted the evening.) The brand-spanking-new Opry House gleamed with polished modernity. It was the centerpiece of Opryland, U.S.A., the family entertainment park in which it was situated. Though the park was closed in 1997, the Grand Ole Opry itself remains in the same location. For three previous decades, the Opry's home had been the historic Ryman Auditorium in downtown Nashville. The new Opry House could accommodate bigger crowds, had better parking facilities, and was much more comfortable with its cushioned seats and air-conditioning. In addition, it boasted many technological improvements—better lighting, improved sound equipment, and modern television capabilities. There were many, however, including me, who felt that the new building wasn't nearly as "holy" as the old Ryman Auditorium, which had been popularly considered the "Mother Church" of country music. The fact that the Ryman was originally a tabernacle may have helped to create this sense, but the real reason for the sentiment was the long string of country music legends that had performed there. (The Ryman was renovated in 1993 and reopened the following year as a performance hall and museum.)

The date of my first night at the Opry was Saturday, September 21, 1974 (only two days after my audition). Kenny Baker gave me directions to the performers' parking lot. I gave my name to the security guard at the gate, proudly saying that I worked for Bill Monroe. After I got my car parked, I walked into the artists' entrance. Inside I found Norman Van Dame, a long-time Opry staff person, sitting at the desk where all entertainers checked in as they arrived. Mr. Van Dame had been with the Opry for so many years he had become a fixture—and a beloved friend to all of the performers. He always took time to visit with the entertainers for a while before directing them back to their dressing rooms. I informed Mr. Van Dame that I was playing with Bill Monroe. After looking over his list, he told me which room had been assigned to Bill and the Blue Grass Boys.

Backstage, the halls and dressing rooms were buzzing with activity. Opry square-dance girls in brightly hued skirts tapped up and down the backstage hallways in their dancing shoes. Country singers in colorful costumes walked about on their way to and from the stage. Porter Wagoner was there, wearing a sequin-covered suit with pictures of wagon wheels on it. Ernie Ashworth, whose song "Talk Back Trembling Lips" had received lots of radio airplay, sported a suit decorated with giant red lips. I quickly realized that Bill Monroe and the Blue Grass Boys were among the most conservatively dressed performers at the Opry. Plain suits and ties were normal stage attire for Bill and his band. I often heard him say, "I was the first man to wear a suit and tie on the Grand Ole Opry." He had always tried to fight the hillbilly or clown image often associated with country music. Acoustic string band music (in which bluegrass was deeply rooted) was especially prone to the hillbilly label, and Bill wanted his music to be respected. That was part of the reason he had such a solemn demeanor on stage—he wanted his audiences to think of bluegrass as a serious and bona fide musical art form. (I could only imagine what he would have thought of the names of the bluegrass bands I had cut my teeth on—the Scottsville Squirrel Barkers and Homer and the Barnstormers.)

I found my way to the dressing room designated that night for Bill and the Blue Grass Boys. In those days, dressing room assignments at the Opry changed from week to week, depending on who was performing on any given evening. (The only exception was dressing room #1—closest to the stage. That one was permanently assigned to Roy Acuff.) We tuned up in our dressing room and rehearsed until it was time for Bill's portion of the show.

Walking out on stage, we stood behind the closed curtain and waited for Bill to be introduced. My nerves were as taut as the strings on my banjo. When the curtain opened I felt a rush of excitement, and then the spotlight was on us. I heard the thunder of countless numbers of hands clapping. Ralph Lewis picked out three lead-in guitar notes, low, strong, and deliberate, before Kenny Baker began to play his fiddle. The tune was "Watermelon Hangin' on the Vine"—Bill Monroe's Opry theme song—and Kenny led us through it above the chop of Bill's rhythm mandolin. As was always the case when I was on stage with Bill, it seemed that my banjo played itself. The notes rolled out with unstoppable momentum. There was no way a musician could stray from Bill's rhythm. It was clear, dominant, and driving. The tune charged on toward its quick conclusion, setting the tone for Bill's portion of the show.

After the applause died down, Bill announced the names of all the Blue Grass Boys. He introduced me as "Bob Black, a wonderful banjo player

Bill Monroe and the Blue Grass Boys on stage at the Grand Ole Opry, Nashville, Tennessee, September 28, 1974. *Left to right:* Kenny Baker, Bob Black, Bill Monroe, Randy Davis, and Ralph Lewis. Photo by Les Leverett. (Used by permission.)

from the great state of Iowa, where the corn really grows tall!" We played "Monroe's Hornpipe"—a fast tune in the key of A that has lots of melody notes and quick chord changes. It was one of my favorite tunes, and I was in heaven when I played my solo and heard the applause from the Opry audience.

Leaving the stage after our portion of the show, I was awestruck at the sight of some of the biggest stars in country music mingling around the stage area. Hank Snow, Ernest Tubb, Roy Acuff, Minnie Pearl, Grandpa Jones, Little Jimmy Dickens, Porter Wagoner—all standing close enough to touch. It seemed unbelievable to me, and I was aware that they all knew and respected Bill Monroe and the Blue Grass Boys. I wouldn't have traded places with anyone that night.

We played the Opry many times while I was with Bill and the Blue Grass Boys. One of the most memorable nights for me was Wednesday, October 15, 1975, when we played at the Opry's 50th birthday celebration. After the shows, all the performers came out on stage and stood together before taking a final bow. I was proud to be standing among the legendary Opry stars. The evening was a real musical milestone for me.

One evening, at the end of our portion of an Opry program, Bill turned to me and said, "Play the 'Pike County Breakdown'" (a tune Bill had written, he said, in honor of the town of Pikeville, Kentucky). I knew we only had a minute or two of time left, so I jumped right into the tune as fast as I could. Unfortunately, I wasn't in the right key—I was still in B, the key of the previous song. We finished the tune, and then played the theme song, closing our part of the show. As we walked offstage, Kenny Baker said to me, "You didn't even know you were in the wrong key, did you?" He was laughing. That's when I first realized it. The entire band had improvised to match the key I was in, but Bill never said a word to me about it.

I can still picture the evening Bill showed up at the Opry missing the upper plate of his dentures. It seems he had been getting them repaired and had sent a boy to go pick them up. The kid dropped them, the plate broke, and Bill had to perform on the Grand Ole Opry with half his false teeth missing.

It was at the Grand Ole Opry that I first introduced Bill to my parents. Mom and Dad had made the eleven-hour-plus drive to Music City, and I took them both to our Opry performance. They sat right on stage, at the back, among other special guests. When I took them to meet Bill, I felt just like a schoolboy at an open house, introducing my parents to my teacher. During the course of his conversation with Bill, my dad, aware that Bill had performed in Shenandoah, Iowa, mentioned the fact that Ike

Bill Monroe and the Blue Grass Boys on stage at the Grand Ole Opry, October 16, 1974 (the Opry's forty-ninth birthday). *Left to right:* Kenny Baker, Bob Black, Bill Monroe, Ralph Lewis, and Randy Davis. Photo by Les Leverett. (Used by permission.)

Everly had recently passed away (October 21, 1975). Dad remembers Bill reflecting on the news for a few moments before saying, "It comes to us all." Everyone who knew Bill could see that thoughts of death frequently occupied his mind. He wrote many songs about the passing of loved ones, the approach of old age, or the prospect of eternal life hereafter. One of his most often-used expressions was, "Time waits for no man."

During our Opry performances we often played old-time fiddle tunes that Bill had learned from his Uncle Pen. (Many of them were recorded on Bill's 1972 album, *Bill Monroe's Uncle Pen* [MCA 500].) Tunes such as "Methodist Preacher" with its relaxed, meandering melody, and "Goin' Up Caney" with its ghostly minor chorus crowned by Bill's powerful falsetto, were featured many times in our shows. One fiddle tune, "Poor White Folks," had words that Bill sang to me after we finished playing it one night:

> Poor white folks ain't treatin' me right.
> Ain't gonna get no supper tonight.
> I'm getting' mad, I'm gonna fight.
> Poor white folks ain't treatin' me right.

After one of our shows at the Opry I asked Bill if his theme song, "Watermelon Hangin' on the Vine," had words. (This was before I realized that the Monroe Brothers had recorded it in the 1930s.) Bill sang a verse to me:

See that watermelon smilin' through the fence?
How I wish that melon was mine.
White folks they am foolish or they haven't got a lot of sense,
Or they wouldn't leave that melon on the vine.

Years later, when I heard the rest of the words, I realized one of the verses was about stealing watermelons:

Went to get that melon, was on one Sat'day night.
The stars they had just begun to shine.
When I left that old man's field I left there on the run,
But I didn't leave that melon on the vine.

Talk about your apples, your peaches and your pears.
Simmons am very very fine.
Bless your heart, my honey, you am the gal for me,
But I'd rather have that melon on the vine.

(Chorus)
Hambone am sweet, chicken am good.
Rabbit am so very, very fine (good to me).
Gimme, oh, gimme, oh, how I wish you would
That watermelon hangin' on the vine.[1]

The honor and distinction of performing on the Grand Ole Opry far outweighed for me the meager pay I received. The standard wage for sidemen was thirty-three dollars per show, with two shows being the norm for a Saturday night. (We picked up our checks later at the Musician's Union building.) Despite the low pay, the thrill of stepping on stage in front of a capacity audience and hearing the thunderous roar of the applause, as well as the satisfying sense of belonging to a part of country music's most prestigious gathering of artists, was ample reward in itself.

## Bluegrass East, South, and West

October 1974 started with a trip to Florida, where we performed at the Third Annual Florida State Bluegrass Music Convention in Middleburg. We were back in Nashville on October 16 to play at the Early Bird Bluegrass Show in the Grand Ole Opry House. Also called the Early Bird Bluegrass Special, the concert was held every year at the beginning of the annual DJ Convention in Nashville. It featured many of the top bluegrass bands in the country, and gave them a rare chance to appear on the Opry stage.

On October 19, we went to Steele, Alabama, to play at the Horse Pens Fourth Bluegrass Festival. The place the festival was held had gotten its name during the Civil War, when settlers kept their horses in natural sandstone pens to protect them from Union soldiers. The forty-acre area became known as Horse Pens Forty. It got quite chilly the evening we performed, and even Bill had trouble moving his fingers.

Southern California was next on our October agenda. Bill Monroe's Second Annual Golden West Bluegrass Festival was held in Norco, at a place called Silver Lakes Park. We drove there in a motor home belonging to Bill's son, James Monroe, and were thankful to make the long trip in something other than the cramped station wagon.

Bill was working on a great new tune he had just written, and he played it a lot on our way to the California festival. I was having a difficult time learning it. Bill had a tricky way of jumping in ahead of the beat at the beginning of the second part, and then holding an A note with a tremolo

Bill Monroe and Marty Stuart playing a twin mandolin solo at Bill Monroe's Second Annual Golden West Bluegrass Festival, Norco, California, October 1974. *In the background:* former Blue Grass Boy Byron Berline (*left*) and Bob Black (*right*). Photo by John Averill. (Used by permission.)

Gospel grand finale at Bill Monroe's Second Annual Golden West Bluegrass Festival, Norco, California, October 27, 1974. The group includes Bill Monroe and the Blue Grass Boys, Ralph Stanley and the Clinch Mountain Boys, and the McClain Family. Photo by John Averill. (Used by permission.)

(a playing technique that involves moving the pick up and down to pluck the string many times in rapid succession) until the rhythm caught up. I was still working on it after we arrived at the festival site in Norco.

A young mandolin player by the name of Marty Stuart, who was to achieve major fame as a country singer in the early 1990s, was at the festival. He was a member of Lester Flatt's group the Nashville Grass, and he was a strong admirer of Bill Monroe. He dropped by the motor home for a visit, and Bill played his new tune, asking Stuart if he had any ideas for a title. "Why don't you call it 'The Golden West'?" replied Marty. "Okay, that'd be fine," said Bill. He played the tune a lot for the next several weeks, and I finally learned it on the banjo. Today I perform it on many shows, but I still don't jump ahead of the beat in as slick a way as Bill did. Bill recorded it long after I left the band—it can be heard on his 1985 album *Bill Monroe and Stars of the Bluegrass Hall of Fame* (MCA 5625).

On October 31, while we were traveling near Payson, Arizona, I asked Bill if he would write a banjo tune for me. To my delight, he put together a real gem of a song. The melody had a lively, happy feeling, like a wild horse running free. He named it "Racin' Through Payson." After Bill played it for me, he said, "Now Bob, whenever you play this tune you should always say, 'This here's a tune about a hoss race through Payson, Arizona, called "Racin' Through Payson"'." And that's how I always introduce it.

That Payson, Arizona trip had some logistical issues that made it different from the other journeys we took. Bill was putting on a festival there himself, which he called the First Annual Arizona Bill Monroe Bluegrass Festival. It took place November 1–3. Bill was scheduled to perform there on November 1. He was also booked to play November 2–3 at a bluegrass festival in Fort Pierce, Florida. There was no way we could drive the motor home to Florida in time to play at the festival in Fort Pierce if we all took part in Bill's show at Payson. We dropped Bill and Kenny (Bill's sideman of choice) at the festival in Payson on October 31, and the rest of the Blue Grass Boys drove down to Florida. Bill and Kenny later took a plane to Florida to join the rest of us in time for our shows in Fort Pierce.

Ralph, Randy, and I had fun traveling to Florida: we were on our own—without the boss around—driving across the country on Interstate 10 in a cushy motor home. I can still remember the beauty of the mountains near Las Cruces, New Mexico, gilded by the early morning sunlight as we passed south of them before stopping in El Paso, Texas, for breakfast. Another highlight of that trip was a restaurant near New Orleans, where we enjoyed some genuine Cajun food.

Back in Payson, Bill asked other musicians to fill in for his missing Blue Grass Boys. He got Johnny Montgomery (who played with Lester Flatt) on bass; Jack Cooke (of Ralph Stanley's Clinch Mountain Boys) on guitar; and Wayne Shrubsall (who had won the banjo contest earlier at the festival) on banjo.

Shrubsall told me an amusing story about the way in which Bill asked him to play banjo on the show. The temperature in Payson was dropping, and it had begun to snow. Bill was warming his hands over a fire where Shrubsall happened to be standing. Bill turned to him and asked, "Have you been playing your banjo a lot lately?" Shrubsall told him yes, he had been. Bill then turned away, ignoring Shrubsall for a few minutes as he continued warming his hands by the fire. Suddenly he turned again, asking: "Does your banjo keep pretty good tune?" Shrubsall said yes, it stayed in tune real well. Again, Bill didn't say anything for a long time. He continued nonchalantly warming his hands. Then he turned a third time, asking: "Would you help me out on the show?" Shrubsall's jaw dropped in surprise before he enthusiastically agreed.

Shrubsall remembers that show well. At one point in their performance, Bill asked him to kick off the song "Molly and Tenbrooks." Shrubsall mistakenly began playing a different tune, "Big Ball in Boston," which he had heard former Blue Grass Boy Del McCoury perform at a festival in Hugo, Oklahoma shortly before that. He was a little confused because he didn't know what key Bill was moving into until the last moment, when Kenny whispered hoarsely to him, "Quick—get into B." While Shrubsall was playing, Bill was frowning—but he smiled too. Shrubsall asked Kenny why the band wasn't playing the same chords, and Kenny told him that it was because he was playing "Big Ball in Boston." Abashed, he waited until Kenny played a fiddle solo on the song, and then he said to Bill, "I'll get it right this time coming around." Bill just nodded. Shrubsall did get it right on the next banjo solo, and Bill said with a grin, "*Now* you got it." Later in the show, Shrubsall played a banjo solo on "Footprints in the Snow," and Bill beamed again, apparently either because he got it right or because he didn't blow it!

The First Annual Arizona Bill Monroe Bluegrass Festival in Payson was also the Last Annual Arizona Bill Monroe Bluegrass Festival. He wasn't very pleased with the small attendance or the cold weather. He did return to Arizona, however, in October 1978, when he played at Old Tucson—a western movie location in the desert outside the city of Tucson. In addition to being a scene for making movies, Old Tucson occasionally served as a venue for bluegrass and western music festivals.

In January 1975 we traveled back to California, performing on the UCLA campus on January 10, and at the Palomino Club in North Hollywood on January 11. Opening for Bill at the Palomino Club that night was the Great American Music Band, featuring David Grisman on mandolin and former Blue Grass Boy Richard Greene on fiddle. Bob Dylan was in the audience, and after our set he came into the darkened backstage area and shook hands with all the Blue Grass Boys. "I heard you out there," he solemnly told me. Dylan had been a Bill Monroe fan for a long time, and he especially liked the early recordings of Bill and his brother Charlie. I overheard him talking to Bill about possibly traveling around with the Blue Grass Boys at some future date. I'm sure he assumed that the Father of Bluegrass had an operating tour bus. It would have been awfully crowded in the station wagon with six people. (I've sometimes wondered how Bob Dylan would have liked sitting on the "apple"of the back bench seat.)

Fiddler and former Blue Grass Boy Byron Berline was also present that evening. He told us that Jerry Garcia of the Grateful Dead had really wanted to attend the performance, but his tour schedule wouldn't allow it. He said Garcia had been a bluegrass banjo player for some time and was a big fan of Bill Monroe's. He had even expressed a desire to become a Blue Grass Boy himself.

We paid a visit to the famous clothing store called Nudie's on Lankershim Boulevard in Hollywood. Founded by tailor Nudie Cohn, Nudie's Clothing Store is the place where distinctive outfits have been purchased by numerous movie and country-music stars since the 1950s. Some of Nudie's more famous customers have been Elvis Presley, Gene Autry, John Lennon, Hank Snow, Hank Williams Sr., and Ronald Reagan. (Nudie passed away in 1984, at the age of 81.) At Nudie's, Bill purchased a leather Kentucky-style hat. He wore the hat for quite some time after that, becoming very fond of it. Once he left it in a restaurant, and sent a couple of us back almost a hundred miles to retrieve it. When we got to the cafe we couldn't find the hat, so we asked a waitress if she'd seen it. Pointing to the top of the jukebox, she said, "Is that it?" We saw Bill's hat sitting there—someone had placed it in a fitting location! In May 1976, *Country Music Magazine* published a cover story on Bill, entitled "Bill Monroe, the Bossman and His Blues." Bill was wearing this same hat in the cover photo.

On November 23 we performed out west again—at the Armadillo Club (also called Armadillo World Headquarters) in Austin, Texas. The opening act was a group called Greezy Wheels. The audience was spirited and enthusiastic, and the smell of marijuana was quite noticeable—although Bill never said anything about it. During our performance we could hear thunder outside, and the sound of rain pelting against the roof. Several inches of rain fell and the entire area got flooded. When the show was over we had to wade through water standing knee-deep in the parking lot to get to the bus. Of course, we never took our shoes off—we knew Bill wouldn't like it if the Blue Grass Boys were seen going around barefoot.

## A Cluster of Pickers

One very special feature of every Bill Monroe festival was the grand finale. Bill's show was usually the last one on the program; after we finished our set he would get many of the bands that had performed earlier to join us on stage to play some bluegrass favorites. It was a massive onstage jam session, and everyone, singers as well as musicians, would get a turn at the microphone. Bill always wanted the Blue Grass Boys to maintain a highly visible presence during these finales. He let me know this once during a show when there were a particularly large number of banjo players. I was trying to be considerate, allowing all of them to get a chance at the microphone, so I moved to the back of the stage. Bill gave me a sharp look and said something like, "You're not helpin' me any." I think Bill wanted the Blue Grass Boys to remain up front to convey the impression of being in charge—even though the entire segment was mostly ruled by disorganized chaos.

During the confusion there would often be two, three, and even four banjos playing an instrumental break at the same time, some in harmony with the others, on tunes such as "John Henry" or "Swing Low, Sweet Chariot." The fiddlers would all play their breaks together as well, and sometimes other mandolin players would join Bill in a multi-mandolin chorus.

The grand finale would always end with an extended gospel medley that usually included a few standards such as "Will The Circle Be Unbroken," "I'll Fly Away," and "I Saw The Light." Bill would clap his hands and the audience would clap along. Then Bill would draw the audience into the chorus by raising his arm and beckoning to them with a motion of his hand, and they would start singing along. When the last chorus was reached, Bill would warn the audience that the song was about to slow down and come to an end by using a very effective hand signal: he would reach up into the air and pretend to be pulling a brake lever on a train. Audiences always loved that.

## Bluegrass Goes to Japan

Bill Monroe had a large international following, and nowhere was there a greater outpouring of affection for him than in Japan. Several Japanese bluegrass bands had made appearances in the United States prior to Bill's first trip to that country, including Crying Time in 1972, the Lost City Cats in 1973, and Appleseed in 1974. One of the earliest Japanese bands to perform in the United States was Bluegrass 45. Formed in 1967, Bluegrass 45 had performed as the house band in a small club called Lost City in Kobe, Japan. They made a self-produced album in 1969 titled *Run Mountain*. In 1971, Bluegrass 45 toured the United States from June through September. They played at Bean Blossom that year, in addition to other festivals, and recorded two albums for the Rebel record label (*Bluegrass 45* and *Caravan*). After their 1971 American tour, Bluegrass 45 banjo player Saburo Inoue and his brother Toshio (who played bass for the group) started B.O.M Service, a record sales company that today does business all over the world. Another member of Bluegrass 45, fiddler Hsueh-Cheng Liao, joined Saburo in becoming part of the staff of the first Japanese bluegrass magazine, *June Apple*. In 1983, Saburo started another acoustic music magazine, *Moonshiner*, which is still flourishing today.

I was fortunate enough to visit Japan twice during my stint as a Blue Grass Boy. The first trip took place during December 1974. It was Bill's first visit there, and it was my first trip *anywhere* outside of the United States. November was spent making preparations for the trip. We had jobs to play that month as well, including the South Louisiana Bluegrass Festival in Folsom, Louisiana; the South Georgia Bluegrass Festival in Waycross, Georgia; and the Fifth Annual South Carolina State Bluegrass Festival in Myrtle Beach, South Carolina.

I had to get my passport before leaving for Japan, and Bill arranged for the photo to be taken by Les Leverett, one of Nashville's finest country music photographers. I don't think I've had a passport photo since then that looked as good as that one! Vaccinations were also required prior to international flights back in those days. Bill, Kenny, and I went to a Nashville hospital together to get ours.

We flew coach class. (Bill never flew first class, at least while I was with

Bill Monroe rehearsing backstage with the Blue Grass Boys at Kyouritsu Hall, Kanda (in Tokyo), Japan, December 10, 1974. *Left to right:* Kenny Baker, Ralph Lewis, Bob Black, Randy Davis, and Bill Monroe. Photo by Nobuharu Komoriya. (Used by permission.)

Bill Monroe and the Blue Grass Boys in concert at Kyoto Kaikan Hall, Kyoto, Japan, December 12, 1974. *Left to right:* Kenny Baker, Bob Black, Bill Monroe, Randy Davis, and Ralph Lewis. Photo by Nobuharu Komoriya. (Used by permission.)

him, and somehow I respected him for that.) Ralph and I checked our instruments through to Tokyo, while Bill and Kenny stowed theirs in the overhead luggage compartments. We all had our hats with us, which were also placed in the overhead bins. Smoking was allowed on the flight, and there were quite a few empty seats on the longest leg of our journey—from Honolulu to Tokyo—so the trip was reasonably comfortable for us. We did run into a freakish air disturbance at one point, which caused our plane to lose altitude at an alarming rate. We experienced what seemed like a plummeting free fall for several seconds, and one of the passengers screamed. Shortly afterwards, the plane began to climb again and we all breathed easier. I noticed how much the wings seemed to flex up and down during flight, which I remarked on to Ralph. He replied, "Yeah, they're floppin' like a turkey buzzard."

The day we arrived in Japan, Bill wrote a beautiful tune called "The Tokyo Moonlight Waltz," which we played on several of our concerts. The melody had a quiet, meditative feeling that conjured up impressionistic images of Japan. The overall mood of the piece was distinctively Japanese.

I still perform that waltz today with my wife Kristie, who plays guitar and sings in our band, Banjoy.

We played five shows in Japan on our first trip (six if you include an impromptu performance to a standing-room-only crowd at the Hillbilly Coffee Shop in Osaka). Two performances took place in Tokyo, one at Kyouritsu Hall on December 10 and another at Sugino Hall on December 14. We played twice in Osaka; both shows were held at Mainichi Hall, on December 11 and December 13. We also played in Kyoto on December 12, at Kyoto Kaikan Hall.

Each show was sold out in advance. The American group Crosby, Stills, Nash, and Young was performing at the same concert venues, one day ahead of us at each location. (They were having a reunion tour—one of several they conducted during the mid-1970s.) Ticket prices were higher for Crosby, Stills, Nash, and Young, but the Father of Bluegrass was also filling the auditoriums. Each of Bill's shows sold out within two days, even at a ticket price of fifty-five hundred yen (around forty dollars)—quite expensive for that time.

Bob Black at Mainichi Hall, Umeda (in Osaka), Japan, December 13, 1974. Photo by Nobuharu Komoriya. (Used by permission.)

We heard several wonderful Japanese bluegrass bands. A few groups were opening acts on our shows. Others played at restaurants, coffee shops, and hotel lounges where we stayed. The group members were truly excellent musicians, and they included many of Bill's songs in their shows. One banjo player impressed Bill so much that he brought him over to show me the "right" way to play "Molly and Tenbrooks."

Everywhere Bill and the Blue Grass Boys went in Japan, we were given royal treatment. At the end of every show, young women walked on stage and presented each of us with bouquets of flowers. It wasn't long before our hotel rooms were overflowing with sweet-smelling blossoms. Crowds mobbed us both before and after each concert, and the security staff often had to lock us in our dressing rooms for our own protection.

Serving as our guide on that trip was Everett Lilly, of the famous Lilly Brothers duo from Beckley, West Virginia. They had brought their close-harmony singing and traditional mountain-style bluegrass to Japan before—in 1973—and had become tremendously popular among Japanese bluegrass fans. (The Lilly brothers weren't the first Americans to play bluegrass in Japan. Groups from the United States who performed on

Bob Black and Bill Monroe at Sugino Hall, Meguro (in Tokyo), Japan, December 14, 1974. Photo by Nobuharu Komoriya. (Used by permission.)

earlier tours in that country included Flatt and Scruggs in 1968, and the Country Gentlemen in 1972.)

Everett Lilly introduced Bill and the Blue Grass Boys on stage at most of our shows. He was down-to-earth, likeable, and talkative. He spoke with pride of how he had converted one of the tour's principal promoters, Robert Tainaka, to Christianity. Tainaka was an entrepreneur who owned several businesses, among them a department store in Tokyo. He gave us a tour of that business one afternoon, and presented each of us with a Seiko watch from the jewelry department. The other major promoter of the tour was Jerry Tainaka, Robert's brother. Both Robert and Jerry were bluegrass and mountain musicians—among Japan's earliest practitioners of those musical art forms. They had also brought to that country such top bluegrass and acoustic music acts as Jim and Jesse, J. D. Crowe and the New South, and Doc Watson.

We were given many other gifts in addition to the expensive Seiko watches, including colorful umbrellas constructed of wood and paper, silk scarves, and beautiful dolls dressed in traditional Japanese attire.

At one point during the tour, Bill told us, "I did something last night I've never done before." We were all ears, waiting for him to continue. Then he said, "I washed a shirt out by hand in the sink." Though our tour was mostly organized quite well, keeping our clothes laundered was a problem that hadn't been adequately addressed. We never saw a single Laundromat. We had to wash out our socks and underwear by hand, hanging them to dry over radiators and lampshades. Randy rolled his socks in a towel, and then twisted the towel up tightly. When he opened up the towel, the socks were almost dry.

Bill and the Blue Grass Boys experienced many aspects of Japanese scenery, customs, and culture during our time there. Our tour included several visits to historic shrines such as the Gold Pavilion near Kyoto—built in 1397 and reconstructed in 1964. We discovered the uniquely introspective quietude found in Japanese gardens. We saw Mount Fuji, the highest mountain in Japan and one of the most well-known symbols of that beautiful country.

We were impressed with the efficiency of Japan's mass-transit system. During our travels between performances we were introduced to Japan's high-speed railways. The lightning-fast "bullet trains" reached speeds of over two hundred kilometers per hour. (Every passenger car had a large analog speedometer displaying current velocity.)

We enjoyed superb western-style dining at the hotels in which we stayed. Delicious curries and seafood were often served, and I discovered that I loved prawns. We also ate several traditional Japanese meals, during which we took our shoes off and sat in our stocking feet on the floor around low tables as the food was brought to us. (This time we didn't worry about being shoeless—we weren't in Austin, Texas, anymore.) I first learned to eat with chopsticks at one of these traditional meals. We all tried using them. Randy Davis was the best chopstick handler among us. Bill was pretty successful with them too, but he, like the rest of us, found forks and knives more to his liking.

We experienced a minor earthquake while staying at the Okura hotel in Osaka—it only lasted a few seconds, but we felt our room shake and saw the curtains waving back and forth over the windows. (I guess I was too young to feel any sense of danger during the earth tremor—if it happened today I'd probably go running from the building.)

We made many friends and created lifelong memories on our first trip to Japan. Bill was pleased to count the Japanese people among his most sincere and enthusiastic fans.

Bill never walked out on stage with a script. His musical performances weren't planned out ahead of time. Many entertainers (including me) write themselves a list of the songs they intend to play during their show, along with the key in which each song is to be played. Performing came naturally for Bill, however, it was as much a part of his life as eating or sleeping. He never told us what key the songs would be in before he announced them to the audience. He just introduced the title and away we would go. I'm indeed grateful that he had the consummate sideman, Kenny Baker. Kenny started, or "kicked off" almost every number, and he very seldom forgot what key the song was supposed to be in. I guess that's one reason Bill called him the Greatest Fiddler in Bluegrass.

Randy Davis's bass playing was something the whole band could always count on too. Unfamiliar numbers never seemed to faze him. He had an inherent spontaneity that carried him over any rough spots the rest of us might encounter. He never lost his cool, and he possessed a great deal of rhythmic precision—important when playing Bill's music. Wrong notes may sometimes go unnoticed as long as they're played with the proper timing. Though Randy generally remained in the background, he played the crucial role of maintaining a smooth flow throughout every performance. During shows, he communicated verbally with Bill off-microphone, suggesting what songs to do next, letting him know how much time was left, and making private little jokes to ease the tension.

One problem associated with live stage performances involves keeping the instruments in tune. To make it easier to play in different keys, most banjoists and guitarists use a gadget called a capo—an adjustable clamp that goes across the fingerboard. Since I wasn't always certain in which key Bill would want to play the next song, I sometimes had to scramble to get my capo placed in time before Kenny started playing a number. Banjos are notoriously hard to keep in tune, and placing a capo across the strings often makes the instrument go sharp. To make matters worse, the banjo's fifth string, which is shorter than the other four, has to have a separate capo. This can be either a special fifth-string capo, which is what I used, or a small set of hooks (model railroad spikes) placed in the fingerboard under which to slip the string in order to raise its pitch. In a perfect world, there would be plenty of time between songs to make fine adjustments in the tuning when a capo is used on the banjo. However, as a Blue Grass Boy I had to learn to be quick—sometimes at the expense of accuracy. Fortunately, I got better at it as I went along.

Dealing with minor emergencies became commonplace for me. One afternoon at the Bean Blossom festival I knelt down beside a tree to uncase my banjo. I was on my way to the stage; our show was scheduled to start about five minutes later. When I opened my banjo case I discovered, to my horror, that the tailpiece—the metal bracket behind the bridge to which all the strings were attached—had come loose. The nut that held it in place had disengaged and fallen inside the banjo. That meant that the bridge, located on the front of the instrument and normally held in place by the taut strings that crossed over it, was free to shift around or fall off completely. The band we were following on the program had only a couple of songs left to do in their show. In frantic haste, I removed the thumbscrews attaching the resonator to the back of my banjo in order to retrieve the small tailpiece nut. I found the nut and reattached the tailpiece to the banjo, tightening it by hand. Then I retuned all the strings and ran up on stage just as Bill was being introduced. I had some tuning problems on the show due to my jury-rigging of the tailpiece, but at least I was able to get through the performance.

Bill always warmed up his voice backstage right before the shows by singing notes softly to himself, in his upper range. The sound he made was like a plaintive wail. Once, his voice took on a much different tone than usual. It happened at a concert in a high school gym in Lafayette, Indiana (March 22, 1975). Because he had a cold, his vocal chords produced nothing more than a low growl. He went ahead with the show anyway, by singing everything in a lower key than usual. During that performance he sounded very somber and quiet, almost delicate. Instead of soaring on top of the instruments, his voice seemed to creep underneath them. The emotion was still present, however, and the hollow, echoing sound produced by the acoustics in the gym added impact, commanding the attention of every listener.

Bill nearly always started the shows with "I'm on My Way Back to the Old Home," and he also included most of his best-known numbers such as "Uncle Pen," "Footprints in the Snow," "Blue Moon of Kentucky," "Mule Skinner Blues," "Blue Grass Breakdown," and "Raw Hide." At many performances, he was called upon to play two sets, and on the second, he would ask for suggestions from the audience. This invariably sparked an enthusiastic chorus of voices from the crowd, calling out titles of songs. Many were older numbers he hadn't performed in a long time. If Bill didn't want to play a certain song, he turned a deaf ear to that request, pretending not to hear it. He had a phenomenal memory, and could remember the lyrics to almost any song he had ever recorded. When he heard a request for a song he wanted to perform, he would acknowledge it by repeating the title and launching into it. I sometimes got a little nervous during those moments, fearing I would have to play an instrumental I didn't know very well such as "McKinley's March" or "Virginia Darling." Ralph Lewis was the one who was really on the spot, though, because he often had to sing the lead part on some of those more obscure vocal numbers. If I had been in Ralph's shoes, I would have been forced to make up lyrics on the spur of the moment.

## The Blue Grass Special

Bill's bus had seen better days. It was called the Blue Grass Special, but it was so old and dilapidated that some of the Blue Grass Boys secretly called it the Blue Grass Breakdown. It had been owned and used by several other musical groups before Bill had taken possession, and it had lots of miles on it. The transmission wasn't very good anymore, and it was hard to shift without grinding the gears.

The bus had been manufactured by the Flxible Company, which was founded in 1912.Originally a producer of motorcycle sidecars with a flexible connection to the motorcycle, the company later made hearses, ambulances, and buses. During World War II, Flxible manufactured parts for blimps including rudders, fins, control cars, and nose cones. The Blue Grass Special seemed old enough to have come from the age of the blimps.

Though worn-out buses such as Bill Monroe's Flxible are usually troublesome and expensive to keep in operation, Bill could afford it because his performance fees were higher than those of most other bluegrass groups. However, I've seen less-successful bands willing to squander large sums of money on such vehicles in order to maintain what they perceive as an air of "professionalism." These groups feel their public image would be compromised if they were seen arriving at a performance venue in any vehicle other than a large tour bus.

At one time the Blue Grass Special had sported a set of steer horns on the roof, near the front. These had long since been removed, but the mountings were still in place. There were no sleeping compartments for the Blue Grass Boys, but we had bunks located on both sides of the center aisle near the middle of the bus. Bill had his own private sleeping compartment. Surprisingly, it was clear at the back—a bad location for several reasons: it was close to the noisy engine; the grinding of gears was especially audible; noxious exhaust fumes were frequently present; and it was where all the bumps in the road could be most easily felt. A popular story among Blue Grass Boys recounted how Bill—without leaving his sleeping quarters—could tell by the feel of the highway whether the Blue Grass Special was on the correct route. (Years of traveling the roads undoubtedly led to that skill, but it wouldn't have been nearly so well developed if Bill had been sleeping in the middle of the bus, where the ride was much smoother.)

We did take the Blue Grass Special out on trips a few times while I was with the band. Kenny Baker or Ralph Lewis did most of the driving. I sometimes traded places with Ralph behind the wheel while we were rolling down the highway. We'd switch drivers right on the interstate—I'd hold onto the steering wheel while he slipped out of the driver's seat, and then I'd sit down and keep it between the ditches for a good many miles. I never had to shift gears that way.

It was always cold on the bus in the winter. To augment the insufficient heating system, a single propane heater was attached to a portable twenty-pound liquid propane tank and placed up front, next to the driver. After lighting it with a match or cigarette lighter, we pointed it down the center aisle and held it in place with a bungee cord to keep it from falling over and causing a fire. The heater was missing the wire guard in front, so there was nothing to prevent a coattail or trouser leg from brushing up against the flame. Though it was unsafe, to say the least, it didn't seem to concern any of us that much, and the heat really felt good on cold winter nights as we traveled down the highway.

I like to tell the story about the time we took the Blue Grass Special to a festival in Missouri. After getting it parked, Ralph decided it needed to be moved to a more convenient location nearer the stage. Searching around, he found the perfect spot and slowly began backing the bus into a narrow area between two trees. Bill emerged from his sleeping quarters to see what was going on. I thought Ralph needed a little guidance, so I got out and walked to the rear of the bus, attempting to direct him by waving my arms left and right in the air. I guess I wasn't much help, because Bill stuck his head out the window and said (without cracking a smile), "What's the matter? Mosquitoes botherin' ya?"

## Of Baseball and Bluegrass

I never was very good at baseball. When I was about eight years old, I got hit right between the eyes with a flying hardball while trying out for Little League. I never mentioned this to Bill as we played catch beside the old Blue Grass Special. While waiting for his next pitch, I realized I was lucky he no longer required the Blue Grass Boys to be good ball players as well as good musicians and singers. That's the way it was in the 1940s, when Bill had his traveling tent show. Back then, the local baseball team was challenged to a match with the Blue Grass Boys in every town where the band performed. The ball games were a good way to promote the show. The Blue Grass Boys would play baseball in the early afternoon, and then perform that night in the tent show. Other acts on the show sometimes included Grand Ole Opry stars Uncle Dave Macon, who entertained audiences by singing novelty songs and playing the banjo in the "frailing" style (a pre-bluegrass technique using plucked single strings along with strummed multiple strings); Sam and Kirk McGee, who had performed with Fiddling Arthur Smith as well as with Uncle Dave Macon; and DeFord Bailey, the Harmonica Wizard.

Bill often told me how, back in those days, his selection of band members would be based more on their baseball talent than their musical ability. I knew about this before I joined the Blue Grass Boys, but when I saw the baseball equipment on the bus I realized that Bill's interest in the game had never really faded. He often told us stories about what a good pitcher Clyde Moody was. (Clyde Moody was a guitarist and singer who had worked for Bill and had written a lot of memorable songs, including the bluesy bluegrass standard, "Six White Horses," and the country classic, "Shenandoah Waltz." He was nicknamed the Hillbilly Waltz King.) Stringbean had also been a good ball player, according to Bill.

I understood why Bill liked baseball so much. The game had several things in common with bluegrass music. Teamwork is crucial to success in both activities. If a lead musician plays an incorrect part, or a singer stumbles over the words, the other musicians must be quick enough to adapt to the change, rather like making a double play at second in a baseball game. There is another obvious similarity: taking an instrumental solo is like taking a turn at bat—you can never really be certain if it will turn out to be a home run or a strikeout.

## Bluegrass Goes to Europe

On April 22, 1975, we left the United States for a twenty-five-day European trip that included performances in Britain, Scotland, Ireland, the Netherlands, Belgium, and Germany. It was Bill Monroe's first major European tour. The principal organizer was Bill Clifton, an American bluegrass

Autographed cover of souvenir program booklet for Bill Monroe's 1975 European Tour. (From the personal collection of Mitchell Wittenberg.)

Kenny Baker and Ralph Lewis performing "Scotland" on twin fiddles at Greyfriars Monastery, Uddingston, Scotland, April 25, 1975. Photo by Alex Dunn.
(Used by permission.)

pioneer who had been living in England since 1963. His knowledge and
experience of performing in Britain and Europe made him very good at
showing us around and making us feel comfortable. He also made guest
appearances on some of our shows, singing duets with Bill on songs like
"Sweetheart, You Done Me Wrong," and "Little Cabin Home on the
Hill."

On April 25 we played at Greyfriars Monastery in Uddingston, near
Glasgow. The monastery, situated in the beautiful Scottish countryside,
was a stone building encircled by pine trees. Inside, a fireplace warmed the
concert room where tables were placed for listeners. At one point in the
program Ralph and Kenny used twin fiddles to play a beautiful rendition
of "Scotland,"[1] a tune Bill wrote in honor of the country of his heritage.

While we were there we also visited Edinburgh, where Bill was presented with a sample of the Scottish Tartan of the Munro clan. He was indeed proud to receive the gift, and he folded it carefully and carried it around with him the rest of that day, showing it to everyone.

In Northern Ireland, we put on a concert in Belfast in which Bill sang "Danny Boy" as a part of the show. (Bill had recorded that song in 1961. It was released in 1962 on the Decca label, as a part of the album *Bluegrass Ramble* [DL7 4266].) The audience at the Belfast concert was subdued but very appreciative. I was disappointed that we didn't get to stay longer in Ireland. We flew in and out on the same day, and consequently didn't get to see any of the Irish countryside.

While visiting England we stayed in a rural bed and breakfast, the Crutherland Country House, where we were awakened in the morning by a gentle knock on the door and presented with a tray of tea and biscuits. It was a very British way to start the day, and I was won over by the courtesy and hospitality of our hosts. I even made up a tune in honor of the place. I called it "The Country House Reel."

Our performance venues in England included the Philharmonic Hall in Liverpool, on April 28; the Digbeth Hall in Birmingham, on April 30; and the BBC studios in London on May 2. During our shows in England, we had a little comedy routine worked up whenever we played Bill's instrumental number "Raw Hide." (Bill's original recording of "Raw Hide" was made in 1951. It was one of his most-requested numbers.) Right after Bill introduced the tune, Kenny would play a quick shuffle in the key of C on his fiddle, as though he were setting the pace to kick off the tune. Bill would immediately swat out a very authoritative C chord on his mandolin, sending the message: "I'm the one who starts this one off!" Kenny would act very irate, saying, "He always starts this one!" At one point, Bill had me step up and verbally chastise Kenny, telling him he was supposed to let Bill kick off the tune. If we got an encore on "Raw Hide," the same thing would happen before Bill played it again. Sometimes Bill would strum his C chord several times, and sometimes Ralph Lewis would strum a quick C on his guitar as well. It was very much like a pack of race horses at the starting gate, impatient for the race to begin. After ending the tune for the second time, Kenny would often play an additional little shuffle in C—just for an added laugh.

Bill had some souvenir songbooks he was selling at shows on the England tour, and they got to be cumbersome for us to carry around from one destination to another. One day the books accidentally got left on a train. They were never recovered. Bill seemed a little suspicious about that.

He may have assumed we left them on purpose because we were tired of lugging them around. It really was an accident—as far as I know.

Several times, after Kenny had finished playing "Grey Eagle," Bill would dedicate that traditional tune to all the old-time fiddlers in England, Scotland, and Ireland. That was his way of acknowledging the rich musical heritage of those countries. He recognized that the roots of American traditional music originated in that part of the world, and he wanted to pay tribute to those who were still keeping the old tunes alive.

The most memorable part of our 1975 European tour was the trip to Germany. It was our first visit to that country, and we played around ten shows there. Richard Weize, owner of Bear Family Records (a major German independent country and bluegrass label), had booked the performances. We traveled all over the country in a van called a Bedford Blitz, driven by banjo player Rolf Sieker, who accompanied us the entire time. Sieker picked us up at the airport in Amsterdam, Holland, at the start of the tour and dropped us off at the airport in Bremen when the tour was finished. (Rolf Sieker now lives in Round Rock, Texas, near Austin. There he composes and teaches, as well as performing with his wife, Beatte Sieker.)

As we traveled about the countryside, Bill remarked at how beautiful and well kept the farms were. Coming from a farm background, Bill respected and admired German agriculture a great deal, often commenting on the quality of the cattle being raised. He was also impressed by the excellent wooden fences built by the farmers. They were designed with beauty as well as function in mind. Bill always did admire a well-built fence. To this day, I can't go by a good-looking, straight fence without thinking of Bill.

Rolf Sieker remembers Bill passing time on the road by demonstrating his talent for making string figures—an ancient children's game still played the world over. Using a loop of string, the player forms designs with the fingers of both hands. The patterns—which number in the thousands—have names like Twin Stars, Jacob's Ladder, and Cat's Cradle (which is actually the first in a series of string figures made by two players.) I watched Bill create this string art many times myself. He was very good at it, and it was fascinating to watch his large fingers nimbly grasping the lengths of string in well-practiced sequences to form pretty patterns—without making tangled snarls.

The German high-speed autobahns (highways) made us a little tense. We often had to travel long distances between shows, making it necessary for Sieker to push the Bedford Blitz to the upper reaches of its speed capabilities. At one point Bill told him to slow down, explaining that his back was bothering him. (In 1953, Bill was involved in a car wreck that left him with numerous broken bones, including pelvic and spinal fractures. Back pain was something he had grown accustomed to, but he wasn't quite up to the challenge posed by the shock absorbers in the Bedford Blitz.)

We performed in towns including Hamburg, Tübingen, Berlin, and Neusüdende—home of the Neusüdende Bluegrass and Old Time Music Festival, which has been going since the early 1960s, making it the oldest and most important festival of its type in Germany. ("Neusüdende" translates to "Newsouthend.")

On many of the shows Bill sang the song "Fraulein," which the audiences loved. He got a standing ovation every time he performed it. Bill wrote a tune at a hotel in Oldenburg, near Neusüdende. As we left the hotel in the morning, he asked me if I could think of a title for it. I named it "Oldenburg Farewell."

During one of our trips between shows, we stopped for a short time at Rolf Sieker's home in Loehne, Wesphalia, to refresh ourselves with some apple juice. (Bill really liked that.) While some photos were being taken of the band, one of Sieker's neighbors came over to visit. Years later, Bill recognized the woman when he saw her again in Nashville. An ambassador in every sense of the word, Bill never forgot the friends he made during his travels.

Our visit to Berlin was something none of the Blue Grass Boys will ever forget. To get to the city we had to travel through a portion of communist East Germany, on a highway that was fenced in on both sides. We were told land mines had been placed beyond those fences. That was difficult to believe—the countryside seemed so tranquil and inviting.

All of us were glad to get to Berlin, and while we were there we visited some important historical sites. We went to the Brandenburg Gate, which had been commissioned in 1791 by Friedrich Wilhelm II as a structure to represent peace. Located in the no-man's-land between East and West Berlin, by 1975 the Brandenburg Gate had become a symbol of Berlin as a divided city. We also saw the Reichstag, a large, domed building, originally built in 1894 by Kaiser Wilhelm II to house the German Parliament. The Reichstag is best known for having been the center of Hitler's government during World War II. It made me think of my father, who had fought in Germany back in 1945—with the 116th Infantry, Twenty-ninth Division. He had been wounded twice: first in Normandy (by shrapnel), and again in the German city of Aachen (by a bullet in the leg). He was awarded a Purple Heart with an oak-leaf cluster, three bronze battle stars, and a combat infantry badge.

The Berlin Wall made the deepest impression on our group. Looking at it, I was reminded that the Cold War was still very much alive. The collapse of communism and subsequent tearing down of the Wall would not take place for another fifteen years. The massive concrete barrier stretched out in front of us, topped with strands of barbed wire. It was covered with colorful graffiti, and though I couldn't understand most of the spray-painted messages, I had no trouble sensing the outrage being expressed in the bold letters. As we stood on a raised platform which allowed visitors to view the other side, Bill quietly said, "Come on boys, we don't belong here." Then he turned away and left. Rolf Sieker later asked Bill what he thought of the Berlin Wall. Bill told him, "It's a bad thing that happened."

The Kurfurstendamm provided a striking contrast to the Berlin Wall. An elegant shopping area containing two miles of luxury hotels, restaurants, art galleries, and department stores, the Kurfurstendamm was an exciting place for us to explore, shop, and sightsee. Everyone turned around and stared at us as we walked down the street in our suits and western hats. Bill must have assumed they all knew who he was, because he kept waving at them.

Bill wrote several tunes on that European tour. One was the "Black Tulip of Holland," which we played in Utrecht, Netherlands. A few taped copies of our show in Utrecht are still floating around today in Europe and the United States, and I've run into several people who either play or know of the melody "Black Tulip of Holland." It's very pretty!

After the tour was over, organizer Bill Clifton gave me one of his recordings, which I kept as a souvenir. He signed it with the following message: "Bob: great to have you and your banjo as traveling companions across Britain and Europe this summer.—Bill Clifton."

## Hard Work Builds Character

I experienced lots of firsts during my two years with Bill Monroe. One such experience involved working with him on his farm outside of Nashville. He would call me up at about 7 A.M., saying, "Are you awake?" Sometimes I wished I hadn't picked up the phone! (Many times I'd been up late the night before jamming with friends, but I never told Bill because I figured he'd disapprove.) Then Bill would ask me to meet him at one of his favorite restaurants—usually a place north of Nashville called Mason's—where he'd buy us both breakfast. He liked fried potatoes, eggs, dry toast, and coffee. He never ate cold cereal. The jukebox in the restaurant contained several Bill Monroe songs. The management always loved it when Bill came in. Most of the local patrons knew Bill, and he also enjoyed joking with the waitresses.

After breakfast I'd go with him out to his home place, where he taught me old-fashioned farm work. I helped him plant potatoes in his garden, which he plowed with a team of mules. I helped him haul fence posts —he cut them himself from the timber on a nearby hillside. I dug postholes for him, and stretched barbed wire. Once I stretched the wire too tight, and it broke and cut my hands. I always wore gloves after that. Bill loved building fences. He always took pains to build his own fences with high-quality woven wire, stretched good and tight, with two or three strands of barbed wire on top. When Bill Monroe built a fence, it was a showpiece that was made to last.

I also went with Bill to Beaver Dam, Kentucky, near his home town of Rosine, where he had purchased a piece of land for a bluegrass festival; he called the place Monroe's Bluegrass Musicland Park. There, he put me to work doing the same kinds of chores that I did on his farm. I also contracted vicious cases of poison ivy and got covered with mosquito and chigger bites. Ah, the memories!

I remember hauling a truckload of fence posts up to Beaver Dam with Bill. We loaded the posts on the flatbed of the truck and "boomed 'em down," using what he called boomers—steel levers that tightened the chains (or ropes) around the load. Bill often talked about the times when, as a teenager, he hauled crossties that his father sold to the railroad. I'm sure he'd loaded and hauled the crossties the same way we did the fence posts—only back in those days he'd used a wagon and horses. As I was driving the truck, I noticed in the side-view mirror that one of the chains holding the fence posts was loose. I told Bill I thought one of the boomers had come unhooked. We stopped the truck and searched the highway ditches on foot for a distance of perhaps half a mile, looking for the boomer that had fallen off. Bill hated to lose it. Unfortunately, we never did find it.

I looked on Bill as a parent figure in those days—and not always in an amiable way. I disliked the early morning phone calls and the daily injunctions to come and help him on the farm. I misinterpreted his motives. I thought he wanted me to prove myself by showing him what a good worker I was. In reality, he was just giving me an opportunity to improve my self-confidence and assurance. He was treating me exactly like a father would treat his son.

I skipped many a late-night party because I was worried that Bill might call me early in the morning. I didn't want to be hungover and tongue-tied when I answered the phone. (I did manage to attend my share of all-night jam sessions, though.) My musician friends couldn't understand the strange power Bill had over me. Many of them thought it seemed funny that I always worried about pleasing him, even when I was on my own time.

One night at the Grand Ole Opry, I approached Bill backstage and said: "I'm planning on going on a fishing trip tomorrow, if you don't need me." "I don't need you." He turned away. His answer seemed sharp and abrupt. My insecurity immediately took over, causing me to worry he really *didn't* need me—for music or anything else. Was he just doing me a favor by keeping me in his employ? After all, there were lots of other banjo players waiting to take my job. One of the first things I learned in Nashville was that every musician is replaceable.

After I thought very carefully about my true worth as a sideman in Bill's band, the rational side of my brain regained control, and I realized he obviously hadn't hired me just for cheap labor on his farm. Bill wasn't out to take advantage of anyone. He knew I was single and had no other source of income, so there was no reason why I couldn't work for him and make some extra money. To Bill Monroe, work was an important measure of a man, a revealing personality trait. No amount of knowledge, social sophistication, or academic background could take the place of hard, physical work.

This is what Bill said about lazy musicians in one magazine interview: "You have more trouble today than you ever had. I don't have no trouble with the fiddler or the guitar man or the bass, right today, but the banjo pickers are gettin' maybe a little bit lazy and they want to stay at home, stay nice. When someones got wives, of course their wives is the boss and they have to stay at home. . . . Course I think we can always find good musicians that'll go along and be a Blue Grass Boy. . . . (But) they're more lazy today than they've been in a long time. They want to sit at home and play a little in front of somebody, and maybe their wives works, you see, and keeps the musician up. And that's the way with a lot of them today, they like to play around home, or clubs, but the money's out on the road. But it's work out there, you know, and I believe in working."[2]

He wasn't talking about me when he mentioned lazy banjo pickers! That interview took place nine months before I went to work for Bill. However, the quote does illustrate Bill's belief that anyone who was lazy deserved no respect, no matter who they were or what position they held. I wanted Bill's respect. He gave me plenty of chances to earn it by working for him on his farm.

Bill cared a lot about his music, and I wanted to make a serious and lasting contribution to the genre he had created. I began to realize that bluegrass was more than just a collection of musical sounds—it was an expression of Bill's own personality. Truly, the best way to become a part of bluegrass was to get to know Bill personally by working beside him on a day-to-day basis. He gave me a chance to do that. Working for Bill wasn't always easy, but it did make me feel a close kinship with him. For the rest of his life, he always spoke of me as a "fine man, a good worker, and a wonderful banjo picker."

Although I didn't realize it at the time—or for some years after—all the hauling and farm work I did for Bill actually had solid psychological benefits. By keeping me busy, he prevented me from becoming too preoccupied with music, about which he knew I was very passionate. It was necessary and healthy to keep a good balance between bluegrass and other facets of life, in order to maintain a proper perspective. The work also had another benefit: it helped me sleep like a rock at night.

## A Flurry of Festivals

We played bluegrass festivals, lots of them—all over the country. Some were well organized, some were primitive, and some were downright scary. In those days bluegrass festivals attracted many types of people, everyone from educated intellectuals who studied bluegrass as a serious musical art form to moonshine-drinking rednecks who enjoyed getting into fights. In May 1975, we played Ralph Stanley's Fifth Annual Memorial Bluegrass Festival at the old Stanley home place on top of a mountain between Mc-Clure and Coeburn, Virginia. There was a lot of white lightning (homemade whiskey) present on the festival grounds, and after sundown many of the fans were whooping it up. We had to move the table where we were selling Bill's records, to prevent it from being knocked over by two quarrelsome drunks who got into a fistfight nearby.

Hippies showed up at many of the festivals, often getting high on marijuana and boogying in front of the stage during performances. A blue haze of smoke hovered in the air above the scene. Bill talked privately about the pot smoking more than once. One of his comments to me was: "I know what that stuff does to a man—it makes him get his mind on just one thing and he can't think about nothin' else." He also took a dim view of the hippies' casual dress and unwashed bodies. He didn't seem to mind their long hair, though. His own hair was quite long and shaggy in back, hanging down over his collar. "I was the first man in the country to have long hair," he often said. Bill knew that the hippies liked him and his

Bob Black at the Fourth Annual Indian Springs Bluegrass Festival, Indian Springs/Hagerstown, Maryland, the last weekend of May 1975. Photo by Carl Fleischhauer. (Used by permission.)

"Watch your timing." Bob Black and Bill Monroe performing at the Brown County Jamboree, Bean Blossom, Indiana. Photo by Thomas S. England. (Used by permission.)

music, and he respected that. He was glad to count them among his fans. In private though, Bill often voiced his disgust with the unclean appearance of many of the hippies, even though decent shower facilities often did not exist at bluegrass festivals (including—at that time—Bill's own festival in Bean Blossom, Indiana). Because of this, I never really understood Bill's negative reaction to unwashed festival attendees. Fortunately, Bill always provided the Blue Grass Boys with motel rooms when we were on the road, so we were never without showers.

Most bluegrass festivals were beautiful, memorable events. One such occasion took place on my birthday, June 14, 1975, at Merrimac, West Virginia. I sat for hours in a crowded camper jamming with Kenny Baker and a few other musicians, playing tune after tune, and feeling as though I existed in both the past and the present, as though a part of tradition was alive and well within me. Later, I observed Bill Monroe gazing off into the hills, playing notes on his mandolin as though they were carried to him on the breeze. The tones of the music were old-time and ancient, moving through him with a life of their own. The experience inspired me to write a tune—I called it "The Mountains of Merrimac."[3] Over twenty-five years later, the melody remains with me.

## Bean Blossom

The Bean Blossom festival was Bill's pride and joy. Friends and fans from all over the country attended his Ninth Annual Bluegrass Festival at Brown County Jamboree Park in Bean Blossom, Indiana, from June 18–22, 1975. It was a joyous reunion of kindred souls. I was excited about performing there for the first time with the Father of Bluegrass.

We Blue Grass Boys arrived several days ahead of time to get the place ready: repair concession stands, fix fences and gravel roads, set out trash cans, and so forth. We set up Bill's PA system by hanging speaker columns in the trees around the concert seating area, then connecting them with speaker wire. After the festival opened, one of my jobs was to go around to every campsite in the morning and wake people up so they could show me their tickets. Early morning was chosen for this duty because that was when most people were sure to be at their campsite. I can't remember running across a single person who hadn't paid their admission, and many had been up jamming all night, so they weren't too happy to have me rousting them out at dawn with the words, "ticket man!"

My time at the festival didn't all seem like work, though. One enjoyable part of the Bean Blossom festival was the dance show in the Brown County Jamboree Barn. (Located near the entrance to the park, the barn was used from early spring through late fall for shows featuring country and bluegrass performers, many of whom were regular members of the Grand Ole Opry. At the bluegrass festival, the barn was used for talent contests as well as shows.) Every year, Bill and the Blue Grass Boys would put on a performance in the barn, featuring fiddle tunes. The concert was billed as a dance. Actually, nobody danced, even though Bill encouraged it. The audience members all sat and listened with rapt attention. Bill danced occasionally during the show. His movements had a professional look about them, fluid and well practiced. I could see why he and his brothers Birch and Charlie were considered good enough to be part of the WLS radio exhibition square-dance troupe in the early 1930s. The WLS National Barn Dance, broadcast from Chicago, featured two square-dance teams. One set of dancers performed on the radio broadcast and the second, to which Bill and his brothers belonged, danced on the road. They performed in theaters all over the upper Midwest.

I loved playing fiddle tunes, so I was thrilled to get a chance to perform a whole bunch of them with Bill, Kenny, and the rest of the Blue Grass Boys. We dusted off melodies on those dance shows that we never got to play at any other time—tunes like "Katy Hill," "Methodist Preacher," "Paddy on the Turnpike," "Heel and Toe Polka," "Sally Goodin," and

"Stoney Point." (Bill always called that one "Wild Horse from Stoney Point.") I could tell Bill really enjoyed himself. He loved to play the old-time dance tunes, as evidenced by his body movements and the sparkle in his eye. He had wonderfully distinctive mandolin interpretations of every tune—for instance, he played "Katy Hill" the way Georgia fiddler Clayton McMichen did, with a sustained high B note, accomplished by picking the string repeatedly. It reminded me of an eagle soaring high on an updraft, transported by pure joy. The way Bill played the song really made you want to dance! Those shows in the barn sometimes lasted well beyond the designated fifty-minute time slot, because none of us wanted to stop playing.

A musical frolic unlike any other took place one special evening during the festival. It was the Sunset Jam, in which Bill led a picking session made up of anyone who wanted to take part, professional or otherwise. A huge crowd of musicians participated, and every bluegrass instrument

Bill Monroe and the Blue Grass Boys performing in the Brown County Jamboree Barn, Bean Blossom, Indiana, June 1975. *Left to right:* Kenny Baker, Bob Black, Bill Monroe, Randy Davis, and Ralph Lewis. "Post-A-Photo" postcard. Photographer unknown.

was represented. It seemed, however, that there were more banjos present than anything else. The sound of dozens of banjos all playing "Blue
Grass Breakdown" filled the park with a spirited, raucous clamor. Bill sang
"Uncle Pen" as the sun sank low, and a multitude of fiddlers added their
final touch by joining together on the old familiar tune, "Jenny Lynn." All
the musicians shared a warm sense of camaraderie stemming from their
unanimous devotion to bluegrass music and its founder.

Strange things always seemed to happen at Bean Blossom. That year
I witnessed the shocking and bizarre spectacle of a gospel singer being
hauled off in handcuffs. Emmett Sullivan, the banjo player for the Sullivan Family (an Alabama bluegrass and gospel group), was apprehended
and escorted through the audience by two uniformed police officers. The
policemen loaded him into a squad car and drove off toward the park
entrance. I found out later what the fuss was all about. James Monroe
had played a trick on Sullivan in response to a practical joke the previous
fall at the Third Annual Alabama Dixie Bluegrass Festival in Chatom,
Alabama. At that time, James Monroe had been served with a phony
child-support suit arranged by Sullivan. To get his revenge, he talked his
secretary, Becky Galyon, into posing as Sullivan's jilted girlfriend. While
the Sullivans were performing their show, Galyon approached from the
audience with two festival police officers, who attempted to serve Sullivan
with a fake paternity suit. Jumping from the stage, Sullivan tried to escape
into the woods, but the officers caught him, handcuffed him, and hauled
him into their waiting squad car. The police later released him at the park
entrance.

In the summer of 1975, *People* magazine printed an article about Bill
Monroe that contained photographs taken by Thomas England at Bean
Blossom that year. (England also took pictures in Nashville, Kentucky
[around Rosine] and at James Monroe's bluegrass festival in Cosby, Tennessee.) Being featured in such a high-profile publication was a feather
in Bill's cap, but it also provided an important showcase for his music,
which was making greater inroads into the public consciousness than ever
before. Bill tried making another inroad shortly after that—into the field
of mass-market radio advertising.

## Drink Dr Pepper

The Dr Pepper radio jingle the Blue Grass Boys recorded with Bill must
have been well written, because it's stayed with me for almost thirty years
now. Here's how the chorus went:

It's not a cola, it's something much, much more.
It's not a root beer—there are root beers by the score.
Drink Dr Pepper, the joy of every boy and girl.
It's the most original soft drink ever in the whole wide world.

Part of a 1970s advertising campaign for the world's oldest soft drink, the Dr Pepper song had several verses and a complex musical score. It had been recorded by many country singers, including Maybelle and the Carter Sisters, Waylon Jennings, Hank Snow, Roy Acuff, Grandpa Jones, and Doc Watson. We studied the sheet music, which didn't help because none of us could read music well enough to be able to use it. After listening closely to a tape supplied to us by the Dr Pepper people which featured Maybelle Carter's rendition, we learned it by ear, simplifying a few of the chords here and there as we went. Bill had to change the key to make it more suitable for his voice. It was a complicated song, not suited to bluegrass at all. At the studio, we put the song down on tape in the same way Bill always recorded—live with no overdubs—but it took us far longer than any of the songs we had ever done for albums. Take after take went by and still there were mistakes that had to be corrected. The word "originality" appeared in the lyrics, and Bill kept pronouncing it "original-ality." It was a painstaking and time-consuming process, and I don't think we ever did

Bill Monroe and the Blue Grass Boys rehearsing in Bill's office for the Dr Pepper radio commercial jingle, summer 1975. *Left to right:* Randy Davis, Bob Black, Bill Monroe, Kenny Baker, and Ralph Lewis. Photo by Thomas S. England. (Used by permission.)

get it quite right. Toward the end of the song, Ralph Lewis had the idea of putting in a G run on guitar, like the run played at the beginning of Bill's song "Uncle Pen." It gave the song a nice touch, bringing it back to the bluegrass fold after it had strayed pretty far from Bill's style. After all that work I only remember hearing the song once on radio, and it contained just a small portion of what we had recorded.

Bill himself was fonder of RC Cola than Dr Pepper in those days. RC Cola had an advertising campaign that spoke to the "me" generation with its slogan: "Me and my RC." Bill repeated that slogan a lot whenever he drank an RC. He sometimes drank Coca-Cola too. (He pronounced it "Co-Cola.") We were all big on caffeine drinks: I drank huge amounts of coffee, Pepsi, and sweetened iced tea—a very popular drink all over the south. I think the caffeine gave most of us a lot of heartburn, because Rolaids were also a very high-consumption item with Bill and the Blue Grass Boys. Kenny Baker often joked about one useful purpose for heartburn. He said when he drove late at night, he liked to pull over at a truck stop and get a bowl of chili—he thought the heartburn that resulted helped keep him awake behind the wheel.

## A Hat Act

I never did like to wear a hat very much. Bill always wanted the Blue Grass Boys to wear them—he felt audiences expected it. Since the music we played was directed toward country folks, western hats seemed very appropriate. The only time we didn't wear them on stage was during Sunday morning gospel shows. In the summer we wore straw hats, and in the winter we wore felt hats. Though I thought they looked pretty good, hats always felt uncomfortable to me. Besides, they gave me "hat hair." They were a nuisance on the road, prone to getting smashed when we traveled in the close quarters of a station wagon. We often stacked all our hats on top of each other and stowed them behind the rear seat to save room, and they sometimes got dented and misshapen as a result.

Bill always wore his hat, both on stage and off. I think it would have pleased him very much if all the Blue Grass Boys had done the same. He once said to me: "If I was from Iowa I'd wear my hat all the time." Wearing a hat on stage does help a musician hear and play better because the wide brim captures sound waves—kind of like cupping your hand around your ear. Kenny Baker especially appreciated this advantage. He has told me it's one of the reasons he still wears a hat today when he performs.

Bill Monroe taught me another use for a hat. On June 5, 1975, we performed at the first anniversary of the Spare Room, in Somerset, New Jersey. The show also featured the Caffrey Family, and had been sold out a week in advance. During our performance, Bill suddenly turned to me in the middle of one of Kenny Baker's fiddle solos, saying: "Hit him with your hat." Though it seemed crazy, I obediently took off my hat and swiped it at Kenny. I guess I got carried away because I really swatted him hard, knocking his own hat askew and totally screwing up his instrumental break. He must have been flabbergasted—I'm sure he never expected something like that from me! It was clear out of left field. People started chuckling in the audience, and when I looked at Bill I saw his shoulders shaking up and down with laughter. After our set was over Kenny told me I had come dangerously close to getting slugged right on stage.

I think Bill told me to hit Kenny with my hat in order to see someone else get it for a change. In the past, I had accidentally knocked Bill's hat askew—not once, but twice. During one show I stepped in close to the microphone to take a solo, and my banjo neck bumped Bill's hat, knocking it down over his face. At another show I did the same thing, shoving his hat sideways down over his ear. I was really embarrassed—it seemed I was pretty dangerous at close range.

Bill met the same misfortune at the hands of Bob Jones, who replaced Ralph Lewis in February 1976. Bob was a left-handed guitar player, and he stood on Bill's left during performances. That meant the neck of his guitar was always pointed toward Bill. Unbelievably, he accidentally knocked Bill's hat off with the neck of his instrument a couple of times as well. Bill got it from both sides: from me on his right, with my banjo neck pointed toward him, and from Bob Jones's guitar neck on his left. He couldn't win.

I'm also a little embarrassed about telling another hat story. The Blue Grass Boys needed some straw hats for summer stage wear. Bill decided we should all wear matching hats, so he sent me to Loretta Lynn's Western Wear store just outside of Nashville to buy them. Inexperienced at buying hats, I came back with four that were unblocked. The crowns were rounded, just like Hoss Cartwright's hat was on the old *Bonanza* TV series. I thought the Blue Grass Boys could block them to please themselves, but they wouldn't shape very easily, nor would they hold their shape once they were formed. We all wore them for one or two shows, and then the rest of the Blue Grass Boys went out and bought their own hats. After that, Bill didn't seem to mind whether they all matched exactly or not.

## 4. BLUEGRASS 101

I thought I was a good banjo player when I first joined the Blue Grass Boys. I quickly found out, however, that I didn't know as much as I had thought; to quote Ralph Lewis: "I thought I knew all the answers, but I didn't even have the questions right." To Bill Monroe, rhythm and timing were all-important, and I found I really had to work to meet his expectations. When I had performed with bluegrass bands back in Iowa, we played our musical passages comparatively slowly and deliberately, giving each note an individual expression of importance. We concentrated on the *melody,* rather than the *timing.* I found that Bill's musical philosophy placed less importance on individual notes and more importance on the flow of the music as a whole. On occasion Bill was heard to use the expression "cutting corners" when describing his playing. That meant he was willing to leave out some of the less important notes in order to give a more powerful forward motion to the music. (This concept reminds me of the way Bill used to drive at night in the early days: by straightening the curves, or cutting corners in much the same way as when playing melodies on his mandolin.)

He never dropped the tempo or timing when he played—they were so strong that you were never in doubt about their dominance in the overall sound. This may have been the result of Bill's early background playing for dances with his uncle Pen. The fiddle tunes they performed together were done at quick, lively tempos. The dancers were energized by the *rhythm* of the music; the melody was of secondary importance.

Bill was a great lover of old-time fiddle music, and he enjoyed playing these traditional tunes on his mandolin. I liked fiddle tunes too, and had learned to play many of them on the banjo. My Iowa City friend Alan Murphy had taught me quite a few, and I had picked up tunes from such Midwestern fiddlers as Lyman Enloe (1906–97), who lived in the Kansas City area at that time, and Delbert Spray (1923–2001), from Kahoka, Missouri.

Bill had strong opinions about how the old tunes should be played. "You ought to play the tune the way the man wrote it," he would often say. "That tune's been around longer than you have, and it'll be around a long time after you're gone." He spent some time teaching me his way of playing "Dusty Miller," which he claimed was the only right way to play it. It moved a lot faster than other people's versions. I really had to pay attention because he wouldn't slow it down—he just played it over and over again at the same quick tempo. Kenny Baker told me he didn't like that tempo—if it had been just a little faster, or a little slower, he could have done a better job of playing it. Of course, anything Kenny played sounded great to me. Bill's "Dusty Miller" was a true challenge: it had a distinctive way of drifting seamlessly from a major to a minor key, and the result was, to me, almost spiritual.

Bill also "rehearsed" me a lot on "Sally Goodin," his personal favorite of all fiddle tunes. He told me that most banjo players played it the way Earl Scruggs had recorded it on his 1961 classic album of banjo instrumentals, *Foggy Mountain Banjo*. However, Bill didn't like that version. He said it didn't have good enough tones. By "tones" he meant long, sustained notes—often on open (unfretted) strings. "You've got to study your instrument to find out where the best tones are," he told me. I worked on "Sally Goodin" for a long time before I could play it to Bill's satisfaction. Bill must have changed his mind later about Scrugg's version of "Sally Goodin," as evidenced by the fact that Bill recorded the tune with Earl Scruggs on the 1995 Byron Berline album *Fiddle and a Song*. (That album—[Sugar Hill SHCD3838] featured the first studio reunion of Bill Monroe and Earl Scruggs in over fifty years.)

Another tune Bill used to enjoy playing was "Cumberland Gap." I had already learned that one the way most banjo players played it. It's considered a standard for the banjo, but Bill did it differently. He put another part into it that didn't sound a bit like any banjo version I had ever heard. He told me that he played it the old-time way—the way it was really "supposed" to go. His brother Birch played it that same way on his fiddle. I still remember the Bill Monroe version; banjo players are often surprised when they hear me play it that way today.

Bill played everything very fast. Southern-style dance music, he claimed, had a much faster tempo than styles from regions such as Iowa, Texas, or Missouri. His rhythm had a forward lean. Each note fell at the front edge of the beat, giving the feeling that the music was gaining in speed from moment to moment, even though the tempo never really changed. This is what Bill meant when he said a tune could be "fast" or it could be "quick"—those two adjectives didn't necessarily mean the same thing. The tune was always boss. It carried you along with it, and all you could do was hang on and ride it out. Bill believed the melody was a living thing, existing in its own reality. When it was not being played, it was still "out there," waiting to be brought forth, like a genie from a lamp.

## *"The Old Brown County Barn"*

Hundreds of artists' signatures, going back to the early days of country and bluegrass music, lined the walls of the backstage area of the Brown County Jamboree Barn. The long, low-roofed barn had been the home of the Brown County Jamboree in Bean Blossom, Indiana, since the early 1940s, and shows had taken place there every weekend from spring through fall each year since. The building was old, weather-beaten, and filled with memories.

Bill Monroe and the Blue Grass Boys put on four or five Sunday afternoon concerts a year in the Brown County Jamboree Barn. Bill's brother Birch, who resided in nearby Martinsville, was the manager. He had a reputation for being somewhat thrifty. When the weather was cool, the barn was heated with rows of woodstoves. Birch would split the wood (but not too much!) and build fires in the stoves before performances (but not too soon before!). The seats in the barn were a hodge podge. Birch must have found them wherever he could. They included both metal and wooden folding chairs from funeral homes, old school chairs with metal frames and flat wooden seats, theater seats, and a few bleacher-type seats. There was a low wooden stage at one end of the building, constructed to look like the porch of a rustic log cabin. An antique grain cradle and a few wooden straight-back chairs gave it a real old-time country look.

Bill usually opened the Brown County Jamboree shows on Easter Sunday, and closed the season in November. Jim Peva, a longtime devoted fan and supporter of the Brown County Jamboree, told me Birch would buy and color only about a dozen eggs for the Easter opening. He'd then give them to Jim's young daughters to hide for an Easter egg hunt for the other kids.

Bill's programs in the Brown County Jamboree Barn often included another big-name act on the same show. Once it was Ernest Tubb and the Texas Troubadours. (Bill always pronounced his name "Tubbs.") Other artists I remember seeing there included Roy Acuff and his Smokey Mountain Boys, and the Stoneman Family. (Right before that concert, Donna Stoneman came into the backstage room where I greeted her by saying, "How are you?" She must have thought I said, "Who are you?" because she replied, "I'm Donna.")

For a couple of weeks before each show, Birch Monroe could be seen traveling about Brown County, always wearing a hat, white shirt, and tightly knotted tie, nailing up posters for the event. Often, the posters came from Hatch Show Print in Nashville, a very old company that has been producing posters for country, vaudeville, minstrel, and gospel shows since 1879. (On occasion, Bill would send me to Hatch, located near the Ryman auditorium, to pick up those posters. The cluttered print shop reminded me of the old letterpress room of the *Shenandoah Evening Sentinel*.)

Sometimes Birch got his fiddle and played a tune on stage with us in the Brown County Jamboree Barn. Usually it was something like "Durang's Hornpipe" or "Boatin' Up Sandy." Occasionally he played "Owensboro." He said it had been composed by a condemned fiddler shortly before going to the gallows. He always enjoyed playing "Down Yonder," and during that tune he would give the guitar player a little solo of about a half-dozen notes every time the second part came around.

Stories about Birch's penny pinching were numerous. Once, it was said, there was a big crowd at the Jamboree, and the concession stand ran out of hot-dog buns. Reportedly, Birch ran over to the local IGA store but purchased only one package. Another time, when they were low on hamburger meat, Birch told his cook to cut holes in the centers of the meat patties so they could make and sell more burgers. During one of our shows in the Brown County Jamboree Barn, a storm came up and the power went off, plunging the building into total darkness. Birch didn't let that stop the show, which would have meant giving refunds. Instead, he set up two wooden folding chairs on each end of the stage and placed flashlights on them, aiming the beams toward us while we finished our performance. I don't remember anyone asking for his or her money back.

Today, the Brown County Jamboree Barn exists only in the memories of those who played or attended shows there. It was razed in 1986; according to many accounts, this was because the county declared it unsafe. It's said the barn resisted the efforts of those attempting to bring it down, and that it finally had to be burned. A few local people kept the woodstoves as souvenirs. The backstage walls, along with the hundreds of signatures that covered them, were burned. The Bill Monroe Museum and Bluegrass Hall of Fame is now located in the general area where the barn once stood.

In 1985 Bill recorded a fond tribute to the building that held so many musical memories for him: "The Old Brown County Barn." Released on an album called *Bluegrass '87* (MCA5970), the tune received a Grammy nomination that year for best country instrumental.

## Bloody Breathitt

Bill Monroe's Sixth Annual Kentucky Bluegrass Festival (August 8–10, 1975) was held in a little hollow in the hills of Breathitt County, Kentucky, near the town of Jackson. I drove Bill's flatbed truck to the festival a day before it opened, because he wanted me to haul a load of rough wooden planks to place on cinder blocks in front of the stage as audience seating. (I didn't envy those who would be sitting for hours on those rugged, splintered boards.)

Breathitt (pronounced Breth'-it) was a dry county, which meant it was illegal to possess alcoholic beverages within its borders. It earned its nickname, Bloody Breathitt County, because of feuds and violence that had taken place there, especially in the period between 1890 and 1930. The Blue Grass Boys discovered it still lived up to its nickname. On Saturday evening, while people were watching the show, local law-enforcement officials sent a young boy around to the various campsites to peek into coolers, checking for beer and other alcoholic beverages. Later, when people had retired for the night, the police moved in and arrested those with coolers of beer by forcibly removing them from their tents. One young man was dragged out of his van by the hair and struck with a billy club. Bill tried to reason with the lawmen, but they were unmoved by his protests and closed down the festival then and there. A group of visitors from France was so terrified that they followed us back to the motel where we were staying, feeling safer in the company of their musical hero, the Father of Bluegrass. Only a few months earlier (March 4, 1975), Bill had presented a fund-raising concert for the local police force in a little coliseum in Jackson. By shutting down the festival, the Jackson police department seemed to indicate it didn't care about the money raised through Bill's efforts. (I suppose no one could accuse them of showing favoritism.) We felt a great sense of relief when we crossed the county line on our way back to Nashville. Bill gave up his plans for a seventh annual Jackson, Kentucky bluegrass festival.

## The Dark Cloud

Bill Monroe often made up nicknames for people he was fond of. He began calling Ralph Lewis Wolf Man, because Ralph's black, curly hair would sometimes hang down over his forehead and give him the appearance of a werewolf. The Wolf Man nickname stuck. Later it got shortened to Wolfy, and the name caught on among a few fans. On July 10, 1975, we were performing at a Milwaukee music festival sponsored by several area breweries. My friend Al Murphy had performed there the previous day with Longshot, a country and swing band. Several members of that group stayed around to watch Bill's performance, which took place on the Schlitz Country Stage. During the show they began yelling "Hey, Wolfy!" from the audience. They could see Bill chuckling every time he heard them.

Bill's nickname for me was the Dark Cloud, partly because I took things so seriously back then, and partly because I looked a little like a Native American. (Kenny had two other nicknames for me: Bad Bob, and Geronimo.) Because of my trusting, sometimes gullible nature, I was very easy to play tricks on. One day James Monroe was playing at the same festival as Bill Monroe and the Blue Grass Boys. My friends Alan O'Bryant and James Bryan played in James Monroe's band, the Midnight Ramblers. They came up to me, looking sad, saying James Monroe had just fired his entire band. Believing them, I became very concerned, asking, "What're you gonna do now?" and "Is there anything I can do?" I really felt bad for them. After an entire day of this, they told me it was just a joke. They were good-natured about it, though. I was so easy to fool, people couldn't resist pulling my leg.

At the Fourth Annual Alabama Dixie Bluegrass Festival in Chatom, Alabama (September 5–7, 1975), the weather was quite hot and the humidity suffocating. Bill Monroe sat inside the station wagon with the motor running and the air conditioner on high. (He always ran the air conditioner full blast in the summer, and the heater the same way in the winter. It was all or nothing for Bill.) Before long, he was fast asleep, and that's where he stayed all afternoon. Bill wasn't feeling very well that day because he was worried about his brother Charlie, who was ill. Wanting to leave him in peace, the rest of the band hung around the record table, visiting with festival attendees. After the show that night, I drove the station wagon out of the park while Bill rode behind in another vehicle with some folks he had met. We were traveling along a sandy patch of gravel road, less than a mile out of the park. It was dark and deserted. Suddenly the station wagon chugged to a halt; the gas gauge read "empty." I got out and walked sheepishly back to Bill. He rolled down his window and stared at me with his mouth open as I told him, "It's out of fuel." (If I had known Bill was going to run the engine all afternoon, I would have filled the car with gas before we got to the festival.) We both knew there were no gas stations in the area open at that hour. He said, "You wait here and we'll bring back some gas." They all left, and I sat there for a long time in the dark, waiting. Finally, about an hour later, the car came back carrying only Kenny Baker and Ralph Lewis. The rest of the band had gone on to the motel and checked in. Kenny and Ralph had been to several places looking for gas. The most they had been able to get was about a half a gallon, in a coffee can, barely enough for me to get back to the motel. After I had parked the station wagon, Kenny motioned to me. Boy, did he look angry! I was certain he was going to cuss me out for not filling the gas tank earlier, and making him and Ralph go traipsing all over to look for fuel. Then he said, "I want to see you in my office." That's when I knew he was joking. He and Ralph had some beer inside their room, and I joined them for a couple of bottles. Ralph opened them with his pocketknife—prying up the edges of the caps with his blade before popping them off. The next day we returned to the festival, where Bill was booked for a second day. Word had gotten around about us running out of gas the night before, and in a solemn ceremony on stage, the MC presented Bill with a siphon hose.

## *"Pie, Please!"*

We never went hungry on the road. Stopping to eat often was a priority. Bill didn't like to miss any meals, and he never hesitated to make his wishes known in a restaurant. When a waitress was slow about coming to take our order, Bill would sometimes yell out, "Pie, please!" or "Coffee, please!" That would usually get her attention—and everyone else's too. Once, a waitress came to our table and asked, "Are you all a band?" Bill answered, "Yeah, we're a rock band. This here's the Wolf Man." He nudged Ralph Lewis, saying to him, "Show her how you howl!"

We seldom ate in fast-food places. Bill always liked a sit-down meal, with meat and vegetables served on a china plate. He did express a liking for Kentucky Fried Chicken, but I think he actually enjoyed it more for its name—it was another connection to the Bluegrass State. (Bill had met Colonel Sanders, the founder of Kentucky Fried Chicken. The two were introduced at the Grand Ole Opry in May 1966, when Sanders appeared there as a guest.)[1] I do remember we Blue Grass Boys going into a Mexican fast-food restaurant and buying Bill a burrito. When he bit into it, it oozed out all over his hand; enough said.

Bill rarely ate dairy products. Ice cream and pizza were about the only foods containing milk that I ever saw him enjoy. (While we were in Japan we had anchovy pizza, which none of us enjoyed very much. Bill told me once that pepperoni was his favorite pizza topping.) I don't know if milk disagreed with him, or if he just didn't like the taste. Many singers don't drink milk—supposedly it can have a detrimental effect on the voice due to its throat-coating properties—but I don't think that's the reason Bill avoided it. Caffeine drinks are bad for the singing voice too, and Bill drank lots of coffee—sometimes right before going on stage. He drank it black, with sugar, and very hot.

Breakfast was a meal we never skipped. Bill always ordered dry toast. If the waitress brought it to him buttered, he would send it back. Grits were a common breakfast dish, especially in southern restaurants. Randy liked to put sugar on his—a practice Kenny always made fun of. (I tried them that way too, and I thought they tasted pretty good.) Kenny loved country ham and redeye gravy (a mixture of ham drippings, water, and a little black coffee). We all liked biscuits with sawmill gravy (made from flour, milk, and sausage or ham fat). Kenny usually ordered his gravy on the side. If it arrived already poured over his biscuits, he would say, "It looks like it's already been eaten."

Many times, while waiting for our food, I noticed Bill rolling the thumb, index, and middle finger of his right hand against the tabletop. He seemed to be keeping time to some secret melody he heard in his head. I asked him about that once. He said he was practicing his banjo rolls. I never heard him play the banjo, but it wouldn't have surprised me if he could.

On another occasion as we waited for our order to arrive, I saw Bill pick up a napkin and write down the names of radio stations where he'd played. He said he could remember every one, and proved it by covering both sides of the napkin with call letters of radio stations. Then he began telling me the slogans that accompanied many sets of call letters. For example, WSM in Nashville (owned at that time by the National Life and Accident Insurance Company) had the slogan, "We Shield Millions." Bill often joked that it also meant William Smith Monroe. Another station, WJKS in Gary, Indiana (where Bill and his brothers had played in the early 1930s), had call letters that stood for "Where Joy Kills Sorrow." WLS in Chicago, founded by Sears, Roebuck, and Company, meant "World's Largest Store," and KFNF, the station in my childhood hometown of Shenandoah, where Bill and his brother Charlie had begun their full-time musical careers, stood for: "Kind Friends Never Fail."

On rare occasions, Bill chose to sit at a table by himself in a restaurant. That always surprised and worried us. It was so out of character, we found ourselves wondering what could be on his mind. We left him to his own thoughts during those moments.

Usually, however, Bill not only sat with us but would often pick up the tab for everyone—including fans who came to eat with us after a show. After we had played, the members of the band were really hungry—performing took a lot of energy and we were ready for a big meal afterward. Ralph sometimes said: "I'm gonna order a steak the size of Bill Monroe's mandolin."

After polishing off our meals, all of us except Bill would return to the station wagon (or bus), and figure out whose turn it was to drive next. We'd sit there waiting for our boss, who was usually at a pay telephone, talking with a promoter, friend, or fan. He always made at least one call at every stop. Eventually, he'd rejoin us and we'd hit the highway again. After only a few miles, Bill would nod off, dreaming of his next piece of pie.

## Stick to the Melody

Banjoist Tony Trischka is highly renowned for his progressive picking style. He has influenced numerous talented banjo players at the cutting edge of acoustic music. Yet he is also deeply rooted in tradition, retaining a profound interest in the history of the banjo. He stretches both ends of the musical spectrum.

Trischka has always been a huge fan of Bill Monroe, and in September 1975 he asked me for help in arranging an audition with Bill—not to replace me, but with the hope of becoming a Blue Grass Boy at some future date when the job opened up. I agreed, setting up a meeting with Bill for him at the Grand Ole Opry.

Trischka had just gotten back from California on the Friday of his audition. He was dropped off at the Opry that evening, but unfortunately it was some time before I could be there to meet him. As he waited next to the guard booth outside the artists' parking lot, he watched various Opry stars drive up and chat with the guard before proceeding into the parking area. Eventually Trischka saw Bill Monroe arrive in his Pontiac station wagon, barely nodding to the guard before being motioned on through. A little while later I showed up and we both went in.

While Trischka waited outside the dressing room, I informed Bill that he had just arrived for his audition. Bill said that he could do it right after the show—which is what I told Trischka. Later on, when our portion of the show was over, Bill said that he should return instead the following day. I told Trischka he was going to have to wait until Saturday night for his audition, but he couldn't do it then because he had to leave town. I went back to Bill, saying that the audition would have to be that evening. Bill then agreed to give Trischka a listen.

Entering the dressing room, Trischka saw Bill sitting in a chair, reading some fan mail. Bill asked him, "Do you have a guitar man?" (He was asking if Trischka had brought along a guitarist to play some accompaniment for him.) Trischka said "No." Ralph Lewis, who was also in the dressing room at the time, was assigned the job. Trischka opened up his case and took out his banjo, revealing an issue of *Time* magazine that had been lying underneath the instrument. The magazine's cover showed a picture of Patty Hearst with her right arm raised in a clenched fist. She had just been arrested due to her alleged involvement with the Symbionese Liberation Army. Trischka began wishing he had closed the lid of his banjo case, because Bill kept staring at the magazine cover during the entire audition.

Trischka played a couple of tunes for Bill: "Molly and Tenbrooks" and "Little Rabbit." He did his utmost to perform each number in a very traditional manner, rendering both melodies with absolute stylistic conservatism—using none of the progressive embellishments for which he was so well known. When he finished Bill told him, "You pick good, boy, but stick to the melody."

## Bill's Quirks and Moods

One question I'm often asked is, "Was Bill Monroe very hard to work for?" The answer is this: anything worth doing is not usually easy, but it's very satisfying when accomplished. Ideas about old-fashioned values seem to surface all the time when I talk about Bill Monroe. He had a rural background and was used to hard work. He expected the Blue Grass Boys to work hard too. He said of one former band member: "He was the laziest man that ever worked for me. He didn't believe in workin', you see?" At the core of bluegrass was Bill's concept of bringing the music to hard-working country folks. He thought that a lot of country music poked fun at people who lived in rural areas. He wasn't going to have any part of that—his kinship and loyalty remained steadfast with that group of folks, and his music reflected it. His commitment was demonstrated by his willingness to perform in small schoolhouses in rural areas for very little money, even at the height of his popularity.

His music and what it meant was all-important to Bill Monroe. It wasn't just a means of making money, or a vehicle to propel him to stardom. For many performers, even those in bluegrass, hunger for fame and fortune far outweighs love for the music. That wasn't true with Bill Monroe. He had a genuine passion for what he was creating, and he never let anything divert him from the musical course he had chosen to travel.

He had his quirky days, though. Once we were sitting in a restaurant booth waiting for our meal. Bill began drawing on a piece of paper with his ballpoint pen. First he drew a circle; then he made a face by adding two dots for the eyes, a dot for the nose, and a very short straight line for the mouth. It was similar to a "smiley face" without the smile—totally expressionless. Finally he wrote a caption underneath his cartoon: "Hi. I'm Bob, the banjo boy. I have really got it. Hell!" It was a joke, of course—but an unsettling one that made me wonder if there was a deeper meaning attached. (That was one of the first banjo jokes I ever experienced. Jokes about banjos and banjo players have been cropping up for a good many years now. Here's one example: A child tells his mother: "I want to be a banjo player when I grow up." His mother replies: "Son, you can't do both.")

From time to time Bill expressed very conservative opinions about the world around him. Many hippies who attended bluegrass festivals where we performed wore blue jeans and work shirts. More than once, Bill said of them: "They dress in work clothes to make everybody think that they work, you see?"

He didn't like sunglasses. Whenever he saw an entertainer wearing them onstage, he would say: "He's just wearing those sunglasses to hide behind." He didn't like colognes or hairdressings either. Often, when one of the Blue Grass Boys spent a little too much time getting spruced up before a show, Bill would say something like: "He's fixin' his hair again," or "Don't bother him now—he's puttin' on his perfume."

He never allowed the Blue Grass Boys to wear blue jeans, even on the road while traveling between jobs. He didn't feel they were appropriate anywhere except doing work such as farm chores. Perhaps Bill was trying to maintain an image free from the hillbilly stigma often associated with country music. He was very fond of telling people that he and the Blue Grass Boys were the first group to wear suits and ties on the Grand Ole Opry.

Bill's mood was often directly affected by the tension caused by occasional "sick headaches" (his name for them). These caused him to become quiet and withdrawn. He usually took Goody's or BC headache powders when they came on. I think his sinuses bothered him quite a bit in those days, too, because he often used nasal spray. Once he sent me to retrieve a bottle he had left in his motel room.

Bill sometimes didn't explain very clearly what he wanted from a musician. For example, he told me many times that he wanted me to choke the strings more often. To me, "choking the strings" meant bending them over the fingerboard, slurring the notes like blues guitarists often do. That's what I would do, but he kept telling me I wasn't choking the strings enough. This went on for months, until I realized that what he really wanted me to do was play more rhythm chops on the upbeat, as he did on the mandolin. I thought I had been doing that quite a lot, especially behind Bill's solos, but not enough to suit him, apparently.

On September 27, 1975, Bill's brother Charlie passed away. I wasn't aware of this until after our show was over that day. We were playing in an outdoor amphitheater in Memphis—a place called Going To Market. Bill suddenly nudged me away from my microphone, saying, "This is *my* microphone. I want everybody to hear *me*." Was he telling me I was playing too loud, or being overbearing with my backup? There was another microphone at the far left of the stage, one the announcer had been using. I walked over and played into it, because I didn't know what else to do. If he didn't want me to have a microphone, why had he even hired me to play the show? I couldn't believe he didn't fire me over that one, but nothing was mentioned about the incident afterwards.

Of course, now I know what the real problem was: Bill was emotionally distraught over the passing of his brother. He hadn't talked about it at all, but his behavior on that day spoke volumes. A few days later, we Blue Grass Boys joined our boss in Rosine to pay our respects to Charlie Monroe.

## Farewell to Charlie

Bill never went to church much while I was with him. He often spoke of his conviction that singing gospel music on shows was enough to release him from the obligation of church attendance. Nevertheless, I had the impression that he felt kind of guilty about being a backsliding Christian. Going to church had been a part of his upbringing—as a child he had gone to the Methodist church in Rosine, where he first heard many of the songs that were later to play such an important part in his music.

The death of Charlie Monroe brought Bill back home again to the Rosine Methodist Church to attend his brother's funeral. Charlie had passed away after a long bout with cancer, and his body was brought to Rosine to be laid to rest.

The Blue Grass Boys were present at the memorial service too. Dressed in our matching stage suits, we surrounded Bill on all sides as we proceeded up the center aisle. Bill wanted his Blue Grass Boys around him partly for comfort, and partly as a buffer between him and Charlie's widow, Martha (sometimes called Mert), with whom he didn't wish to speak. There seemed to be a degree of friction between them. In part, this was because she and Bill had dated prior to her marriage with Charlie. According to Bill, she had been sitting with her deceased husband in the funeral home day and night, just to prevent Bill from seeing his brother alone for the last time. Of course, this was Bill's impression of the situation. Jim Carr, who played several shows with Charlie Monroe as a member of his band, the Country Pardners, told me that Martha was a "sweet lady who collected antique tea cups and had nothing but the warmest feelings toward Bill."[2] Bill and Charlie hadn't wished to see each other for a long time—whether this was due to jealousy, country pride, or other factors may never be known, but toward the end of his life Charlie expressed a wish for Bill to come and visit him. The visit never took place, though. Kenny Baker told me that Bill had been very worried about his brother for quite some time. My own observation is this: I sat behind Bill during the funeral service, and whenever he turned his head sideways, I saw tears on his cheeks. It was the only time I had ever seen him cry. It was obvious to me that Bill cared very deeply for his brother.

## I Quit

Approximately a year after I joined the band, I turned in my two-week notice. I felt like a child under strict, constant supervision, never allowed to unwind and just be myself. Even if I did a job that satisfied Bill, he said nothing about it. It seemed as though the only feedback I ever got was negative. I began to feel that Bill wasn't satisfied with my playing, and I developed the notion that he considered the banjo strictly a show-off instrument. I asked him about that one time because it was really bothering me. He replied, "Banjo pickers are all show-offs." I don't know if he was just kidding or trying to aggravate me, but at the time I took him seriously. It really affected my self-esteem. I began to have serious doubts about my playing ability. Every time he looked at me during a show, I thought he was expressing dissatisfaction with the job I was doing. Yet at other times, he would speak of various banjo players and list my name among such greats as Rudy Lyle and J. D. Crowe. I became confused and decided to call the job quits.

Bill Monroe and the Blue Grass Boys performing at the Grand Ole Opry's fiftieth anniversary, October 15, 1975. *Left to right:* Kenny Baker, Bob Black, Bill Monroe, Randy Davis, Ralph Lewis. Photo by Les Leverett. (Used by permission.)

I thought I had good reasons to leave, but ended up withdrawing my resignation, primarily because of something Bill's sister Bertha said to me. Bertha, who was in her mid-sixties, rode with us on a couple of trips when we had the bus. I liked her very much, and because she seemed rather frail, I tried to help by running errands for her. (Once she sent me into a grocery store to get her a half pint of cream, which she drank straight out of the carton. She said it gave her strength.) She knew I had turned in my resignation, and tried to convince me to stay, saying Bill had told her he liked my playing and he didn't want me to quit. Bertha's comment was what made me change my mind about leaving. Later, when we were alone backstage at the Grand Ole Opry, I told Bill I wanted to stay if it was all right with him. Looking away, he said, "yessir."

## Blue Grass Boy as Clinch Mountain Boy

In October 1975, I had the distinct honor of filling in for Ralph Stanley at Bill Monroe's Fifth Annual Lone Star Bluegrass Festival in McKinney, Texas. Ralph couldn't make it to one of the shows, and I was asked to perform in his place with his band, the Clinch Mountain Boys. I was proud to do so, and I tried my best to reproduce the crisp, driving tone of Ralph's banjo style.

At that time the Clinch Mountain Boys consisted of Ricky Lee on lead guitar, Jack Cooke (whom Ralph often introduced as "the ex-mayor of Norton, Virginia") on bass, Keith Whitley (a powerful singer who became highly successful in country music before his untimely death in 1989) on rhythm guitar, and Curly Ray Cline on fiddle. Curly Ray was a wild man on stage. He always gave a spirited performance while playing his fiddle—grinning and jumping around in front of the microphone, using lots of body language to punctuate his instrumental solos. My father, who loved watching performances by Ralph Stanley and the Clinch Mountain Boys, once told me that Ralph and Curly Ray "seemed to battle each other with their instruments." Dad thought it funny the way they appeared to glare at one another and "get into each other's faces." Curly Ray must have been trying the same act with me. Standing next to him was a little dangerous, as I quickly found out. At one point on the show I got poked right between the eyes with the tip of his fiddle bow. I stayed out of his way after that.

Bob Black performing with Ralph Stanley's band, the Clinch Mountain Boys, at Bill Monroe's Fifth Annual Lone Star Bluegrass Festival, McKinney, Texas, October 1975. *Left to right:* Curly Ray Cline, Ricky Lee, Bob Black, Keith Whitley, Jack Cooke. Photo by James Rae. (Used by permission.)

## The Fiddler from Kentucky

Cool night breezes are beginning to rustle through the trees around the bluegrass festival campground, carrying with it the sounds of banjos twanging and doghouse (stand-up acoustic) basses thumping. A large crowd is gathered among camping trailers that have festive electric lanterns strung across their awnings. All eyes are focused on the fiddler standing in the center of the group. His face is expressionless as he plays a tune that hasn't been heard on any of the stage shows. His bow arm moves with fluidity never before seen, as though it were made of rubber. Some listeners are holding cassette recorders, others have cans of beer, all are listening with fascination and awe—eagerly absorbing the melodious strains as they flow outward with their unquestionable air of authenticity. The tune reaches its conclusion and everyone knows that it has been played *right*. Spontaneous applause ripples through the crowd. Next, a few voices are making requests: "Hey, Kenny—play that 'Hollow Poplar.'" "How does 'Say Old Man'[3] go, Kenny?" "Do you still play 'Rocky Road to Dublin,' Kenny?" This is Bill Monroe's fiddler—he's the best there is—and everyone knows it.

There's no question about it. Kenny Baker is the pick of the fiddlers— "the Greatest Fiddler in Bluegrass," to use Bill Monroe's words. The tone of his fiddle is astonishingly smooth, every note exacting in its precision. The number of tunes he knows is staggering. I once heard him play the fiddle while riding in a camper all the way from Denver to Nashville, never playing the same melody twice. Now that's a lot of tunes!

Kenny told me he learned to play the fiddle when he was eight or nine years old. His father, T. E. Baker, played the fiddle (he also made several fiddles), but would only let Kenny play guitar to accompany him. Therefore, Kenny would sneak up on the roof of the house and play his dad's fiddle while he was gone.

I first got a chance to jam with Kenny Baker two years before I joined Bill Monroe's band. The jam took place at a bluegrass festival in Knob Noster, Missouri, in 1972. My parents attended that festival (at my suggestion) and saw Bill Monroe and the Blue Grass Boys for the first time. My mother was quite taken with Kenny's fiddling, saying, "His arm gracefully guided the bow across the strings, bringing out haunting music that was hypnotic." After the stage shows were over, Kenny joined a group of jammers that included my friend Al Murphy on guitar and me on banjo. We had just been playing with Lyman Enloe, one of Kenny Baker's (and our) favorite old-time fiddlers, when Kenny decided to take a turn at the

Kenny Baker. Photo by Thomas S. England. (Used by permission.)

bow. Jamming with him was an exhilarating experience, and Kenny often turned the melody over to me so I could "take a ride." (I first heard that expression from Al Murphy. It refers to playing a solo, or break. Sometimes Kenny would ask me, "Do you want to break this number?") I discovered later—after many jam sessions with Kenny—that he really believed in letting a musician show what he could do. He was a lot like Bill Monroe in that respect. And I could tell he liked the banjo. Some other fiddlers I had met didn't appear to have a lot of respect for the banjo. A few of them even exhibited an attitude of smug superiority. I remember an event that illustrates this: When I was living in Nashville I went to the Tennessee State Fair with some friends. While strolling around the grounds, we came upon a boy playing the fiddle, for tips. His case was open on the ground and people were throwing money in it. I asked him if I could join him on the banjo just for fun—I didn't want any of the money. He replied, "Nope, I ain't playin' with no banjo." I didn't know whether to feel amused or insulted.

Our musical get-together at Knob Noster marked, for me, the beginning of a long series of informal jam sessions with Kenny Baker that took place at many different locations around the country. Once Al Murphy, Celia Wyckoff, and I traveled all the way to Myrtle Beach, South Carolina (which is approximately a twenty-two-hour drive from Iowa City) mostly to jam with Kenny Baker. He invited us to a motel room where a large picking party was going on. Among the many musicians present was Tommy Jarrell. Jamming with Kenny was an experience that Al, Celia, and I always looked forward to eagerly. We hated to put our instruments back in their cases once we got started—it went against our principles to be the first ones to quit picking. Often our jam sessions lasted until daybreak.

One all-night jam session occurred at Bean Blossom in June 1973. Al Murphy played his guitar for so long that the skin broke on the index finger of his left hand. Each time he played an F chord, his B string would lay right inside the cut. It became painful for him to continue—but continue he did. (At one point during the jam session we discerned Bill Monroe standing some distance back from the crowd of listeners, attentive to the music we were playing. I pretended not to notice him, but inside I was bursting with pride to think that the Father of Bluegrass was listening to us.) Among the variety of tunes Kenny played, a handful kept reemerging in the jam session. These were tunes he was getting ready to put on an album; when he asked Al and me to record them with him, we eagerly accepted.

As soon as the festival was over, we cut Kenny's album in a room at the Orchard Hill Motel, a few miles south of the festival site. Kenny told us not to change our strings because they were broken-in well from the jam sessions of the previous few days, and he wanted to keep them sounding the same. He also told us to be alert and in good mental condition (that is, *not* hung over). John Kaparakis came in from Washington, D. C., to join us on guitar for the recording session; Lonnie Feiner, who had been a member of the California bluegrass band High Country, played bass. (Feiner had also participated in the jam sessions.) The title of the project was *Dry and Dusty* (County Records 744, 1973). It was the first album I ever played on, and I was filled with keen enthusiasm and high spirits during the entire session. Produced by County Records founder Dave Freeman and using portable recording equipment, it was engineered by Paul Gerry over a period of two days. We placed mattresses against the walls to deaden sound in the room. Though the weather was very hot, the air conditioner had to be turned off during takes because it was too noisy. Al Murphy managed to rise above the pain in his finger to do a superb job of guitar playing. Dave Freeman played rhythm mandolin, a fact not widely known. Kenny asked him to "chop mandolin" on the sessions and he was happy to do it, although modesty prevented him from adding his own name to the credits on the liner notes. I don't know if Bill Monroe ever heard the album *Dry and Dusty* or not, but I would have been proud if he had—the recorded tunes ended up with just as much energy and sparkle as they had when we were jamming on them earlier.

I was fortunate to be able to record several other albums with Kenny after *Dry and Dusty*. In November 1974—shortly after I joined the Blue Grass Boys—we cut *Grassy Fiddle Blues* (County Records 750), a record that featured Joe Stuart on guitar, Randy Davis on bass, and Ralph Lewis on guitar and mandolin. (Ralph also played twin fiddle with Kenny on one of the tunes, "Lazy Liz.") Kenny often played the title song of that album on stage shows with Bill Monroe, and I always added my banjo break. "Grassy Fiddle Blues" was fun to play on the banjo—it reminded me a little bit of an old-time tune called "Cotton Patch Rag."

In October 1976, I recorded another album with Kenny called *Frost on the Pumpkin* (County Records 770). It also featured the great guitar work of Joe Stuart. Playing mandolin on that recording was Sam Bush, who performed at that time with his band, the New Grass Revival. County Records recently rereleased *Frost on the Pumpkin* on compact disc (in 2002), and I was asked to write the liner notes. That gave me a chance to talk to Kenny again, because I needed information about how he had named some of the tunes on the album. One of the more interesting titles is "McClanahan's Reel," which came about this way: One of Kenny's hobbies was raising and fighting gamecocks. I remember seeing some fighting roosters that he kept in separate wire coops on his farm. As a child, Kenny met a fellow named Willie B. McClanahan, who was a fiddler and cock fighter and had started his own breed of chickens. Kenny admired the breed, so he named the tune in Willie's honor.

Later in 1976, we recorded Kenny's tribute album to his boss and inspiration, *Kenny Baker Plays Bill Monroe* (County Records 761). Bill returned the favor by sitting in on the session. We all agreed that with the Father of Bluegrass playing on it, the album had to be good.

Kenny played a fiddle that was a given to him by Roy Acuff. (Acuff was a fiddler himself. When he first worked on the Grand Ole Opry, he fiddled for the square dancers, playing tunes like "Turkey Buzzard" and "Cacklin' Hen.") Roy was a big fan of Kenny's. There was always a picking party going on in Acuff's dressing room at the Opry, and Roy always invited Kenny to join in the festivities between shows.

In addition to playing "Grassy Fiddle Blues" on stage, Kenny also occasionally included "Grey Eagle" on the shows. I recorded that tune with him on *Dry and Dusty*, and my break on the banjo was always featured. Kenny's favorite song to play with Bill Monroe was "Mule Skinner Blues."

His fiddle solos were unique and powerful, and he never backed off during Bill's vocals. (I quickly found out that Kenny would stay right on the microphone during the course of each number, and that I had to be very aggressive about adding my banjo parts to the ensemble.) Kenny's solo parts were so self-confident and definitive that you couldn't imagine any other version being the correct one. Once I attempted to copy Kenny's solo on the song, "Workin' On A Building," because it seemed like the notes he was playing just had to be the right ones. Bill quickly called me on that after the show. He said: "You shouldn't try to copy Kenny. You've got to play that number in your own style." I worked up my own banjo solo on it—but I still think Kenny Baker played it better!

Kenny told me that no one was more surprised than he was when I first joined the Blue Grass Boys. (Maybe he didn't think I would be willing to cut my hair and put on a suit and hat.) Getting to play with Kenny Baker

Kenny Baker. Pencil sketch
by Bob Black.

was one of the best things for me about working in Bill Monroe's band. He taught me lots of tunes, and set a positive example by the serious view he took of the music.

Kenny's sense of humor helped make road trips easier for the Blue Grass Boys, because he always had plenty of jokes to tell and amusing recollections to share with us. He sang a few songs, too; one went: "When you're dead and in your grave, no more biscuits will you crave. I'll be glad when you're dead, you rascal you." He gave me advice on how to get along in Bill's band, such as where to stash things on the bus, when to wear casual offstage attire ("no dungarees!"), and how to be discreet about consuming alcoholic beverages on the road ("don't let the Chief find out!"). Kenny gave me practical recommendations—for example, he explained that when sleeping on the moving bus it was important to have your feet pointing forward because, he claimed, there was then less chance for injury in case of a collision.

Kenny was always a good friend to me. He invited me out to his farm for jam sessions with people like Joe Stuart and Dale Sledd (a fine vocalist and instrumentalist who played with the Osborne Brothers for many years). Kenny also cooked me breakfast numerous times (he was a good cook). He even made his own sausage from hogs that he raised himself—and let me tell you, it was tasty!

## Curb Jumping

I was driving Bill down Interstate 24, toward Chattanooga. We were on our way to Georgia to check on a used Silver Eagle bus he had been negotiating to buy. As we approached a Union 76 truck stop, Bill remarked, "A piece of pie'd be good about now, wouldn't it?" Bill loved pie. I replied, "Yes it would," and I swung into the truck stop, pulling up to one of the cement parking curbs in the middle of the lot. When we finished our pie and coffee, I got back behind the wheel and gave the powerful Pontiac station wagon some gas. It leaped forward over the curb, which I'd forgotten was there. The front wheels came down hard on the other side, and the station wagon bottomed out on the parking curb. I didn't know what to do. If I backed up, we'd have to run over the concrete again with the front wheels, and if I pulled forward, we'd have to run over the concrete with the back wheels. Either way we'd continue to scrape bottom. Bill stared at me with his mouth open, as though I was out of my mind. I felt it was best not to speak. I decided to keep going forward, so I hit the gas again, bumped up over the curb with the rear wheels, bottomed out once more, and then drove on. Bill never said a single word to me.

## 5. THE CHILDREN OF BLUEGRASS

Because Bill Monroe was the Father of Bluegrass, his songs could appropriately be called the Children of Bluegrass. Their ancestry is traceable to the traditional musical influences to which Bill had been exposed from early childhood. Modern-day descendants of old-time melodies, Bill's compositions were his own personal link with the past. He searched for what he called "ancient tones"—sounds that reflected time-honored tradition and gave a sense of immortality to the music that was his progeny.

Many times we Blue Grass Boys were witness to the genesis of a new Bill Monroe tune. He often composed melodies while riding on the bus. Many of these songs seemed connected to the countryside through which we were traveling. Tunes like "Racin' Through Payson," "Ashland Breakdown," or "Tallahassee" were written about real places, and they convey an image or mood associated with those locations. One melody, the "Reelfoot Reel," was written about Reelfoot Lake, in northwestern Tennessee. Bill wrote another tune while riding on the Pennyrile Parkway in Kentucky—he named that one the "Pennyrile Breakdown." "Tombstone Junction" was another tune Bill created about a real place.

It was fascinating to listen while Bill played and wrote tunes on the bus. As we pulled out of Nashville, he would first sit down with a stack of fan mail, opening the letters one by one with his pocketknife. (He kept that knife sharp, often honing it on a little sharpening stone he always carried with him.) He was usually very quiet while he did this. I sensed he was a little stressed-out, possibly from all the responsibilities—business and otherwise—that he faced while spending time around Nashville. Going on the road helped him to relax, and his mood would change after we had been traveling down the highway for a while. That's when he would take out his mandolin and begin tuning it up. Often, he wasn't satisfied with the bridge placement. Improper placement of the bridge will make the strings sound out of tune when they are pressed against the frets of the fingerboard. Bill would lay the instrument down on his lap and slide the bridge back and forth until he felt it was in the correct location. Finally he would pick it up and begin to play, and nothing was more inspiring than listening to the stream-of-consciousness music that Bill produced while he rode down the highway and watched the landscape go by. Old-time fiddle tunes, ragtime pieces, and blues all formed part of Bill's travel repertoire.

As he got warmed up, Bill became more creative. He liked to experiment with harmonics, creating very pretty bell-like sounds by resting a finger of his left hand lightly across the strings at certain frets. He would then strike one or two of the strings with his pick, quickly removing his finger to allow the "chimes" to ring. Most stringed instruments will chime nicely at the fifth, seventh, twelfth, seventeenth, and nineteenth frets, but Bill could also make chimes that sounded good at the fourth and ninth frets. Once he showed me how he could make a chime by laying his finger across the nut (the grooved piece of bone that the strings stretch across near the tuning pegs). He was very precise about it, and when he did it just right there was no denying that a definite chime could be heard.

Often, while searching for new sounds, Bill found himself playing a pleasing or evocative string of notes purely by chance. Those few notes would become the foundation of a brand new tune, and he would work with them, playing them this way and that, polishing them until he was pleased with the overall sound. He never forced the notes, and he never slowed them down. He always let the music come out at its own natural tempo. Bill believed every song was born with a life and energy all its own.

During one bus trip I sat listening to Bill playing tune after tune, far into the night, as we traveled down the highway. At one point he began playing some slow blues lines, and I realized he was making up a song. It was unlike anything I had ever heard him play, a sort of blues melody with a bluegrass accent. I committed its distinctive melody and phrasing to memory, and the next day when I had time, I worked it up on the banjo. It was very good, I thought, so I took it to Bill. "Here's a tune I heard you playing last night," I said. "I think it should be called 'Monroe's Blues'." He listened as I played for him, and told me he liked it. Soon we began playing it on shows. I had a bluesy little "hot" lick that I put in toward the end of my solo, and Bill always cocked his ear down close to my banjo during that part. A few years later, after I had left the band, he recorded the tune. In 1979 I included it on my first solo album, *Ladies on the Steamboat*.

Bill once told the Blue Grass Boys how he had come to write a tune called "Bill's Dream." (Bill recorded this number on February 3, 1964.) He had been dreaming one night of his foxhounds—he could hear them barking and they sounded strange, as though they were in trouble. He searched and searched, following the sounds they made, until he came upon a well. He realized the dogs had fallen in the well. The tune he wrote recreates the sounds of his foxhounds barking down at the bottom of the shaft.

At least one of Bill's compositions was in all likelihood inspired by physical pain. He told me that he wrote "Roanoke" one evening while suffering from a toothache. He had been performing at a theater in that city when the tune was born. Reminiscent of a well-known old-time melody called "Turkey in the Straw," "Roanoke" is a fast-moving, almost frantic-sounding breakdown. The mandolin sets a furious pace right at the start with a breakneck string of introductory notes.

Bill Monroe and the Blue Grass Boys discussing a song arrangement backstage at the Grand Ole Opry, November 22, 1975. *Left to right:* Bob Black, Kenny Baker, Bill Monroe, Ralph Lewis. Photo by Robert Black Sr. (Used by permission.)

Bill was also willing to experiment with new and different ways of writing vocals. While we were touring Germany he wrote down lines and phrases as they occurred to him, using scraps of paper that he stuffed into his pockets. Those scraps of paper consisted of anything he could find, such as pieces of envelopes or empty cigarette packages we gave him. His intention was to later assemble the scraps like a puzzle to form songs. (I don't know if it worked, but it was an intriguing idea.)

In the dressing room at the Opry one night, Bill made up an electrifying tune in the key of D minor. It had an intense, rolling melody, with a signature line on the end that he played by sliding his fingers downward from a high position to a low one. When he noticed me listening, his enthusiasm picked up, and he turned his body in my direction to let me hear him play it more clearly. He stood with his back to the dressing-room mirror, and went over and over the tune until it was time to do our show. The melody stuck with me, and I learned it on the banjo when I got home that night. It has remained with me ever since. There have been times down through the years when this tune leaps to the front of my brain, demanding to be played, and other times when it lies dormant, but I never completely forget it. My wife Kristie and I play this song on our shows these days. We call it the "Unnamed Monroe Tune." I'm not sure if Bill Monroe ever played it again after that night at the Opry long ago, but the melody lives on in our shows.

Surprising things often found their way into Bill's music. Once, while we were in Germany, Bill sat in his hotel room and began imitating, with his mandolin, a songbird just outside his window. Bill and the bird seemed to be doing a call-and-answer pattern and the song Bill played on his instrument was surprisingly similar to that of the bird. I was inspired by this idea years later when I wrote a tune called "The Chickadee Waltz."[1] (I guess, since I'm a Blue Grass Boy, you could call my melody an adopted child of bluegrass.) It's based on the two-note call of a chickadee I heard outside my home near North English, Iowa. The chickadee was singing in B-flat, so I chose that key to write the tune in. I'm sure Bill would approve.

## Back to Japan

Japanese bluegrass fans have immense respect for Bill Monroe. His music has always had a unique way of transcending cultural and language barriers, touching the hearts of listeners no matter what part of the world they're from. Bill was profoundly moved by the warm and enthusiastic reception given him by the Japanese people on our first visit there, and

Videotaping at NHK, Tokyo, Japan, December 7, 1975. *Left to right:* Kenny Baker, Bob Black, Bill Monroe, Randy Davis, Ralph Lewis. Photo by Nobuharu Komoriya. (Used by permission.)

when a return invitation was extended he happily accepted. We flew out of Nashville on December 6, 1975 for an exciting two-week tour.

Booked by a bigger promoter, Itoh Ongaku Jimsho, our second trip to Japan included shows in Tokyo, Osaka, Nagano, Matsumoto, Yamagata, Kyoto, and Nagoya. The concert ticket price was three thousand yen—less than the previous year's price, but still high (around twenty-five dollars). We also taped a couple of TV shows and a radio show while in Japan.

The crowds were large at every venue except Matsumoto and Nagano, where the audience numbered around 120 people at each concert. Those two shows consisted entirely of audience-requested numbers. The fans were extremely knowledgeable about Bill's music, and they asked for many older numbers like "I'm Going Back To Old Kentucky" (written by Bill and recorded by him twice: first in 1947, then again in 1961) and "Sally Jo" (written by Rusty and Doug Kershaw and recorded by Bill in 1957).

Bill and the Blue Grass Boys visited many of Japan's smaller towns, especially in the northern part of the country where the landscape is filled

Advertising poster for two Bill Monroe concerts in Tokyo, Japan, December 15, 1975, Yubinchokin Hall, Shiba (in Tokyo), and December 17, 1975, Nakano Sun Plaza Hall.

with beautiful mountains. Ralph Lewis said they reminded him of the Great Smoky Mountains close to his home near Asheville, North Carolina.

In Matsumoto we were presented with brand new musical instruments, made by Ibanez, as promotional endorsements. (The Ibanez company belongs to Hoshino Music, a family-owned business from Nagoya that is nearly one hundred years old.) Several Artist model mandolins were given to Bill, and a Blue Bell model banjo to me. Designed after a model by Gibson, the banjo was made of beautiful natural-finished maple. I immediately fell in love with it and proudly played it on stage the evening after I received it, at our concert in Nagano. Later I was told an unfortunate mistake had been made and I was to be presented with a different Ibanez banjo model—the Artist—because the Blue Bell was sold only in Japan. The Ibanez Company wanted me to endorse a model that was distributed in the United States. The Artist was also quite beautiful, and it boasted an intricate mother-of-pearl vine inlayed in the fingerboard. I played it for the rest of my days as a Blue Grass Boy. (Approximately a year and a half later, I was forced to sell it during a period of financial hardship.)

We were taken on a tour of the Fujigen factory in Matsumoto, where Ibanez musical instruments were made. At the Fujigen factory, we were lucky enough to meet the person who built the mandolins, Mr. Kosakabe,

Bob Black and Bill Monroe shopping in a Japanese clothing store, December 1975. Photo by Nobuharu Komoriya. (Used by permission.)

Bill Monroe, Bob Black, and Kenny Baker riding on a train after shopping in a Japanese clothing store, December 1975. Bill is holding his purchase. Photo by Nobuharu Komoriya. (Used by permission.)

as well as the banjo luthier, Mr. Sugimoto. We were shown several more of their exquisitely crafted banjos and mandolins in various stages of construction.

The Ibanez Company was very serious about improving their already first-rate line of bluegrass instruments. In Nagano, representatives from Ibanez met with Bill and examined his mandolin to get ideas and take measurements for a new line of Blue Bell mandolins.

During a sound check before one of our shows, photos were taken of us playing the Ibanez instruments, and several of those photos were later used in advertisements promoting the Ibanez Company. (Nearly thirty years later I ended up in possession of a print of one of those photos. It was presented to me by author and historian John Boothroyd in Harrietville, Australia, where Kristie and I were performing. Boothroyd had bought the photo in the 1970s in a Melbourne music store, Fretted Instruments, which still exists. I have the print framed and hanging in my living room.)

Bill had been given a large number of gifts in Japan, and when we got ready to leave the country he placed them all inside a huge box to be checked through at the airport for the flight home. Our luggage had to be

An after-dinner jam session in Japan, December 1975. Photo by Nobuharu Komoriya. (Used by permission.)

examined by airport security; one official began pulling Bill's mementos out of the box, one by one, asking whether he had purchased the items or received them as presents. Bill kept telling the man they had all been given to him. The pitch of Bill's voice rose and his tone became defensive. I could tell he was getting exasperated since it was taking such a long time. Many of the items he had been given were quite expensive. These included watches, jewelry, figurines, and musical instruments A line of impatient people was growing behind us. We were on a tight schedule, and it soon became apparent that we were going to miss our flight. Fortunately, another airport official approached the person who was hassling Bill and said, "Just expedite him on through. We've already postponed the plane's takeoff long enough."

On our way back to the mainland United States, we stopped over in Honolulu, staying at the historic Moana hotel on Waikiki beach. The Moana, famed for being the oldest hotel in Waikiki, is an elegant Victorian building dating back to 1901. Its Banyan Court, which faces the sea, contains a large banyan tree underneath which Robert Louis Stevenson is said to have written poetry. Bill wanted to surprise the Blue Grass Boys by treating us to a vacation for several days in Hawaii, but I was so weary of traveling that I spent just one day and night at the Moana and then headed back to Nashville. If that seems stupid now, I can only explain it this way: when you've been on tour for a long time and you're lonesome for familiar surroundings, it doesn't matter if you're in the most beautiful country in the world or staying at the most luxurious hotel—you just want to go home. During my day and a half in paradise I did find time to watch a Hawaiian dance performance and to see a little bit of Honolulu. I relaxed on the beach as well—so I didn't miss out on the important things.

Bill was given two Ibanez mandolins on each of our trips to Japan, a total of four instruments. They were all very fine mandolins, but he couldn't use that many. After we got back to the United States he got the idea to give one of them to Ralph Lewis's son Don, who was ten years old and played bluegrass with his dad and his brother, Marty. Bill decided to present the mandolin to Don backstage at the Opry. In the dressing room between shows, Bill handed the instrument to the boy, asking him what he thought of it. Don played on it a little bit and told Bill he thought it was a fine mandolin. Bill then surprised him by telling him it was his to keep. Don Lewis still owns the mandolin today, and he's very proud of it and of the fact that it was given to him by Bill Monroe.

Bill's trips to Japan were among the high points of his career. He went back to that country three more times after I left his group (in 1977, 1984, and 1989). The affection Japanese fans displayed for Bill was never surpassed by any other audiences. Bluegrass music seemed to stir them in a deep way, and they responded with a degree of passion and excitement that surprised even Bill.

It was in touring Japan that I first witnessed the astonishing power of Bill's music and became aware of the significance of his relationship with the audience—he was one of them, sharing in their joys and heartaches and celebrating the experience of life. There, he was able to successfully communicate with people at a fundamental and universal level. I think Bill's own realization of this unique quality of his was crystallized during his first two visits to Japan. International acceptance affected his demeanor in many positive ways. He grew more comfortable with his role as musical patriarch. His art form became a life form, of which he was the chief ambassador. Though Bill didn't change his stern, dignified bearing, he became more approachable. He mellowed because more people were realizing what he had known all along: bluegrass music was valid and meaningful. The world was finally beginning to listen to him.

## Recording with Bill Monroe

I wasn't given any idea of Bill's plans for his upcoming recording session. I had a clue we might be doing "Watson Blues" and "Jerusalem Ridge," but beyond those two numbers I was completely in the dark. Unlike most other headliners in Nashville, Bill Monroe used the same personnel on his recordings that he used in his band. He felt if a musician was good enough to be a Blue Grass Boy, he was good enough to record with him. That's one reason Bill's albums each have their own unique character and personality. Many recordings done in Nashville use the same select group of session players, a practice that often results in a certain generic predictability of backup sounds, dear to the hearts of recording executives who wish to stick with proven formulas for success. Band members, who are frequently used and discarded as though they were replaceable modular units, are not highlighted nor featured on these recordings.

*The Weary Traveler* (released January 3, 1976) was the first and most widely distributed of Bill Monroe's albums in which I took part in the recording. It was Bill's twenty-second album for MCA Records. In addition to all the Blue Grass Boys, the recording featured James Monroe on guitar and Joe Stuart on fiddle. (Joe, who originally came up with the idea of naming the album *The Weary Traveler,* had worked with Bill on and off for many years.) We recorded at a studio called Bradley's Barn, located a few minutes east of downtown Nashville. Founded in the 1960s by famed record producer Owen Bradley, Bradley's Barn has been the scene of recording projects by such famous artists as Webb Pierce, Loretta Lynn, Ernest Tubb, Merle Haggard, and George Jones.

The band had heard some of the songs Bill chose to include on the album; a few we had even performed on stage. One was a George Jones number, "The Old Old House." Another was a tune of Bill's that I had heard him play on the Opry before I joined the group, "Ashland Breakdown." We recorded all the numbers in the studio by playing together at the same time; that is, we didn't go back and fix anything by overdubbing or rerecording certain portions to spruce them up. In those days lots of bluegrass albums were recorded live, the way some of the best jazz albums have been; it gives the final product lots of vitality, as well as spontaneity. I am very proud of my part on the *Weary Traveler* album—I think my playing holds up well in comparison to the work done by banjo players on Bill's other albums. I'm happy he gave me a chance to show what I could do.

I played on three additional albums with Bill. One was the Kenny Baker album, *Kenny Baker Plays Bill Monroe*. Kenny had hired me to play on several of his other albums, but this was the first time Bill Monroe had ever shown up at one of the sessions. It was a pleasant surprise; Bill's playing was easy and relaxed. All the musicians did a better job because he was there. Some of the numbers we recorded on that album later reappeared on a 1994 four-CD retrospective set of Bill's music released by MCA, *The Music of Bill Monroe from 1936 to 1994* (MCAD411048). John Rumble, of the Country Music Foundation, told me that when he was compiling songs for the CD set, he discovered there was a shortage of good instrumental recordings by Bill Monroe in the MCA vaults from the mid-1970s. Consequently, MCA obtained permission to use recordings from the album *Kenny Baker Plays Bill Monroe* to complete their set. Bill had played lead solos on most of the tunes, and one of the album's highlights was the first recorded solo mandolin break by Bill on "Jerusalem Ridge." On his first recording of the tune—part of *The Weary Traveler* album—Bill didn't play any solo; only the fiddle was featured. It's interesting to note the differences between Kenny Baker's interpretation of the tune and Bill's mandolin version. Some of the minor chords that sounded good behind Kenny's solo didn't necessarily complement Bill's solo (although we used the same chords behind both). It's a good illustration of how the author's concept of a tune can differ from the final version recorded by other musicians.

In 1975, Bill Monroe and the Blue Grass Boys—minus Kenny Baker—recorded an album of fiddle tunes with Birch Monroe. It was called *Brother Birch Plays Old-Time Fiddle Favorites* (Atteiram 1516). One of the selections on that album was a waltz that Birch had written. He hadn't been able to come up with a title, so Bill named it for him: "The Beautiful Red Rose Waltz." The last line of that tune bore a marked similarity to the last line of Bill Monroe's song "Kentucky Waltz." Bill's versions of some of the tunes on the album differed from Birch's. On "Carroll County Blues," for example, Bill played a mandolin solo that lasted half a measure longer than Birch's fiddle solos. On "Durang's Hornpipe," however, both solo versions were roughly the same. When the album came out, I was disappointed that the sidemen weren't given any credit on the liner notes. The backup musicians were listed simply as the "Blue Grass Boys."

Birch was fun to play music with. We often backed him up on stage at Bean Blossom, and during those times he was at his most charming. He often told his listeners: "You're a great audience. I'd like to buy you all a Coke, but I don't think one would be enough to go around."

Birch's onstage charm had a way of evaporating when we were working with him around the park grounds. At those times he could be a bit rude, shoving people out of the way if he felt they were driving a nail too slowly, or grabbing the hammer out of their hands, or in general treating them as though they were lazy slackers. Nevertheless, I was pleased and proud to get the chance to record with him because I respected his fiddle playing. He knew some wonderfully authentic old-time tunes, and I loved his tempo and timing. I could forgive some of his other less-desirable personality traits. Birch's music had a great feeling that harked back to the old days.

Another recording I did with Bill was a live radio show for the CBC Radio Network series *Country Road* (the title is *Bill Monroe, Live Radio*—Country Road CR-02). It was recorded near Nashville, at Nugget Recording Studios, and the program was later broadcast in Canada. (Two days after our session, Bill loaned me to Wilma Lee and Stoney Cooper so they could use me on their show for the same series.)

I was also involved in recording a few TV shows with Bill. One was the long-running, syndicated *Porter Wagoner Show*. The segment we videotaped was a celebration of Bill's thirty-five years on the Grand Ole Opry. Wagoner's band, the Wagon Masters, included fiddler Mack Magaha, whose lively stage performances could have given Curly Ray Cline a run for his money (Magaha passed away in 2003). We recorded another TV program, *The Carl Tipton Show*, which was broadcast in the Nashville area on WTVF, Channel Five, on weekdays at 5:30 A.M. and Sunday mornings at 7:30 A.M. I sometimes watched the early morning music program after jamming all night. Our goal at many jam sessions was to stay awake long enough to watch *The Carl Tipton Show*.

## Rattlesnakes and Old Wood

One afternoon, after the band had finished playing an Opry matinee, Bill handed me his mandolin, asking me to keep it for him overnight. I told him I might want to play on it some, and he gave me permission to do so. I carried it to my apartment on Ferguson Avenue. The case was old, travel-worn, and repaired in places with tape. On its lid was a hand-painted picture of a mandolin with a king's crown on top, along with the words: "Bill Monroe—Original Bluegrass Music Since 1927." The case had been made for him by Tut Taylor, who told me that the date had been chosen because Bill said that 1927 was when he first began playing with his brother Charlie. Opening the case, I gazed upon the famous 1923 Gibson Lloyd Loar—serial number 73987. Lloyd Loar worked for the Gibson Company from 1919 to 1924, supervising the manufacture of what are now considered to be the finest and most valuable mandolins ever produced. Bill had purchased it around 1945, after seeing it displayed in a barbershop window in Miami. He had paid about $125 for it. (Years later, after Bill's death, it was put up for sale by his son James, whose asking price was $1.5 million!) It had been used on all of Bill's greatest recordings, and its signature tone was well known by every musician who had ever played bluegrass. The top was covered with scratches. A decorative portion of the peghead called the scroll was broken off due to the instrument having been dropped. There was a deep gouge in the peghead where the mother-of-pearl Gibson logo had been dug out. I had heard stories about how Bill had gouged out the inlay with his pocketknife to express his disgust with a repair job done by the Gibson Company. The incident happened around 1951. Bill sent his mandolin to Gibson to have them repair the broken neck; replace the tuning keys, fingerboard, and bridge; and refinish it. They kept it for four months, and when he got it back, all that had been done was the neck repair. That aggravated him! (Years later Bill and Gibson made up their differences, and he actively endorsed the company.)

When I picked up the mandolin, something rustled around inside. It was a rattlesnake rattle, placed there by Bill to "improve the tone." Many musicians, especially fiddlers, follow this practice. I don't know of any scientific evidence to support the belief that it changes the tonal qualities of an instrument, but why question tradition? (Another reason rattlesnake rattles are placed inside instruments is to keep dust and cobwebs from building up inside.) Bill often bragged that his rattlesnake rattle was the biggest anyone had ever seen: "twenty-nine rattles and a button." It was said to have come from Oklahoma. Some people claimed it was really two rattlesnake rattles joined together, but I never heard any confirmation on that.

Placing the instrument's leather strap over my right shoulder, I took a heavy flat pick from underneath the strings where Bill kept it. Strumming a G chord first, then an A, I was amazed at the resonance the mandolin possessed. It filled my small apartment with deep, throaty tones. I played a few rhythm chops, thinking of all the musicians who had played to the driving beat of this mandolin—powerful as a freight train—"shoving them along," as Bill often put it. It took a heavy hand to play it, because the strings were very high above the fret board, but its projection was astonishing. I played some simple tunes, very much aware of the trust Bill had placed in me by letting me take it home, and of the importance of this instrument's role in American music. I slept that night with the mandolin under my bed.

## Spit and Polish

Bill Monroe often bragged to us Blue Grass Boys about how he didn't sweat, and it was true—I never saw any beads of perspiration on him. He must have willed himself to stay cool. He invariably wore his suit and tie on stage, no matter how hot it got. Sometimes he'd allow us to shed our jackets. We wore short-sleeved white shirts and matching ties on those occasions. Nevertheless, we'd still be drenched in sweat. While walking off stage, Kenny would say: "I ain't got a dry thread on me."

The Blue Grass Boys had three matching suits apiece: brown, pale gray, and forest green. We also occasionally wore navy blue blazers with light blue trousers. I can remember only one occasion when we performed in public wearing casual dress. It was Thursday, June 10, 1976, at the official opening of the New Deal (a club founded by Marty and Charmaine Lanham) in Madison, Tennessee, just outside of Nashville. Bill was dressed even more casually than the rest of us—he was wearing blue jeans and an open-collared shirt. (I can't remember why we didn't have our suits, but it was probably because we just didn't have time to put them on.) Every seat in the New Deal was taken the night we performed there. Judging by the audience's response, Bill's Music City fans weren't bothered at all by his casual dress.

Once, while we were standing in a dusty outdoor backstage area waiting to go on, Bill took a Kleenex out of his pocket and bent down to dust off the zipper boots he was wearing. (We all wore zipper boots except Kenny, who usually wore western-style boots.) Then, without saying a word, he handed the Kleenex to me. I didn't think my shoes were that dusty, but Bill had eyes for that sort of thing, I guess.

Sometimes we didn't have time to shave properly before a show; that's when we had to "dry shave." We'd scrape our faces with our razors while we rode in the station wagon—without using water or shaving cream. Kenny sometimes used a little aftershave to wet his face beforehand. Sometimes we'd find a truck stop restroom to shave in. I learned from observing Bill that it was quicker to turn your collar inside your shirt than to take your shirt off.

Bill always got decent motel rooms for us. Usually he rented three rooms: one for himself and two more that were shared by the Blue Grass Boys. Some of the other major groups on the festival circuit didn't have that luxury in those days—they had to sleep on their buses and try to get showers anywhere they could, often at truck stops. Once, when we were pressed for time, Bill rented motel rooms for an hour or so in the afternoon just so we could get showered up. I can almost hear him saying to himself: "It wouldn't be good for the music if the Blue Grass Boys didn't smell clean!"

## Jamming with Bill Monroe

Smokey McKinnis came to Bill Monroe's Tenth Annual Bluegrass Festival at Bean Blossom, Indiana for just one reason: to jam. He had driven all the way from St. Louis with just his fiddle and a few extra clothes, itching to play some bluegrass and lots of old-time fiddle tunes. I wanted to do some jamming with him, but I had been busy working all day at the festival. By nightfall, after the shows were over, Smokey still hadn't gotten into a satisfying jam session, and he was beginning to lose his patience. I finally had time to jam, so we decided to play a few tunes among the parked campers—just with the fiddle and banjo. In a little while, Smokey noticed Bill Monroe walking up through the campground in our direction. He snagged Bill and told him he hadn't been able to find a good jam session all day. Bill said, "Is that right? Wait here, I'll be right back."

We placed some lawn chairs in a circle and sat down, playing a few more tunes. A guitar player came up and joined us. In a short while Bill returned, carrying his mandolin. He very seldom jammed with anybody, and he usually tried to discourage the Blue Grass Boys from doing so. I think there were several reasons for this. Alcohol was often present at late-night jam sessions, and Bill didn't think it looked good for the Blue Grass Boys to be around beer-swilling get-togethers. In addition, jam sessions often lasted until the wee hours—sometimes until daylight—and Bill wanted us to get the sleep we needed to be well rested and fully functional for our shows the next day. A third reason may have been that the quality of the music being played was sometimes corrupted by well-meaning amateur musicians, and Bill didn't want his band to be associated with any kind of music that was less than top-notch.

Now, though, Bill was ready to jam, and as he approached us he looked serious—filled with a singleness of purpose. It was almost as if he was silently telling Smokey, "You said you wanted a jam session—well, get ready now: this jam session's gonna wear you out." The heavy artillery was present, and I began to get nervous. Sitting down, Bill started playing a new tune in the key of C that I had never heard before. I pretended to be busy tuning my banjo, hoping he wouldn't want me to play a solo. The guitar player took a turn at the melody. Quietly, I stood up to leave. "Sit down, Bob," came from Bill. Meekly, I sat back down. The guitar player was close to finishing his solo. "Okay, Bob."

There was no turning back, so I jumped in picking—and I surprised myself. The tune had a nice flow and I held my own pretty well. Bill took another solo on the mandolin, finishing the tune. I started feeling a little more at ease. We played several more instrumentals—then Bill really turned up the heat, launching into "Katy Hill" at a fierce tempo. It was all I could do to keep up. I imagined beads of sweat popping out on my forehead. I squeaked through my banjo solo, thankful Bill didn't make me play it more than once.

He played "Paddy on the Turnpike," also at a fast tempo. His timing was perfect, unchangeable. Even when the other musicians were on shaky ground rhythmically, Bill's beat was rock-steady. He added the syncopated double-stops he always included in that tune, and they possessed an almost visual impact. Listening to the tones was almost like seeing shades of color. The banjo and fiddle took their solo turns and passed the tune back to the mandolin, which took charge again, stating the melody in an absolute and authoritative way.

After the initial burst of musical adrenalin, our jam session settled down and became a bit more relaxed. Bill played "Kentucky Mandolin," placing rich, full chords among the single notes of the melody. "Kentucky Mandolin" was reminiscent of "Paddy on the Turnpike," except that it contained more minor chords, giving it an aged, classic flavor. (I had to retune my banjo in a hurry, just as I had done in my audition for Bill.)

Then Bill sang "Wayfaring Stranger." His voice was clear and high, filled with sustained pathos. I don't think I ever heard him do a better job on that song. He had the enviable ability of being able to switch his voice from normal to falsetto with no apparent effort. (Bill sometimes used the word falsetto when talking about singing—only he pronounced it "false.") When Smokey played his fiddle solo on the song, Bill added backup notes and chords in unexpected places, sometimes ahead of the beat and sometimes behind the beat, creating an interesting counterpoint. His enthusiasm was unmistakably evident.

The music came alive that night—a true bluegrass experience. I was glad Bill hadn't let me sneak off! Playing with him was a challenge—but something intangible had taken over and allowed us to rise above our own abilities. It had truly been magic. And Smokey got his jam session.

## Dueling Mandolins

One bluegrass festival in particular stands out in my memory. In late July 1976, we played at the Berkshire Mountain Bluegrass Festival in Hillsdale,

New York. A furious storm came up following our afternoon show. We were sitting on Bill Monroe's recently acquired Silver Eagle bus. (Bill had purchased the Silver Eagle because he could no longer find parts to keep the old Flxible running.) Suddenly, we were startled by a flash of lightning, accompanied by a heart-stopping crack of thunder. It had been very close, in fact, so close that a man standing next to the bus was struck. Incredibly, he suffered only minor burns on the soles of his feet. His metallic necklace had attracted the bolt of lightning—or was it actually his proximity to the Father of Bluegrass?

Earlier that afternoon, Bill had been "playing up a storm" with a uniquely innovative mandolinist named Frank Wakefield. Possessing an eccentric sense of humor, Frank had entered the bus carrying his instrument and fearlessly announced to Bill, "I'm the only man who can play your stuff just as good as you can." He said it with a big grin, knowing Bill would take the challenge. Uncasing his mandolin, Bill began playing one tune after another with Wakefield, blasting out his original melodies at furious tempos. Wakefield held his own pretty well, answering each devastating musical attack with brilliant flashes of his own, even matching some of the deep richness of tone and effortless drive generated by Bill. They brewed up a storm with their duel, and the heavens couldn't resist joining in the brawl.

## Bill's Favorite Stories

Everything had its place on the Blue Grass Special. Stage suits were hung in a closet at the back of the bus. The bass, and the boxes of records to be sold at shows were stowed in luggage bays underneath. Bill had a spot where he stashed pieces of hardware and other things he had picked up along the road. Bill didn't like throwing away such items—he thought they might come in handy someday. We Blue Grass Boys tried very hard to keep the aisles clear, mainly because of a story that Bill told us more than once: while traveling down the highway one night he stumbled over a pair of shoes one of the band members had left in the aisle while he was sleeping. Bill picked up the shoes and threw them out the window. (I hope the sleeping Blue Grass Boy brought an extra pair of shoes that trip.)

Bill told another great story of how he had once been accidentally left at a truck stop. He was dozing in his sleeping quarters at the back of the Blue Grass Special during a food and fuel stop. None of the Blue Grass Boys wanted to wake Bill, so they let him sleep while they went into the restaurant. Later Bill woke up and left the bus to use the restroom and make a phone call. Meanwhile the Blue Grass Boys finished their meal and boarded the bus again, taking off down the highway. They thought Bill was still asleep in the back. When Bill returned to where the bus had been parked, he realized he had been left behind. He got back on the phone, calling the highway patrol. The Blue Grass Special was stopped at a tollbooth many miles down the road. The tollbooth operator told the driver: "You'd better go back and get your boss."

There was one story Bill could never tell without chuckling. We Blue Grass Boys thought it was so funny that we had a running gag line referring to it the entire time I was in the band. Several years before I joined the band, Bill and the Blue Grass Boys were playing a show in a schoolhouse in Bluefield, West Virginia. Melvin Goins, who performed in a duo with his brother Ray, was on the same program. (Melvin Goins, by the way, has some memorable stories of his own to tell.) The car Goins had driven to the job had a transmission leak that he had been worrying about during the whole trip. He checked into the same hotel where Bill and his band were staying. After he parked his car he found a piece of cardboard to place underneath the car, so he could tell by looking for stains whether any transmission fluid had leaked out during the night. When Goins wasn't around, one of the Blue Grass Boys got a quart of oil and poured the contents all over the piece of cardboard. The next morning, when they went out to get in their vehicles, Goins saw the puddle of oil underneath his car and said, "Well, boys, we're rurnt (ruined)." Bill told that story many times, and we loved it so much that whenever anything went wrong we would always say, "Well, boys, we're rurnt."

Bill often told another story about a time when Earl Scruggs was playing in the band. They were in a hotel when Bill knocked on Scruggs's door. Scruggs opened the door just a crack to see who it was. Bill forced the door open and grabbed him by the arm, dragging him out into the hallway. Scruggs was dressed only in his underwear. As far as I know, no one has ever heard Earl Scruggs tell that story—but I can still hear Bill laughing as he recounted it.

Bill liked oysters a lot. I don't know if their reputed qualities as an aphrodisiac had anything to do with it, or if he just loved the flavor. He often told us about the oyster-eating contests he would get into whenever he and the Blue Grass Boys were in the area of the Gulf of Mexico. (Bill was very competitive in nature.) Whoever ate the fewest oysters had to pick up the tab. Joe Stuart, a Blue Grass Boy with a large appetite, once lost one of these contests to Bill—Stuart ate ten dozen oysters, but Bill surpassed him by eating twelve dozen.

## The Head of the Family

Bill was having a little trouble with his ears. When he asked me to administer some eardrops, I was glad to be of assistance. He lay down on his side on one of the forward bench seats of James Monroe's motor home as I applied the drops, hoping we wouldn't hit a bump in the road that would cause them to spill.

Most of the time Bill Monroe seemed as strong as any of his mules, but at that moment he struck me as being an old, old man. Granted, he did have gray hair, age spots on the backs of his hands, and a few crow's feet around his eyes, but still he was only sixty-three—and he possessed the physical stamina of a man nearly twenty years younger. In truth, I believe Bill cultivated the image of being elderly when it suited his needs. Very much aware of his role as bluegrass patriarch, Bill knew how to use that to his advantage. He seemed more like a father figure than a boss—an image that also carried over into his relationship with his fans. He was always ready and willing to play upon the "aging Father of Bluegrass" aspect of his public persona. When he sang "The Old, Old House," for example, he would look down toward the floor and lower his voice to a mere whisper when he got to the chorus:

When the leaves start to fall in autumn,
And the rain starts to drip from the trees—
There's an old, old man who walks in the garden
And his head is bowed in memory.

It was easy to get the idea that the song had been written especially about him, and he invariably elicited sympathetic responses from audiences with his highly personalized interpretation of the lyrics. By the 1980s Bill had refined his presentation of "The Old, Old House"; he dedicated the song to the ladies in the audience and drooped his shoulders during the chorus, causing his voice to break as though he were struggling to hold back tears. At one concert in Iowa City, he sat down in a chair at the back of the stage after he finished the song, apparently trying to regain his composure after being overcome with emotion. Within a few songs after his heart-wrenching portrayal of old age in "The Old, Old House," Bill might exhibit a youthful strength and vigor, dancing to a fiddle or banjo solo, or singing an energetic version of "Molly and Tenbrooks." He could be both young and old during the same fifty-minute set of music.

When Bill asked you for a favor, he had a way of making you feel good about it—as though he was honoring you by asking. People always wanted to do things for him. He constantly received gifts. Women baked pies and cakes and brought them to him at festivals. (Often, the baker brought two pies —"one for Bill and one for the boys.") Photographs, craft items, and all sorts of memorabilia were offered to him as he signed autographs. Whenever Bill manned the record table with us, fans would swarm around. That was back in the days when vinyl was king, and LPs sold for five dollars apiece. We also sold *Grand Ole Opry WSM Picture-History* books, as well as copies of a recently published volume by Jim Rooney called *Bossmen: Bill Monroe and Muddy Waters* (New York: Dial, 1971). This work drew many comparisons between the personalities and careers of each bandleader.

People always asked Bill to sign their album covers. (Bill pronounced the word "album" with an "n" on the end, as in "albun.") Other people wanted their photos taken with him. (He always removed his glasses before posing for pictures.) Fans invited him to dinner in their homes between shows. Audiences felt true affection for him, which they demonstrated by their enthusiastic applause. They also demonstrated their loyalty by returning to his shows year after year.

Bill warmed the hearts of his fans. Bluegrass was his personal gift to them, and he presented the music in such a dignified way that it promoted a sense of pride in their shared common values. His gift of bluegrass was something to be treasured—a prized family heirloom to be lovingly handed down through the generations. The Father of Bluegrass truly was the much-beloved head of a large and devoted family of followers.

Today, the Family of Bluegrass (like the proud Scottish clan from which Bill's pioneer ancestors descended) is strong, powerful, enduring, and filled with a sense of loyalty to tradition. It owes these qualities to the legacy of its founder.

## Possum Holler

One night after the Opry, Bill Monroe and I put on an impromptu show with just the two of us. The place was Possum Holler, a restaurant in downtown Nashville owned by country singer George Jones. Bill had given Jones the nickname "Possum" (because he thought George's eyes resembled a possum's), and that's how the restaurant got its name. Bill bought dinner for himself and a lady friend, as well as for me and a buddy named Dave Lynch. (Dave had just hitchhiked in from Iowa and joined a carnival out at the Tennessee State Fairgrounds.) After dinner, Bill treated us all to a round of "chicken whiskeys," the house specialty drink. It was

Bob Black, playing the Ibanez banjo presented to him in Japan, at Ralph Stanley and Bill Monroe's Third Annual Old-Time West Virginia Bluegrass Festival, Aunt Minnie's Farm, Stumptown/Glenville, West Virginia, August 1976. Photo by Carl Fleischhauer. (Used by permission.)

called that because it didn't contain very much alcohol. That was the only time I ever saw Bill Monroe consume spirits—he detested "beer hogs," often saying: "I don't see how they can drink that old sloppy stuff!" Bill often talked about how he liked the taste of good whiskey—though he seldom drank it. During our trip to Germany, a radio DJ had offered him a bottle of expensive whiskey as a gift, and Bill turned it down. I heard him mention several times that the job of preserving bluegrass music and maintaining his band was one of the reasons he didn't allow himself to drink. (He didn't mind being sponsored by a beer company, however. The Schlitz brewery was the financial backer for one of the Grand Ole Opry segments hosted by Bill.)

While we enjoyed our drinks, the solo artist performing at Possum Holler that night learned that Bill Monroe was in the audience, and asked him to come to the stage and sing a little bit. Bill and I had both brought our instruments, so we got up and played a couple of numbers, just the two of us. It was fun not having to compete for a chance to play some backup licks. I was proud to play the role of Bill's entire band that evening.

## A Band of One

Before one show, all the Blue Grass Boys began jamming backstage. Bill wasn't there—we assumed he was in the next room. After we finished a tune, we could faintly hear Bill's voice drifting toward us from the other side of the closed door. At first I thought he was just softly warming up his voice, singing the high, wailing tones that I often heard him use. This time, however, I could hear words. He was singing "I'm On My Way Back to the Old Home," a song he often used to start his shows. Suddenly, we realized he wasn't in the adjacent room at all, but on stage—all by himself. Kenny said, "Come on boys, he's startin' without us!" We hadn't heard any introduction. We rushed out to the stage. Bill was standing at the microphone, singing and chopping rhythm on his mandolin, with nobody backing him up. We joined him just in time for the last chorus.

## The End of My Apprenticeship

"Bob, I'm changin' the style of my music, and I've got to get me a new banjo player." I heard those words one evening in September 1976, soon after arriving at the Opry House for another show. I walked into the artist's entrance, and found Bill Monroe standing next to the postal boxes where fan mail was picked up. He looked at me very seriously as he gave me the bad news.

I didn't press him on it. I figured his mind was made up, and I would have to go along with his decision. I simply acknowledged his statement and left to get ready to do our show. Entering our dressing room, I told the other Blue Grass Boys I had just been fired. They didn't seem too surprised, although I'm sure they had no prior knowledge of it. They just told me they were sorry to hear it—that was about all they could say. I played the evening show in a trance, but in a way I was kind of relieved. Working for the Father of Bluegrass had been very stressful. Not long after that, Kenny Baker told me something he had learned from Bill: he had let me go because he was worried about my health. I was such a perfectionist that I had been trying too hard and couldn't see the toll it was taking on my nerves. Our heavy tour schedule was causing a steady buildup of anxiety for me. I had very nearly reached a state of nervous exhaustion, and Bill felt certain that my condition would become more serious if I continued working in the band. Therefore he let me go, or laid me off, whichever you choose to call it. The upshot was this: it was Bill's decision that I leave the band, not mine—and I accepted that decision. I trusted him. I had no doubt that he had my welfare uppermost in his mind.

Now my apprenticeship was over. I had spread my wings and I had soared, but it was time to come back down to earth and make my own contributions to the music. The pressure was off. Leaving the band was probably the best thing for me to do. I never felt too comfortable wearing a hat anyway.

## 6.   A TOUGH ACT TO FOLLOW

I was still a Blue Grass Boy—I would always
be one. Playing with Bill Monroe was something that would never leave
me. You could never forget Bill, once you got to know him; he stayed with
you in spirit, influencing your habits and ways of thinking. His concepts
about music left a permanent mark on me; his attitudes, expressions, and
beliefs were always there as a point of comparison in all my ways of thinking. I crossed paths with Bill Monroe many times during the years that
followed, and each occasion was a reminder of what an immense influence
he had exerted on me.

I had been so dedicated to my role as a Blue Grass Boy that my sudden
detachment from the group left me feeling empty and a little bit confused. I
had a hard time processing the fact that I would now be functioning outside
Bill Monroe's sphere of influence. The idea of returning to Iowa seemed
out of the question to me. I had left Iowa City with dreams of becoming a
success in Nashville. My idea of success meant achieving recognition as a
banjo player based on the merits of my own individual style. In my mind,
I hadn't achieved that goal yet, because I had been playing the way Bill
Monroe wanted me to—not the way *I* wanted to. I had an unfulfilled need
for self-expression. I didn't want to return to Iowa until I had satisfied that
need in the public arena. I wasn't ready to throw in the towel yet.

I stuck it out in the Nashville area for two-and-a-half more years after
leaving the Blue Grass Boys. I collected unemployment checks for a few
months before getting a job with Jay Grizzell, Doug Mounts, and the Misty
Mountain Boys. We played several nights a week at a club on Sixteenth
Avenue called the Salty Dog Saloon, which shared the same building as

the Country Music Wax Museum. It was an enjoyable time for me, during which I was able to catch my breath, recuperate, and determine my next course of action. I got along well with Jay and Doug, and Terry Smith, the bass player, was a good friend whom I had known for a couple of years. We had been to a lot of picking parties together. He could play a bass solo on almost any number, and to my mind his knowledge of the fingerboard was unmatched. (Terry later joined the Osborne Brothers, playing and traveling with that band for many years.)

In the spring of 1977, singer and mandolin player Buck White asked me to join his group, Buck White and the Down Home Folks. The band consisted of Buck and his two daughters: Sharon on guitar and Cheryl on bass. The Whites possessed a trademark family harmony that traced its development to singing in church. Cheryl's voice had a husky, earthy quality that was both appealing and melancholy, while Sharon had a higher voice that was sweet, cheerful, and melodious. When all three of the Whites sang together they created a soulful mood that was sincere and emotionally moving.

The Whites were originally from north Texas and their style of blue-grass, though drawing its roots from Kentuckian Bill Monroe, was defi-nitely Texas-flavored—it drew strongly on Western Swing music. The influ-ence of Bob Wills and the Texas Playboys, as well as that of Bill Monroe, could be heard and felt in the Whites' music. The beat was slower and the melodies were jazzier than in Bill's southern style of bluegrass. In addition to being a bluegrass mandolin stylist of considerable note, Buck White is an accomplished honky-tonk piano player. He often played piano on the shows I performed on with them.

My employment with Bill Monroe played an important part in the Whites' decision to offer me a job. They felt that working for the Father of Bluegrass had given me sufficient traveling and performing experience to be an asset to their band. As an incentive to join the group, Buck told me I would be given much more creative musical freedom with the Down Home Folks than I had experienced with the Blue Grass Boys. I was happy to take the job, not only because the pay would be better than it had been with the Misty Mountain Boys, but also because the music would be chal-lenging and fun.

We did fancy tunes such as "Honeysuckle Rose" and "Limerock," and I sometimes got carried away musically, overreacting to the newfound freedom I had been granted. In this respect, Bill Monroe was still influenc-ing me, although not necessarily in a good way. I was like a puppy that had just broken its leash—I ran wild, putting lots of melodic notes into every song. Buck introduced me on stage one time by saying: "This is Bob Black—give him an inch and he'll take a mile."

We played coffeehouses, clubs, and college campuses all over the United States and Canada. We appeared at bluegrass festivals in Ohio, Maryland, Pennsylvania, New Jersey, Oklahoma, Michigan, Missouri, Texas, and New York. (Near Corinth, New York, we performed at a festival held on the banks of the Hudson River. On a foolish whim, I swam across the river and back. Total exhaustion had nearly set in by the time I was finished. Two other young festival attendees accompanied me on the lunatic adventure.) One especially memorable performance occurred at a taping of a TV show in Chicago called *Sound Stage,* along with Emmylou Harris and her band. I remember Cheryl doing a great job of singing "My Window Faces the South" on that show.

We also performed at Bill Monroe's fall festival at Bean Blossom, Indiana. I talked to my former boss there for the first time since leaving the Blue Grass Boys. Bill made me feel very welcome at the festival, and there was no animosity between us. He told me he had been surprised to hear that I had stayed in Nashville. He figured I would go back home to Iowa after leaving the Blue Grass Boys. I guess he underestimated my stubbornness, which really began to display itself during the time I spent with the Whites.

I cut my first solo album, *Ladies on the Steamboat,* while I was a member of the Down Home Folks. Buck had introduced me to Slim Richey, the owner of Ridgerunner Records—a label for which the Whites recorded—and persuaded him to finance and distribute the project. We made the album at Gordon Reed's studio in Nashville. I first met Reed when he played banjo with James Monroe, and his firsthand knowledge of the instrument and the music enabled him to engineer the project with a great deal of expertise. I included Buck on mandolin and Cheryl on bass. (I asked Sharon to play guitar, but she had to go out of town during the recording session.) There were many other featured guests on the album, including Kenny Baker, Norman and Nancy Blake, Alan O'Bryant, Terry Smith, John Purk, and Al Murphy. I found out later (much to my regret) that Bill Monroe had wanted to be included on the album. I hadn't asked him because I assumed that contractual obligations with his label (MCA) prevented him from recording on other labels. I should have known better—if I had been thinking, I would have realized that Bill was free to record on other labels because he had participated on Kenny Baker's album, *Kenny Baker Plays Bill Monroe,* on the County Records label. That regret notwithstanding, I'm still very proud of the album. I included two

Bob Black and Buck White performing on stage at Delbert and Erma Spray's festival in Kahoka, Missouri, August 1977. Photo by Bill Nelson. (Used by permission.)

of Bill Monroe's numbers on it: "Jerusalem Ridge" and "Monroe's Blues." *Ladies on the Steamboat* answered the need I felt to make my own mark in the world of music. The selections, style, and arrangements were mine alone and, for the first time, I felt I was creating a work of art that came from *me*, and not just assisting someone else with *their* creation.

I enjoyed my first year with the Whites, but I gradually became dissatisfied with the job. I understood that the Whites were a family band and that I was a hired sideman, but my lack of power or influence in the group began to affect my attitude. I missed the sense of belonging that had been present with Bill Monroe. Working with the Blue Grass Boys, I had felt I was among equals. We were Bill's "sound," and he used us on every show, no matter how large or small the venue. His band was important to him. Each of us played a vital role in presenting Bill's music to the public. The Blue Grass Boys were a cohesive unit, and the resulting sense of mutual respect was woven into the fabric of the music itself.

With the Whites, I began to feel like an outsider. They were the headliners of the show, and I was the sole sideman. I perceived (perhaps mistakenly) a wall of separation between us that was constantly being reinforced. For example, when the album *The Whites: Poor Folks' Pleasure* (Sugar Hill 3705, 1978) was recorded, other musicians were used on most of it—people I barely knew or had never even met at all. I was included on only three cuts. I was surprised at how little banjo was used, considering that I played banjo on every song in our shows. This was in sharp contrast to the way Bill Monroe recorded his albums. He invariably used all of his band members on every track.

I began to grow sullen on the road. Of course, Buck didn't like my attitude; I can't say I blame him. Our relationship steadily deteriorated. It was inevitable that I would either quit or be fired. The latter happened while we were in Buck's van, traveling through the District of Columbia area on our way to a performance in New York State. Buck told me that he'd been thinking about it very hard, and had decided it was best to let me go.

I didn't take being fired lying down, as I had before. I was angry, but maintained enough control to keep from raising my voice. All the conflicting emotions I had kept bottled came out. I told Buck that it was wrong to fire a man on the road and then expect him to play a decent show that same evening. I demanded that he drop me off at the nearest bus station. Buck tried to convince me to finish out the trip, but I wouldn't hear of it. Unable to reason with me, he finally let me out at a bus depot. I rode a Greyhound back to Nashville, taking only my banjo and leaving my clothes in Buck's van.

I had traveled and performed with Buck, Sharon, and Cheryl for approximately two years. The style of music performed by the Whites changed soon after that. Their bluegrass approach was abandoned in favor of a more country-oriented format. After I was gone, Buck released another recording that included some of my banjo playing. Entitled *More Pretty Girls Than One* (Sugar Hill 3710, 1979), the LP contained music that we had recorded while I was still working for him.

I've seen Buck, Sharon, and Cheryl several times since I left the Down Home Folks. We harbor no grudges or ill feelings. In May 1998, while performing at the Grand Ole Opry with Rhonda Vincent and the Rage, I stopped by to visit Buck in the Whites' dressing room. (It was the same room Roy Acuff had always used—Acuff passed away in 1992.) Reminiscing, I told Buck that I had been just a kid during my Down Home Folks days, and that I wanted to apologize for my immature behavior. He answered that in many ways, he had been just a kid then too.

In retrospect, it's clear to me that neither the Whites nor I understood my yearning for the sense of belonging I had experienced with Bill Monroe. Few people can inspire the degree of loyalty and commitment that Bill could in his musicians; that type of bond is extremely rare.

## Government Cheese

Disappointed and homesick, I decided I'd had enough of Nashville, and I returned to Iowa City in late 1979 to play with my old friends and bandmates Al Murphy and John Purk. We formed a group called Grasslands, playing at such Iowa City establishments as the Mill Restaurant (still the best venue for bluegrass and acoustic music in that town), and Gabe's (a popular local tavern for student residents that hires mostly rock and roll bands). Bart's Place, where I played with the band Grassfire before I left Iowa, hadn't featured bluegrass for a long time—although when I walked by the place I noticed they still had a small sign with interchangeable letters on the outside corner of the building that read "Bart's Place Blue Grs."

Doug Page, from Cedar Rapids, became our bass player. He was an exceptionally good musician—he occasionally performed with the Cedar Rapids Symphony—and I felt lucky to be sharing the stage with him. He could play lead bass solos on practically any number. Warren Hanlin, from Iowa City, was our guitarist and singer. He had his own style—a kind of "sock" rhythm that seemed to be influenced as much by swing music as by bluegrass. Not that it was bad—indeed, Warren had a very unique and individual approach. Fortunately for me, my experience playing with Buck White and the Down Home Folks was a good bridge between the straight-ahead rhythm of Bill Monroe and the "jump" style favored by Warren.

I was anxious for Grasslands to be a success, but I didn't realize how difficult it would be to make a living performing bluegrass in Iowa in the 1980s. The wave of popularity enjoyed by bluegrass during the 1970s had played itself out there. We appeared at local bluegrass festivals around the Midwest, including many hosted by the Tri-State Bluegrass Association and Society for the Preservation of Bluegrass Music of America (SPBGMA). Unable to pay for motel rooms, we usually camped in tents on the festival grounds, which didn't bother me at first, because I always enjoyed camping out. Later on, however, I grew weary of roughing it. I had spent too many nights lying in soaked sleeping bags during rainstorms.

While performing at one SPBGMA festival in Waterloo, Iowa, we agreed to help drum up business for the weekend's bluegrass gala by climbing aboard the back of a pickup truck and playing instrumentals while being driven around town. The promoter, Chuck Stearman, rode with us and used a bullhorn to describe the festival's many splendors to motorists and pedestrians. When we pulled into a strip mall, a local police official drove up in his squad car and ordered us to stop. (Bill Monroe would have argued with him, or at least offered him free tickets to the festival.)

Grasslands had an ill-fated existence and met with its demise after only a short time. We were plagued with a lack of jobs, because booking was something none of us had any experience with or desire to do. Back in the early 1970s we had always had steady club work, but by the time the 1980s arrived we found there were no more club owners willing to hire bands on a full-time basis. Disagreement about musical direction also contributed to Grasslands' downfall. It quickly became clear to me that the band in which I had placed high hopes was going nowhere.

I soon found myself jobless and broke, living in a roach-infested rooming house and going to the local office of human services on a monthly basis to receive rental aid and food stamps. I took some part-time housepainting jobs that paid very little. At that time the Reagan Administration had a program of surplus cheese distribution for lower income citizens. More than once I had my monthly supply of government cheese stolen from the communal refrigerator in my rooming house. (I couldn't believe anyone would like it enough to pilfer it—it had such an unpleasant, artificial taste.)

In my opinion, the year 1980 marked the beginning of nearly two decades of lean, lonesome years for banjo players in general. Though bluegrass music itself was not as popular as it had been during the 1970s, bluegrass instrumentalists—with the conspicuous exception of banjo play-ers—were making inroads into popular music. Musicians I had known and performed with could be heard on commercial radio stations providing instrumental backup for mainstream country artists. It seemed to me that much of country music sounded like bluegrass without banjo. Though considered by many to be an important symbol of American musical culture, the banjo still had not been able to escape the stigma associated with its unfair hillbilly stereotyping. Recording executives, whose primary concern was financial profit, considered banjo to be the kiss of death for any commercially produced project. Banjo players who should have risen to national prominence during the decade of the 1980s either remained in obscurity or quit playing the instrument altogether.

I never could seem to abandon music in those post–Bill Monroe years, even though money was scarce. I had no interest in starting a career out-side of music. The graphic-arts degree I had received at Drake University seemed worthless because the entire graphics field had changed so much. Commercial art was no longer produced manually. Digital technology had replaced hands-on design, layout, and pasteup. Computer software pro-grams made it much easier for graphic artists to experiment with elements of composition. The quality of graphics had undergone a marked improve-ment as a result of these changes, but none of that meant anything to me because I was computer illiterate. I didn't know the difference between a floppy disk and a mouse pad—nor did I have any desire to learn.

Fortunately, I did know a lot of other musicians, and it wasn't long before I became involved with another band. It was called Calliope[1] and was a distinctive ensemble specializing in original, traditional folk, and Irish music. Calliope also performed a few bluegrass numbers, including one written by Bill Monroe called "The Sunset Trail,"[2] a western-style harmony vocal that always received good audience response. (Bill had occasionally performed the song while I was a member of the Blue Grass Boys.)

My experiences in the early 1980s had shown me how cheaply I could live when necessity demanded it. I developed thrifty habits that are still with me today—such as shopping for clothes at Goodwill; buying generic or store-brand items whenever possible; seeking out used appliances and furniture, watching for scratched and dented items on sale, and going to flea markets, clearance sales, and garage sales. Music nourished my soul during those times. I survived and prospered intellectually by getting to-gether with fellow musicians on a daily basis and learning new tunes. Music gained a new status in my existence, becoming an even more important part of my personal identity. I hadn't given up on it, and it hadn't given up on me. The early 1980s also proved to be the perfect time for the birth of a new musical team: Dave Lynch and Bob Black performing together as the Dogs of Love.

## The Dogs of Love

Dave Lynch sings real country music—the kind you used to hear on country-and-western radio stations. He also sings traditional bluegrass, with an energy and vitality reminiscent of Jimmy Martin's most spirited performances. His powerful voice can be heard above a rowdy crowd in any barroom.

In the early 1980s there was a farm crisis in the state of Iowa. Many farmers went out of business, auctioned off their family farms, and looked for jobs in the neighboring small towns. Often, these disaffected people could be found hanging out in local beer joints. These were the places where Dave and I—as the Dogs of Love—went on the prowl, performing bluegrass and country-and-western music. We made our money by passing the hat. We often earned a good haul because we both put a great deal of enthusiasm into our performances.

Dave came up with our modus operandi. We would march into a tavern with our instruments and announce to the proprietor that we played country music. (Everybody in a small-town Iowa bar loves country music.) I'd tell them I had worked for Bill Monroe on the Grand Ole Opry, and that would generally spark their attention. Then we would ask if it was okay to put on a show and pass the hat. Once we had permission, (and we almost always got it) we would launch into a lively rendition of "Night Train To Memphis," or "Jambalaya," or some other equally energetic crowd-pleaser—and the show would be off and running. Dave sang with wild enthusiasm, making eye contact with all the barroom patrons and flashing his devilish, white-toothed grin. He played with a forceful downbeat on his battle-scarred Martin guitar as we strolled about the establishment, serenading one and all and generally making ourselves difficult to ignore. We performed all of the hits: "Rocky Top," "Foggy Mountain Breakdown," "Dueling Banjos," "The Ballad of Jed Clampett," and so forth. We also sang many Bill Monroe songs, including one that Bill had written during the time I was working for him: "Louisiana Love." The most popular Bill Monroe song we did was "Blue Moon of Kentucky."

When our impromptu concert was over, we would pass the hat and leave. At one tavern in Fort Madison, a customer became upset when we passed the hat after playing only two songs. When she persisted in her public denouncement of us, Dave approached her table and dumped all the proceeds out in front of her, saying to the entire bar, "If anyone wants their money back, this lady right here's got all of it." Then we left.

Playing in taverns and passing the hat was enjoyable for the most part, but sometimes one or two of the patrons would get stirred up in a negative way. They would pick fights with other customers, and more than once we had to exit in a hurry when a skirmish escalated into an all-out fight involving the entire bar. We didn't stick around to sign autographs.

For some reason, the Bob Wills number "Corrina, Corrina" was the song we were singing when most of the fights broke out. At the Quart House tavern in West Branch, Iowa, we had just begun singing that song when I suddenly had to dodge a flying beer bottle. Several patrons began fighting, and they were moving in our direction. We ducked out the back door, which was several steps above the ice-covered parking lot. I don't think my feet touched a single one of those steps. Dave doesn't sing "Corrina, Corrina" any more.

At the Purple Cow in North Liberty, Iowa, two women were having a verbal disagreement while Dave and I were playing. Their argument, fueled by alcohol, reached critical mass when one lady shoved the other. "Take your hands off me, you bitch!" yelled the other, shoving back. Suddenly their husbands got involved, knocking over chairs and disturbing other patrons as they wrestled each other to the floor. In a few short seconds, the whole place erupted into battle. We hurriedly cased up our instruments and left. Outside, we could hear bodies slamming against the walls as the brawl intensified. I said to myself: "Bill Monroe never told me there'd be days like this."

Dave and I worked our way to Nashville in this manner later that winter. On our way to Music City, we stopped in many small taverns to put on shows. We played for several days at a tavern called the Red Fox in Paris, Tennessee. The owner was a country musician and bluegrass fan. He took a liking to us, letting us stay in a vacant room above the establishment.

I had a couple of Nashville recording sessions scheduled. One was with Kenny Baker—the album later came out under the title *Highlights* (County Records 785, 1984). I was proud to be included on that recording in the company of such great musicians as Bobby Osborne on mandolin, Joe Stuart on guitar, Roy Husky Jr. on bass, and Charlie Collins (who was a member of Roy Acuff's band) on guitar. The other album I recorded on was by California fiddler Jim Moss. The title song on that album, *Tanyards,* was a Bill Monroe piece that I had heard him play countless times. Bill had named it for a place near his boyhood home. Another featured performer on that project was the famed mandolin player who had invented the style of playing called cross picking—Jesse McReynolds.

After we got to Nashville, I decided to pay a visit to Bill Monroe in his office, which was then located just north of town. He asked me how I had been doing. I told him that Dave Lynch and I had been playing music in taverns and passing the hat. Then I asked him if he'd like to join us one time, just for fun. Turning his head away, he said, "I bet I could get a lot of money in the hat."

## Play It Again, Kenny

After over twenty years of playing fiddle with Bill Monroe, Kenny Baker decided to leave the job on October 12, 1984. The parting took place under unusual circumstances—in the middle of a show at Jemison, Alabama. A combination of factors was to blame; among them was a misunderstanding between Kenny and Bill over a schedule for their upcoming tour, and Kenny's concern for his brother, who was seriously ill. The situation was exacerbated at the show in Jemison when an obnoxious audience member began repeatedly requesting the tune "Jerusalem Ridge." Bill wanted Kenny to play it but Kenny refused, walking off the stage.

As soon as I heard the news, I called Kenny to see if he'd like to play some shows in Iowa with Al Murphy, Aleta Murphy (Al's wife), and me. I knew Kenny liked Al's rhythm guitar playing immensely, and he was sure to enjoy the traditional vocal duets sung by Al and Aleta. I was pleased and surprised when Kenny said yes, and I eagerly looked forward to teaming up once again with my favorite fiddler.

Kenny drove to Iowa in January 1985 for our first couple of shows. We rehearsed in a room at the Airline Motel, on the south side of Iowa City, where Kenny had checked in. Our first performance took place at the Mill Restaurant, where we played to a packed house. Kenny started the show with a tune by Fiddlin' Arthur Smith called "Indian Creek." (He kicked off many of our concerts with that one.) It was a good instrumental to get warmed up with, and we were riding high from that point on. We played lots of Kenny's originals, including "Bluegrass in the Backwoods," "Denver Belle," and one of my favorites, "Last Train to Durham." I was a happy banjo picker that night! The next day, we traveled to Ames, Iowa, to play a square dance for the Onion Creek Cloggers. Somebody at that

Bob Black, Kenny Baker, and Alan Murphy. Photo taken at the Airline Motel in Iowa City, January 1985. Photographer unknown.

show requested "Jerusalem Ridge," and Kenny willingly played it with us, as he did on nearly every one of our performances after that.

On January 26 we appeared at the Chicago Folk Festival at the University of Chicago. Roger Bellows played bass with us there, and Kenny recalled on stage how he and Bellows had recorded together on a 1972 album, along with the Dobro player Josh Graves (who had performed with Flatt and Scruggs from the late 1950s through 1969). That project, entitled *Something Different*,[3] surprised a lot of bluegrass fans, because on it Kenny played lead guitar in addition to the fiddle. His guitar technique is flowing and beautiful, involving both fingerpicking and flat-picking.

During our show at the Chicago Folk Festival, Kenny commented briefly on stage about his relationship with Bill Monroe, and about why he had left the Blue Grass Boys. He expressed his admiration for Bill and the music he had written. He explained that the only reason he had left Bill's band was because he was now fifty-eight years old, and felt it was time to start playing more of his own music. He ended his remarks by saying how much he enjoyed working with Bill, and how much he respected the man. Spontaneous applause rose from the audience after Kenny spoke his words of tribute to his former employer.

One week later, we played on the *Prairie Home Companion* radio show in St. Paul, Minnesota. After driving all night, we arrived early in the morning at a fancy hotel in St. Paul. Our rooms weren't ready yet, so we waited in the lobby with all our instruments and luggage until our rooms were ready. There was a severe cold snap in the twin cities of St. Paul and Minneapolis at the time, and the temperature outside was well below zero. Kenny was wearing only a light overcoat and no hat. When he walked outside, his ears turned bright red in the freezing air.

The *Prairie Home Companion* show took place at the Orpheum Theater in St. Paul, and we shared the stage with singer and songwriter Greg Brown (who also proudly hails from Iowa), as well as the noted musician, composer, and producer Peter Ostroushko. Garrison Keillor, the program's host, introduced Kenny by saying, "If Bill Monroe is the Father of Bluegrass, then Kenny Baker is the Uncle." One memorable moment took place when we performed "Cincinnati Rag" as a part of a medley. Butch Thompson played a ragtime piano solo on the piece, and then Lou Green on cornet and Vince Giordano on bass saxophone played a horn duet. The blend of instruments was considerably different from Kenny's usual sound on "Cincinnati Rag"!

While we were in the Twin Cities area, we played in the Jean D'Arc Auditorium at the College of St. Catherine's (also known as St. Kate's), and at a small club in Minneapolis called Johnny's Liquors. Bass player Gordy Able joined us on those shows, and he lived up to his name by playing able bass backup and even taking a few lead solos. We had loads of fun at Johnny's Liquors. There were lots of musicians in the audience, and they made us feel loose and right at home. After one of several requests had been made, I remember Kenny smiling and saying, "I ain't tipped that one in years." Then he turned his head to the right, and gazed sharply up at the ceiling. His bow started moving and there was the tune, right back on the tips of his fingers, as though it had never left him.

Al and Aleta Murphy and I next went on a Missouri tour with Kenny. One of the shows took place in Hannibal, at the Tri-State Bluegrass Festival. Just before our performance there, Kenny told Aleta: "I'm gonna do the singing on this show." Taking him seriously, she sat down in the audience instead of waiting backstage to be called up. When it was time for the vocal portion of the set, Al had to go out into the audience to retrieve his singing partner. Aleta didn't realize Kenny had just been joking about doing the singing himself!

In Columbia, Missouri, we played at a club called the Blue Note. We also performed on a bluegrass radio show in Columbia called *Chokin' the Strings*. It was broadcast over KOPN-FM, and hosted by a woman named Sister Jenny. We were joined on our shows in both Hannibal and Columbia by skilled bassist Forrest Rose.

Kenny had been receiving calls from many festival promoters, and he booked a number of them with Al, Aleta, and me. We played at a small bluegrass festival in Texas. It was held inside a firehouse in the town of Hardin, near Beaumont. A lot of fiddlers came over from the Houston area just to hear Kenny that day. Of course, they were Texas-style fiddlers, but their respect for Kenny's fiddling transcended all musical styles.

On June 29 and 30, we performed at the Thirteenth Annual New York City Bluegrass Festival in Staten Island. Between our shows, I enjoyed listening to a guitar performance by Jimmy Arnold, the gifted musician from Fries, Virginia, who had inspired me at Bean Blossom back in 1971. I barely recognized him at the Staten Island festival—he was covered with tattoos, including a large image of a wolf's head on the side of his face.

On some of our shows we had bass players, and on others we didn't. Though for the most part they were good musicians, a few of the bass players we hired weren't familiar with Kenny's music. Kenny asked Aleta if she could play bass on the performances, and she agreed to do so. (Prior to that, she had been accompanying herself on guitar.) Her first show as bass player was at Jerry Sullivan's Bilboa Creek Bluegrass Festival in Alabama. Aleta's playing was solid and tasteful, and the rest of us felt completely at ease performing with her.

Kenny always paid us very generously. The money taken in at every show was split evenly. At the Homestead Pickin' Parlor in Minneapolis we offered workshops (classes where students pay to listen to, and ask questions of, professional players), and the money there was divided into equal portions as well—more than fair, considering that Kenny had many more paying students at his workshop than I had at mine.

Later in 1985, Kenny Baker teamed up with Josh Graves, beginning a musical partnership that has lasted to this day. They've called on me to play banjo with them on several occasions, and I've always been pleased to do it. I'm proud to have spent some time with Kenny during his transitional period between leaving Bill Monroe's Blue Grass Boys and beginning his long-time career with Josh Graves.

## *Up in Smoke*

In December 1985, the rooming house where I lived burned to the ground. Owned by Francis Black (to whom I am not related), Black's Gaslight Village was a group of low-rent buildings located on Iowa City's north side. My modest, cramped room was in the L House. Poorly constructed, the interior walls of the dilapidated, two-story firetrap were covered with unfinished wooden planks. The blaze started when a tenant in the second-floor room next to mine got drunk and fell asleep while smoking a cigarette. All the residents awoke in the wee hours of that cold December morning to the piercing sound of smoke alarms. When I opened my door, I saw that the hallway was choked with thick black smoke. I put on my clothes and shoes before rushing out to see what was wrong. I didn't even grab my coat. When I got downstairs, my eyes were drawn to a flickering orange glow being cast on the trees and overgrown shrubbery outside the front door. Walking a few steps out to the parking area, I looked up and was stunned to see that the fire was already spreading with devastating speed throughout the second floor near my room. It was too late for me to go back up and retrieve anything.

Other residents emerged from the building, and we stood watching sparks and flames reaching up through the tree branches above the building. As the smoke alarms continued their shrill whistling, I became aware of another sound: people crying. I stood by numbly, watching the fire devour every square inch of the building. It didn't even register with me how much I was losing until the flames were nearly burned out.

I had left my banjo inside the rooming house, along with my many souvenirs. I lost records, tapes of jam sessions, photos taken while I was in Japan performing with Bill Monroe, a keepsake railroad cap I had received at the birthplace of Jimmie Rodgers in Meridian, Mississippi (where we played for the annual Jimmie Rodgers Festival), and a handwritten note from Bill that he had given to me for my birthday while we were on the road. (I don't remember his exact words, but the sense was that he enjoyed playing with me, and thought I was fun to travel with.) Also lost was the autographed album given to me by Bill Clifton after our 1975 European tour.

I don't think most of us at Black's Gaslight Village had even heard of renter's insurance, nor could we have afforded it if we had. Fortunately no one had been injured, and the Johnson County Red Cross provided us with food and clothing. A benefit to raise money for me was organized by my friends and fellow musicians from around the Iowa City area. It took place at the Mill Restaurant. Donations were placed in an open banjo case near the front door. I felt a warm sense of gratitude for the care shown to me by so many folks. Their contributions didn't feel like charity, and I learned an important truth: friends are worth more than any amount of money.

The funds that were raised from the benefit helped me to make a deposit on another room, and the Johnson County Red Cross purchased a banjo for me—a 1937 Gibson Recording King,[4] acquired by mail order from Elderly Instruments in Lansing, Michigan. I ordered it sight unseen, and it turned out to be a wonderful banjo. I still proudly play it today. More important than the banjo, though, was the faith shown in me by the Johnson County Red Cross. They assumed I was still a professional musician, and their confidence helped me to continue believing it myself.

## Belt Buckle Number 83

The Blue Grass Boys—everyone who had ever played in Bill's band—were going to be presented with a special gift honoring their contribution to the American way of life through music. That was the news I received in a 1987 letter from Doug Hutchens, a Virginia native who had played with Bill Monroe in 1971. He said the idea came from Grant Turner, the Grand Ole Opry announcer and bluegrass fan whose support for Bill Monroe was well known in Nashville. Turner had mentioned that Ernest Tubb created special belt buckles for members of his band, the Texas Troubadours, who also have a loose-knit organization called the Fraternity of Troubadours. In 1986, Doug Hutchens decided to present special Bill Monroe belt buckles to all of the Blue Grass Boys on Bill's seventy-sixth birthday, as a commemoration of our membership in that elite group.

Doug had been organizing birthday get-togethers for Bill since 1982, each year honoring him with a unique gift along with a custom hat designed by Randy Priest of Eagle, Idaho. The first year Bill was presented with a tooled-leather mandolin case. In 1983, the gift was a saddle; in 1984, several plaques for the Bluegrass Hall of Fame; in 1985, a fireplace set. (Later the same year, a vandal broke into Bill's house and used a poker from that fireplace set to smash Bill's mandolin to bits. Many people speculated that a former lover had done it in a vindictive rage, but no one was ever charged with the crime. Bill took the nearly 250 fragments in a sack to Gibson craftsman Charlie Derrington, who spent four months gluing the instrument back together, at times using a microscope to aid him to see the smallest pieces. When he finished, the mandolin looked like new.)

In 1986, Bill was given a clock. And in 1987, he was honored with a silver belt buckle that was number one of a set of 250.

The presentation of the buckles was made on a live television show called *Nashville Now.* Doug had commissioned artist Fred Huffman to create the design, and spent four thousand dollars of his own money to have the buckles manufactured. The two other financial contributors, *Bluegrass Unlimited* (the first bluegrass-music trade publication) and the Grand Ole Opry, provided fifteen hundred dollars each. Of the 250 buckles, six were made of solid silver, six were made of gold and silver plate, and the rest were made of solid brass.

Every Blue Grass Boy was given a numbered solid-brass buckle. On each is a relief sculpture of Bill Monroe playing his mandolin, with a likeness of Bill's uncle Pen playing his fiddle in the background on the left side, and an image of the Ryman Auditorium on the right side. Grant Turner was presented with one of the buckles, which is now on display in the Ernest Tubb Record Shop on Broadway in Nashville. I'm told that

One of the special commemorative belt buckles given to all of the Blue Grass Boys in 1987. Commissioned by Doug Hutchens and designed by Fred Huffman. Photo by Bob Black.

Bill Monroe wore his buckle every day for the rest of his life. The buckle was sold at auction after Bill's death.

Doug Hutchens has done numerous other things to honor the Blue Grass Boys. He recently arranged with the governor of Kentucky to make all of us members of the Honorable Order of Kentucky Colonels. The Kentucky Colonels Commission is Kentucky's highest honor. It is a non-political brotherhood for the advancement of Kentucky and Kentuckians, and carries with it a responsibility to be "Kentucky's ambassador of good will and fellowship around the world."

My Bill Monroe belt buckle is number 83. I wear it with pride almost every time I perform, and I truly believe it brings me good luck. It makes me think of my days with Bill Monroe, of my friendship with him, and of the great music we played together.

## The Iowa-Missouri Sore Foot Tour

Bill was barely able to hobble off the bus. Spring farm work had given him leg cramps, and by the time he and the Blue Grass Boys reached Hannibal, Missouri, Bill was in serious pain. It was a bad way to start his 1987 Midwest tour.

At the Holiday Inn, he met with his old friends Delbert and Erma Spray, who were promoting the tour. (Delbert was a wonderful old-time fiddler, and he and his wife, Erma, had been putting on the Kahoka, Missouri bluegrass festival since 1972.) Erma noticed that Bill had quite a limp, and she asked him what was wrong. He told her he was "all stove up" from working on the farm, and that he needed some quinine for his leg cramps. Delbert got him the medicine, and they all made their way to the Sprays' motel room. Bill also had a terrible sore on the bottom of his foot. He'd been plowing the garden with his mules and had made the mistake of walking behind the plow wearing heavy, stiff work shoes. He took off his shoe, showing Erma an ugly blister. It looked mighty painful.

Erma told Bill to take a hot shower and wash his foot thoroughly while she went to a pharmacy to get some antibiotic salve and gauze. When she returned, he sat down in a big chair and placed his foot up on a stool while Erma dressed his sore. Erma had lived on a farm all her life and had cared for many a blister, but she never expected to be caring for the Father of Bluegrass in this way. It made him feel better, and he went out for a press interview right after that. He enjoyed talking to the TV and newspaper reporters, and he even played a few tunes on his mandolin for them.

Bill was happy to be back in Hannibal again. He was comfortable around Delbert and Erma, because they had a lot in common. Like Bill, the Sprays farmed and raised cattle. Bill, along with Kenny Baker, had once gone to visit Delbert and Erma at their farm near Kahoka to seek help in purchasing some bulls. The Sprays had located some purebred shorthorn stock near Hannibal, and the four of them drove down together to look at them. Bill purchased his bulls, and developed a lasting friendship as well.

Bill stayed with Delbert and Erma in their room that night, sleeping on an extra bed. The next day, they went up to Strawberry Point, Iowa, where Bill and the Blue Grass Boys put on a wonderful show. Bill would never let something like sore feet slow him down. He even wrote a song in honor of the picturesque little town where the band played: "Strawberry Point." (On the same tour, Bill composed another tune in honor of the state of Iowa: the "Tall Corn State Breakdown." He played that one on his show in Iowa City to a very appreciative audience.)

On their way to Iowa City, Bill wanted to stop at a bakery in Manchester, Iowa. He never lost his love for pie, cake, and doughnuts. Before leaving the bus, Erma suggested that they first go shopping for some soft leather shoes for his sore foot. Bill agreed, and they made their way down the street. By happy coincidence, when they turned onto the next block they discovered a first-rate shoe store. The clerk brought out a pair of the softest leather shoes he had, and they fit Bill perfectly. He bought them right away.

The clerk took Erma aside, asking her, "Is that really Bill Monroe?" She told him yes, it was indeed, and he then asked Bill if he would mind waiting a few minutes while the local newspaper photographer came over to take his picture. Bill was happy to oblige, and he walked back to the bus—sore foot and all—to get some photos and other souvenirs to give to the store clerk. That was the true Bill Monroe: always willing to go out of his way to please the kind of everyday, hard-working folks with whom he would always share a common bond.

Bill and Erma visited the bakery after that. "Just pick out whatever you think looks good," said Bill. Erma did just that, purchasing a large box of rolls and doughnuts. When they got back to the bus, Bill's bass player, Clarence "Tater" Tate, brewed coffee for everyone, and they relaxed and enjoyed the pastries. The warmth and companionship they shared made the treats even sweeter.

The band I was playing with, Harvest Home,[5] was the warm-up act on several of the shows during that Iowa-Missouri tour. I had the pleasure of playing with Bill on stage in Monroe City, Missouri, and at McBride Auditorium in Iowa City. I have tapes of those shows; in Iowa City, Bill and I had this amusing verbal exchange over the microphones:

Bill: "Are you glad to be on the show tonight?"
Bob: "I sure am."
Bill: "Well, it's sure good to see you again, and hear you playin'—and you're comin' along fine with that five-string banjo. And you're singin' now.
Bob: "I'm singin' a lot more than I did when I was with you." (There was some laughter in the audience.)
Bill: "'Course you're a lot older too now than you was then."
Bob: "Yeah, age makes a difference. You get a few years on ya—"
Bill (interrupting): "What are you gonna do this time?"
Bob: "The one that I used to do with you all the time, that I used to enjoy playin' a lot, 'Dear Ole Dixie.'"
Bill: "All right, let's go."

We then played the energetic, southern ragtime tune and it transported me back eleven years to my days as a Blue Grass Boy. All my Iowa City friends could tell it was a real treat for me. Bill was at the top of his form, and his spirited mandolin solo drew excited applause from the audience.

In Keokuk, after the last show of the tour, we all went out to eat at a Country Kitchen restaurant. While Bill was waiting for his order to arrive, he stepped up to the lunch counter and, using the microphone belonging to the short-order cooks, sang "Blue Moon of Kentucky" to all of the patrons in the establishment. There were a few surprised looks on the faces of people who didn't know who he was!

Bill returned to Nashville and soon after played on the Grand Ole Opry. He spoke on the show of what a good nurse he had had up in Missouri, mentioning Erma Spray by name. Erma was really proud—she had taken good care of him.

Bill Monroe walked straight into a beam of sunlight striking the stage, bowing his head and raising his arms while the audience roared. Rumors had been flying—it was going to be the last Bean Blossom bluegrass festival. Bill was bringing it to an end—1989 would mark the final year.

That wasn't to be the case, after all. Bill announced from stage that he had just made the decision to continue the festival. Applause cascaded through the shade trees of the concert area. This time, however, the hand-claps and cheers sounded different than those which always followed a musical performance. A sense of profound contentment could be felt. The party wasn't ending, and Bill's fans wanted to show their appreciation.

I was performing at Bean Blossom that year with GroundSpeed, a German bluegrass band I had joined six months earlier. Kenny Baker had been instrumental in getting me the job. He and Josh Graves had toured Europe with GroundSpeed, and when they told him they were looking for a new banjo player, Kenny gave them my phone number. Kenny knew I would love playing with GroundSpeed, and that it would be a great chance to spend some time in Europe.

The group, which included Ulli Sieker (Rolf Sieker's brother) on mandolin and fiddle, Matthias Malcher on guitar, Klaus Gausmann on bass, and Edwin Herkert (who was leaving the group) on banjo, had achieved a great deal of popularity among European bluegrass and country-music fans, according to Kenny. Performing traditional-style bluegrass at clubs and festivals all over Europe, GroundSpeed was a top-notch full-time band that featured not only excellent musicianship and vocal skills, but also superior songwriting capabilities as well. The band had taken its name from a well-known banjo tune written by Earl Scruggs. Scruggs, who was a pilot, had chosen a flying term for the title of his piece. The song "Groundspeed" has become a bluegrass standard, and virtually every bluegrass band in the world plays it. The band GroundSpeed chose that name not only because of the tune's familiarity among bluegrass fans, but also because of the speed and flight associations the term carried with it.

GroundSpeed was already familiar with me from my performances at the Neusüdende festival in 1975 with Bill Monroe. Ulli had appeared there with a band called Bluegrass Express, and he had shared the stage with the Father of Bluegrass. Remembering me, Ulli thought I would be an ideal choice as banjo player for GroundSpeed.

Ulli phoned me from his home in rural Schnathorst, Germany, to invite me to join the band for a minimum of one year, starting in January 1989. My plane ticket would be paid for. He said he would fix up a small apartment in the large house where he lived with his wife, Anke Sieker, and their three children, Marvin, Rouvin, and Charlotte. I could live there, and the rent would be cheap. I could share meals often with his family. We would be performing full time and getting good pay, so I would probably be able to save some money. (That would be something highly unusual for a bluegrass musician!)

It didn't take me long to make a decision. For many years, I had been wishing I could return to some of the places I had visited in Europe when I was a Blue Grass Boy. I had been too young in the mid-1970s to really appreciate the chance to travel to those distant countries. Seeing things through the eyes of a Blue Grass Boy was like having tunnel vision—music and performing were my main concerns at the time. Everything else seemed to be of secondary importance.

My choice was clear. In Iowa City I was depressed, living alone in a dingy rented room, staring at my seldom-used Gibson Mastertone banjo, and feeling my arteries become more clogged with each bite of my daily Tombstone pizza. Would I rather go to a beautiful new country, make money, play lots of music, eat well, and be happy? Of course, I said: "Yes."

I arrived at the Frankfurt airport in January 1989. There, Matthias and Ulli greeted me warmly; their sincerity immediately assured me that I was among kindred spirits. We talked about bluegrass and Bill Monroe, Kenny Baker and Josh Graves, fiddle tunes and banjos— I quickly felt I had known Ulli and Matthias for many years.

I stayed in a very nice apartment overlooking a well-tended cherry orchard. The Sieker family treated me like one of their own, and I settled down to life in Germany feeling as though I truly belonged there. The countryside was beautiful with its barley fields bordered by pine-covered mountains. Every morning dawned bright and sunny, and in the afternoon clouds invariably rolled in. I walked about a mile and a half into town every day to purchase groceries and beer. The beer was great! Occasionally I purchased a bottle of wine or doppelkorn, a liquor made from corn. Several times I hiked up into a nearby chain of hills known as Wiehengebirge to write songs and dictate letter-tapes into a small recorder. Most of the tapes were for Kristie Reynolds, my girlfriend back in Iowa, whom I missed very much. Cupid had fired his arrows all the way across the Atlantic.

I remember my first show in Germany with GroundSpeed. It was at the Nashville Rodeo Saloon in Offenbach. The place featured mostly country music, but its patrons obviously enjoyed bluegrass too. It was surprising to see them line-dancing to bluegrass music. Many wore western-style clothing, boots, and hats. I saw large, sheathed hunting knives hanging from several belts, and I got the feeling they would have preferred to carry six-guns in holsters. One guy had a U.S. dollar bill stuck in his hatband. There were license plates from various American states nailed to the walls. The customers had an obvious fascination with the United States, but their superficial knowledge of the country gave them only a simplistic, Hollywood-style perspective.

We played many shows in Germany, and also performed in Austria, Switzerland, Holland, and Czechoslovakia. We had a five-week engagement aboard a ferryboat called the M/S SVEA that sailed back and forth between Stockholm, Sweden and Turku, Finland. Each excursion lasted a full day, and we put on a couple of shows every trip.

GroundSpeed came to the United States twice while I was a member of the band. Our first U.S. trip took place in June 1989; we played in Ypsilanti, Michigan; Branson, Missouri; and at Bill Monroe's Bean Blossom Bluegrass Festival.

It was exciting to be back in the United States and playing at Bean Blossom once again. At that time there was a sign above the stage that read: "Back Home Again in Indiana," and that's exactly how I felt. GroundSpeed performed on the same program with Ralph Stanley and the Clinch Mountain Boys, the Osborne Brothers, Jim and Jesse and the Virginia Boys, and Bill Monroe and the Blue Grass Boys. Matthias was concerned that we might be a little misplaced among such big shots. I told him, "We have a band as good as anybody."

On one of our Bean Blossom shows, Klaus put on a pair of short German leather britches called Lederhosen and danced the Bavarian "Schuhplattler," clapping rhythm on his legs and thighs. Meanwhile, Ulli sang a Bavarian yodeling song, during which he made up verses using obscene German words.

One especially unforgettable image lives in my memory of Bean Blossom that year—the sight of Bill Monroe riding around the festival grounds on a beautiful white Appaloosa horse named Speck. (Speck had tiny spots of black coloring.) The Father of Bluegrass passed in front of the stage, waving his hat to the audience and stopping every few feet while people snapped photographs. Bill was a singing cowboy that day, just like Gene Autry or Roy Rogers.

Later that summer, Bill Monroe and the Blue Grass Boys traveled to Switzerland and Germany along with the Osborne Brothers, joining GroundSpeed on a couple of shows. Traveling with my old boss, teacher, and friend made thirteen years and thousands of miles melt away. It was just like the old days.

We played at a large music festival in Basel, Switzerland, then headed north for a show together near Oldenburg, Germany. In Basel, Matthias took Bill to a shopping mall. He remembers people staring at Bill Monroe in his white suit and hat. Bill kept lifting the hat and greeting people in all directions (just as he did in our 1975 tour).

After the festival in Basel, all three bands crammed together into two Volkswagen vans to travel to the next show. Sonny Osborne and I shared the same van, and he was in a good mood all the way, telling jokes non-stop. Bill Monroe rode in the other van, and Matthias remembers how he hummed fiddle tune melodies while they traveled up the highway. The van I rode in was leading the way much of the time, and it seemed as though every time I looked back toward the other van, I could see Bill napping in the passenger seat; the top of his white hat bobbing up and down as his head drooped in slumber. Of course, he might have been playing possum again—writing songs in his brain, just like in the old days.

I returned to the United States with GroundSpeed on September 15, 1989. On September 19 we appeared as a showcase band at the International Bluegrass Music Association (IBMA) convention in Owensboro, Kentucky. (The IBMA was formed in 1985 to promote bluegrass music. Its annual World of Bluegrass convention features seminars, a trade show, and a fan fest including performances by many of the top bands in bluegrass.) We spent the following week recording a CD[1] at Fox Farm Recording Studio in Mount Juliet, near Nashville. One of the tunes on that project was the beautiful Bill Monroe composition "Northern White Clouds," which Ulli had learned in 1988 from the Father of Bluegrass. We had been playing it on nearly every one of our shows.

On October 5 and 6 we appeared at the Sullivan Family Festival in Wiggins, Mississippi, and on October 7 we returned to Nashville to perform on the banks of the Cumberland River as a part of a music festival called Riverfest. The next day, I bade farewell to my GroundSpeed friends at the Nashville airport as they prepared to board a plane bound for Amsterdam. It had been a wonderful nine months, filled with priceless memories. They had released me from my commitment to stay with them for a full year. I had a very good reason for wanting to return to the United States: I was in love.

## Return Engagement

In the spring of 1990, I introduced Bill Monroe to my fiancée, Kristie. The wedding date was set. Kristie and I had been writing love letters back and forth during the time I had been in Germany, and we had made so many international long-distance phone calls that her monthly bill was never less than four hundred dollars. (There went the money I was supposed to be saving.)

We were attending another concert at McBride Auditorium with Bill Monroe and the Blue Grass Boys.[2] They had returned by popular demand. Bill was surprised to see me at the show. "I thought you was livin' in Germany," he said. I told him I had come back to get married; that surprised him even more! He was very pleased to meet Kristie and congratulated us both.

Once again Bill asked me to be a guest on the show, so I got up on stage and played "The Pike County Breakdown." This time I did it in the right key! Bill danced a few steps to one of my banjo solos.

My parents were in the audience that night and later, as Bill visited with them, my mother gave him a kiss. Bill Monroe sure did have a way with women! Mom told me the kiss surprised her as much as it did Dad. It seemed to please Bill, too, because he told my folks he'd love to show them around the Opry the next time they came down to Nashville. He said to my dad, "You raised a good boy."

On May 19, 1990 I got married to Kristie—now my musical partner as well as my partner in life. Kenny Baker said it best. When I introduced him to Kristie for the first time, he told me: "Bob, I think you drove your ducks to a good market."

## Elvis's Cadillac

When Kristie and I walked into the lobby of Nashville's Country Music Hall of Fame, we immediately saw Bill Monroe eating at a small table in the corner. He noticed us right away and motioned to us to come over. We had come to attend the October 1994 CD release celebration of MCA's brand-new four-disk set of Bill Monroe's music from 1936 to 1994. Included in the compilation were some of the cuts I had played on (previously mentioned in chapter 5). I had my copy of the CD set with me and I asked Bill to autograph it. As he got out his pen, I asked him if he could make it out to "Bob and Kristie." He looked at me and said, "Oh, so you've got to have your name on it too, huh?"

I had a chance to visit with a lot of old friends and acquaintances, including the man often credited with giving Bill the nickname "Father of Bluegrass"—Ralph Rinzler. (Rinzler, who worked for the Smithsonian Institution for close to thirty years, was a former Greenbriar Boy, a musicologist, and a historian. I first met him in June 1976 at Bean Blossom. He passed away shortly after we saw him at the CD release party.)

There was a table spread with gourmet cuisine, and another with copies of the CD set, which were given to all of the attendees. Several people, including Bill, made speeches. He expressed thanks to MCA for their confidence in him and their long-time support. One of the highlights of the evening was Loretta Lynn's a cappella rendition of "Blue Moon of Kentucky,"[3] with Bill singing spontaneous harmony.

Later, Kristie and I went to view some of the exhibits with Alan and Cathy O'Bryant, Blaine Sprouse, Doug Dillard, Roland White, and several others. Among the Hall of Fame's most popular attractions was a display featuring one of Elvis Presley's Cadillacs. The top rose up to allow a view of the automobile's luxurious interior. It was an early-1960s customized model with many gold-plated gadgets, a refrigerator, tape deck, record player, shoe buffer, and television set. As we gazed at it, I recalled Bill Monroe telling me about how Elvis had followed him around to some of the tent shows he had put on back in the old days. One of Elvis's earliest hits was a song written by Bill Monroe—the one he had sung with Loretta Lynn only a few moments earlier: "Blue Moon of Kentucky."

Suddenly, I noticed that Bill was standing there too, looking at the display with us. Several of our friends asked Bill to climb over the guardrail and get into the automobile with them. We were surprised when he said yes. At the age of eighty-three, Bill still had a few tricks up his sleeve. As they helped him over the barricade, Kristie and I became a little nervous;

we knew he had recently had hip surgery, and a fall would not be good. Everyone climbed into the car safely, however. Bill sat in the back seat. I had never seen him clown around so much. He picked up the telephone. The TV fell over and landed in his lap. Laughing, the others helped him replace it and no harm was done.

## Long Hollow Jamboree

Kristie and I heard that Bill Monroe had been coming out to jam on Tuesday nights at a place called the Long Hollow Jamboree, just north of Nashville. When we paid a visit to Music City again in September 1995, we resolved to catch up with him. Our motel was several miles away from the restaurant and music establishment, and I had no idea what time Bill would be showing up. Just to be sure we didn't miss him, I telephoned the Long Hollow Jamboree early, asking if Bill Monroe was going to be playing there that night. "Sure. He's here now. He'll be playing in a few minutes," I was told.

We had to rush. Kristie had just gotten out of the shower and didn't have time to dry her long, curly hair. When we got to the Long Hollow

Clowning around in Elvis's Cadillac at the Country Music Hall of Fame, Nashville, Tennessee, October 1994. *Left to right:* Blue Grass Boy Mark Kirkendall, Bob Black (shoulder and nose visible only), former Blue Grass Boy Roland White, Debra Ann Hutchinson, Bill Monroe, Julia Labella, and Blaine Sprouse. Photo by Kristie Black. (Used by permission.)

Jamboree, we found Bill sitting at a table all by himself. Unable to figure out why he wasn't surrounded by fans, we approached him to say hello. He seemed changed. We knew he had recently been ill, but we hadn't expected to see him looking so tired and withdrawn. His sense of humor was still present, though. He looked at Kristie and said, "How'd you get your hair that way?" She told him she'd been in a hurry because she didn't want to miss him.

Bill asked us to stay and have a bite to eat with him after the show. He got up on stage a little later with the Boys From Kentucky, a bluegrass band that had been playing, and he invited me to sit in with them. As soon as he began performing, Bill exhibited a startling transformation—he seemed to grow younger before our eyes.[4] Once again he was the Bill Monroe I knew—the Father of Bluegrass, the Grand Ole Opry star, and above all, the master showman playing for people who loved and respected him. On stage was where he truly belonged, doing what he enjoyed most, and it filled him with an inner glow that warmed the entire room.

Bill sang two or three songs, and then he introduced me. I played "Blue Grass Breakdown," putting everything I had into it, and I stayed on stage with him for the rest of the show. We closed with Bill's old theme song, "Watermelon Hangin' On the Vine." Afterward, we sat down to eat with him. He seemed to grow remote once again. Kristie and I noticed that he didn't finish all of his food, and he put most of it in a box to go. A little later we said our goodbyes. That evening was the last time I would ever play music with Bill Monroe, in this life. He passed away less than a year later.

## The Little Community Church

The news of Bill Monroe's death came over the phone. On Monday, September 9, 1996, our friend Randy Escobedo (a wonderful banjo player who played on stage with Bill several times) called to let us know that the Father of Bluegrass had just passed away. Randy told us that radio station WSM in Nashville was doing a tribute to Bill, and that we should tune in. When I turned on my radio, announcer Eddie Stubbs was playing Bill Monroe's old recording of "Lord, Protect My Soul" (written by Bill and recorded in 1950). Tears immediately flooded my eyes when I heard Bill's soaring tenor voice coming in on the chorus:

> Oh, I want the Lord to protect my soul;
> To lead me on to Heaven's goal.
> My life down here will soon be o'er,
> And I want the Lord to protect my soul.

Tributes to Bill were aired on all of the national television networks during the following days. ABC news anchor Peter Jennings said Bill Monroe was a "family name to millions and millions of Americans who love the music they call bluegrass." CBS News presented filmed highlights of Bill's career. Singer and musician Alison Krauss, in an interview aired on ABC, said: "He started it all—he's going to keep influencing bluegrass musicians forever, and (he has) written some of the best songs you'll ever hear."

After making a few phone calls, I found there was to be a funeral service in Bill's hometown of Rosine, Kentucky, that Thursday. I was scheduled to perform in Salem, Illinois that day with Gary and Roberta Gordon (an Illinois folk and bluegrass duo). The Gordons were extremely gracious about releasing me from my commitment so Kristie and I could attend the funeral. It was something I had to do.

A moving public memorial service was held on Wednesday at the Ryman Auditorium in Nashville, where over two thousand devoted friends and fans gathered to pay final tribute to their beloved musical patriarch. Heartfelt prayers were offered and loving stories were told. Emmylou Harris, Patty Loveless, Ralph Stanley, Vince Gill, and many others expressed their love for Bill by singing hymns and sacred songs. At the close of the funeral, a group of Scottish bagpipers encircled the casket to play "Amazing Grace" as Bill was carried from the room. They marched down the aisle in a sad, slow procession. It was said that a shaft of sunlight fell upon the casket as the pipes wailed in mourning. A showman to the end, Bill followed the sun's shining rays—just as he had done on stage at Bean Blossom years before.

Cars were parked all over the little town of Rosine when Kristie and I pulled in on Thursday. We left our van along the highway at the edge of town and walked to the small Methodist church where Bill's funeral was to be held. Throngs of people crowded together outside. We met Kenny Baker in the churchyard, and he put his arms around us in greeting. With him was Doug McHattie, a gentleman from England who had traveled around a lot with Bill and the Blue Grass Boys. I hadn't seen him since the mid-1970s. We reminisced for a little while, and then Kristie and I left to get into the line, nearly a block long, that had formed outside the front door of the church.

The crowd that day was estimated at five hundred, twice as many as the little building could hold. We noticed that speakers had been placed on the lawn to make it possible for those outside to hear the service.

This was the same church where I had attended Charlie Monroe's

The Rosine Methodist Church. Photo by Bob Black.

funeral in 1975. James Monroe greeted us at the door. He remembered me, even though I hadn't seen him in almost twenty years, and he thanked us for coming. Inside, we worked our way to the front of the sanctuary, where Bill Monroe rested in a light-blue and silver casket. Tears flooded my eyes again as I looked upon the man who had been the single most important influence in my musical career. He had followers all over the world, many of whom had made the trip here to pay their last respects. He lay peacefully resting, his white hat placed beside his head. On his lapel was a small cross—one that he had worn for some time—announcing his faith to the world. Bill had become a very spiritual person in his later life. While on a trip to the Holy Land, he had even been baptized in the River Jordan.

Many people were putting quarters along the inside edge of the open casket lid, next to Bill's body, in remembrance of how he had often given quarters to children he was fond of. He used to carry quarters in his mandolin case expressly for that purpose. I laid a quarter down along with all the rest. Later, the Reverend Paul Baggett, who was asked by James Monroe to preach at the funeral, gathered up the quarters and passed them out to the children present—a parting gift from Bill Monroe.

When the service began, Grand Ole Opry performer Ricky Skaggs came to the front of the church and began to sing "Amazing Grace" a cappella. After the first verse, the entire congregation joined in, including singer Kathy Chiavola, whose voice stood out above the rest, clear and melodious. Ralph Stanley, wearing dark glasses, joined Skaggs for the next song, "Two Coats," sung with only guitar accompaniment. A few "amens" drifted up from the congregation. Skaggs then performed "If You See My Savior," an old song written by the reverend Thomas A. Dorsey, and his voice broke several times as he fought back tears. Gospel singer Alma Randolph then performed another Thomas Dorsey song: "Precious Lord, Take My Hand." Nearly everyone in the room was shedding tears.

Wayne Lewis, who had been a Blue Grass Boy from 1976 through 1986, spoke a few words next. James Monroe had asked him to do so less than an hour before the service was scheduled to begin, saying that he thought Lewis could handle it the way Bill would have wanted. Wayne performed the task admirably, officiating with skill and sensitivity. As he spoke he mentioned that there were several Blue Grass Boys in attendance, calling many of them by name. He also sang several songs, including one written about a church that had stood on the same site in earlier years, "Little Community Church" (composed by Bill and recorded by him in 1947).

Two more members of the Grand Ole Opry also spoke: my former employer Buck White, who attended the service with his wife Pat; and

Carrying Bill Monroe's casket into the Rosine cemetery, September 12, 1996. The pallbearer in front is Blue Grass Boy Wayne Lewis. Photo by Bob Black.

Blue Grass Boys (and others) pose around Uncle Pen's memorial in the Rosine cemetery, September 12, 1996. Photo by Kristie Black. (Used by permission.)

the country singing star Skeeter Davis, who spoke of her affection for Bill and his music, saying she had always wanted to be a "Blue Grass Girl."

Reverend Paul Baggett directed much of his sermon to the Blue Grass Boys who were present. He said we would one day get to play bluegrass with Bill Monroe again—when we entered the Kingdom of Heaven, for Bill would be waiting for us just inside the gate, with his mandolin tuned up and ready to go.

After the service, everybody walked the four blocks to the Rosine cemetery where Bill Monroe was laid to rest. Long rows of colorful flowers reached head-high, forming a pathway to the graveside. Many of us reached over and placed our hands on the casket, saying goodbye one last time. Alma Randolph sang "My Old Kentucky Home." Ricky Skaggs and Ralph Stanley joined their voices in a rendition of "Swing Low, Sweet Chariot," followed by a sad, slow version of "Blue Moon of Kentucky," on which the crowd joined in.

When the graveside service was over and the casket covered with earth, many people picked up small dirt clods as souvenirs. A large group of Blue Grass Boys gathered around Uncle Pen's nearby memorial, where Kristie and several other people took pictures. The mourners gradually began to disperse. After the crowd was nearly gone, Kristie and I went to get our van and drove it back to the cemetery. I noticed Ronnie McCoury, the son of former Blue Grass Boy Del McCoury, standing a little way off, playing

Bill Monroe's burial monument in the Rosine cemetery, 2003. Photo by Bob Black.

a Bill Monroe tune called "Old Dangerfield" on his mandolin. I got my banjo out and walked over to join him.

My long-time friend Alan O'Bryant was there, along with former Blue Grass Boy Butch Robins. We all decided to drive up to a place on a timbered hillside just outside of Rosine, where Bill Monroe's uncle Pen had once lived. It was the place Bill had stayed from 1928 until he left Rosine in 1929. There he learned old-time fiddle tunes from his uncle and acquired a treasury of memories that influenced his later life and music. He once wrote: "I can remember those days so very well, there were the hard times, and money was scarce, but also there were the good times. If it was to do over, I'd live them again."[5] Uncle Pen's cabin was gone now; only traces of the foundation remained. But the music handed down at that site was still alive and well. It was what had brought us there.

## Memories Never Die

I have a note and an autograph from Bill Monroe that I prize very much. It's something he wrote on a souvenir booklet he gave me back in 1989, at one of his shows in McBride Auditorium. I never asked for the booklet or the message—he gave them to me of his own free will. The note says: "To my friend Bob Black, Bill Monroe."

I often have dreams about Bill Monroe. In them, I'm usually late for a show, trying to get to the stage on time. I can hear Bill and the rest of the Blue Grass Boys starting without me. Sometimes I can't find my hat. I guess when I get to Heaven I won't have those dreams anymore—I'll finally make it to the stage and be back at my old job once again, playing with the Father of Bluegrass Music.

Bill Monroe's autograph, from the author's collection of keepsakes. Photo by Bob Black.

## Snapshots

Sometimes, when I close my eyes, I can call up visual images that have been stored away in my memory ever since the time I worked for Bill Monroe. Here are some of those scenes I still vividly recall:

I'm at a lively and colorful festival in Carlisle, Ontario. Bill and I are sawing a log with a large two-man crosscut saw, seeing how fast we can cut our way through the thick piece of timber. With spectators cheering us on, we work the blade back and forth. It's my first time using such an implement and I quickly discover that the saw works best when each man takes his turn pulling it toward himself, letting the other man then pull it back. We get an energetic rhythm going that picks up in tempo as the teeth bite deeper and deeper. Bill has done this before, and (as he's already told me) it's a lot of fun! The saw blade begins to sing and Bill is grinning as he pulls his end faster and faster. The slice of wood falls to the ground as we finish. I never would have dreamed it could be that easy and quick.

Bill and I are sitting in the grass to watch a beautiful sunset at Monroe's Bluegrass Musicland Park in Beaver Dam, Kentucky, after spending the day building and repairing fences all around the grounds. We're outside the doublewide mobile home Bill has placed there, stretching our tired legs out on the cool, shady lawn as the sun drops below the horizon. The next day, I discover that my thighs and entire backside are covered with ferocious chigger bites. Bill must have gotten them too, though he never lets on about it.

I'm riding in the station wagon, listening to Bill dream out loud. He tells of his desire to visit the Holy Land, and to see with his own eyes the countries written about in the Old Testament. The ancient pyramids of Egypt intrigue him, and he speculates on how they were constructed. "You know," he states with certainty, "they had to use horses and mules."

The Blue Grass Boys are standing around a campfire at a festival site in Louisiana, near Baton Rouge. It's the night before the festival is scheduled to begin. As the logs crackle, fragrant woodsmoke fills the night air. We turn away from the flames to warm our backs, while Bill tells stories about foxhunting around Jerusalem Ridge when he was a young man. (Bill loved foxhunting, and he kept about fifteen dogs during the time I was with him.) He tells us about how he used to stand around campfires just like this while listening to the foxhounds run. He could recognize each

Bill Monroe tipping his hat to the audience at the Bean Blossom festival, June 1975. Photo by Thomas S. England. (Used by permission.)

hound by the sound of its bark. "Put 'em all together," he says, "it makes a wonderful sound." He could have been saying the same thing about the elements of bluegrass music.

I'm standing on a raised stage, looking out over a sea of faces in the Ernest Tubb Record Shop in downtown Nashville, just around the corner from the old Ryman Auditorium. The band is waiting for the Grand Ole Opry to finish up so the Ernest Tubb Midnight Jamboree can get underway. The impatient crowd is overflowing onto the street, and their anticipation soars as the live radio show finally gets ready to begin. As soon as we're on the air, Kenny leads us into a fast bluegrass version of Ernest Tubb's theme song, "Walking the Floor Over You." After Bill Monroe sings a verse, Ralph Lewis plays the kick-off notes to Bill's theme song, and Kenny and his fiddle take over again. Grant Turner, from a podium on the floor to our left, begins his introduction: *Now, from Ernest Tubb's theme song to the great Bill Monroe's theme song, "Watermelon Hangin' on the Vine," here we are, friends, with a Midnight Jamboree, with the great Bill Monroe—stepping right out of the Hall of Fame in Nashville, Tennessee. . . .* The faces below us are smiling, hands are clapping, and a memory is stamped forever in my mind.

I'm looking at a bumper sticker that reads "Bill Monroe for President" placed on the rear bumper of my car, a 1964 Mercury Comet—purchased for four hundred dollars from Randy Davis. The car is parked at VanAtta's, and Bill Monroe sees the sticker as we get ready to head out to a show. "I think that man would make a powerful president," he says.

Bill is reaching out to shake hands with me, backstage at the Great American Music Hall in San Francisco in 1984—many years after I've left the band. He grasps my hand with a strong grip and pulls me toward him, nearly making me lose my balance. (He did that with a lot of people, as a joke.) Then he asks me to get my banjo and play a tune on stage with him and his band, making me proudly aware of my undiminished status in the brotherhood of Blue Grass Boys.

I have a cherished mental picture, shared by countless others, of the final moment of a show. It could be any show—just after the last encore is played. It's the unforgettable image of Bill Monroe, the Father of Bluegrass Music, lifting his hat to the audience in a proud, stately gesture as he takes his final bow.

# Afterword

Music, when soft voices die,
Vibrates in the memory—
—Percy Bysshe Shelley

I told Bill before I left the Blue Grass Boys that I was going to write this book. At that time, I asked if he would be willing to write a few words as a foreword. He said to me: "I'll be glad to help you any way I can." Bill's endorsement of this book will have to be made later—in the hereafter. I feel sure it will be a good endorsement, however, because I've stuck to the truth. It's taken me almost thirty years to get the book written, and it's been a cathartic experience in many ways. I now realize how much I've grown since those days, and also how much of that growth has been tempered by the power of Bill Monroe's continued presence in my psyche. Though he was often a demanding and authoritarian bandleader, he also had a great deal of respect for those who dedicated their talents to the advancement of his music, and he was always willing to lend his support in any way it was needed. He helped me in more ways than he was probably aware of. He legitimized my career as a musician and songwriter.

Bill Monroe left his mark on all of the Blue Grass Boys by the example he set. His music is a superb illustration of how various influences can be distilled to create something new, exciting, and relevant—but in truth it was his *belief* in his music that set him apart. Bluegrass was the most important thing in the world to him. It was almost like a religion. I once heard him say, on stage: "I started bluegrass music in nineteen and thirty-eight,[1] and now it's the most popular music in the world." Another time, I heard him say: "You know, I'm not braggin' or anything, but I can put a mandolin number, or a fiddle number and some banjo numbers together in half a minute."

People often jokingly refer to Monroe's "ego," "stubbornness," or "delusions of grandeur." But these were the qualities that sustained Bill through very difficult times down through the years.[2] To survive in the music business, a very strong belief in one's own abilities is an absolute

Bob Black rehearsing for the Dr Pepper commercial radio jingle in Bill Monroe's office, summer 1975. Photo by Thomas S. England. (Used by permission.)

necessity. Bill had an unshakable faith in himself; most musicians, who often must struggle for success against formidable odds, admire this attribute of self-assurance. Bill Monroe urged every musician to work hard and to be proud of what he or she did. His example makes performers feel they actually have a chance to become successful if they put in enough hard work—and never stop believing in themselves.

Bill Monroe started something that will be around forever, growing in momentum as each year passes. It's something that speaks to the heart, validates the feelings of the common people, and celebrates the treasure of human emotion that is the very essence of life. It's something he called bluegrass music, and I'm proud of my small contribution to this unique art form. Thank you, Chief!

# Appendix A
## A Record of Personal Appearances

The following is the most complete list I've been able to compile of the shows Bill Monroe played while I was a member of the Blue Grass Boys (September 20, 1974–September 19, 1976).

### 1974

September 20: Asheville, North Carolina (Black Mountain). Bluegrass Festival, Monte Vista Park

September 21: Murfreesboro, Tennessee. Concert at Middle Tennessee State University

September 21: Nashville, Tennessee. The Grand Ole Opry

September 22: Parker's Lake, Kentucky. Tombstone Junction western-style theme park

September 28: Nashville, Tennessee. The Grand Ole Opry

September 29: Bean Blossom, Indiana. The Brown County Jamboree. Hall of Fame Show (third) with Roy Acuff and Ernest Tubb

October 4–5: Middleburg, Florida. Third Annual Florida State Bluegrass Music Convention, Country Music Park

October 12: Nashville, Tennessee. The Grand Ole Opry

October 16: Nashville, Tennessee. Early Bird Bluegrass Show, Grand Ole Opry House

October 16: Nashville, Tennessee. The Grand Ole Opry (the Opry's forty-ninth birthday)

October 19: Steele, Alabama. Horse Pens Fourth Bluegrass Festival, Horse Pens Forty

October 25–27: Norco, California. Bill Monroe's Second Annual Golden West Bluegrass Festival, Silver Lakes Park

November 2–3: Fort Pierce, Florida. Bluegrass Festival at the Fairgrounds

November 7: Lake Charles, Louisiana

November 9–10: Folsom, Louisiana. Bill Monroe's South Louisiana Bluegrass Festival, Bluegrass Park

November 11: Bean Blossom, Indiana. Brown County Jamboree

November 15–17: Waycross, Georgia. Bill Monroe's South Georgia Bluegrass Festival, Speedway Fairgrounds

November 21: Portland, Oregon. Pacific International Exposition Center, Jantzen
    Beach (on a program with the Sawtooth Mountain Boys)
November 23: Austin, Texas. Armadillo Club (Armadillo World Headquarters)
November 24: Bean Blossom, Indiana. Brown County Jamboree
November 28–30: Myrtle Beach, South Carolina. 5th Annual South Carolina State
    Bluegrass Festival, Convention Center
November 29: Salem, Virginia
November 30: Nashville, Tennessee. The Grand Ole Opry
December 10: Tokyo, Japan. Kyouritsu Hall, Kanda (a section of Tokyo)
December 11: Osaka, Japan. Mainichi Hall, Umeda (a section of Osaka)
December 12: Kyoto, Japan. Kyoto Kaikan Hall
December 13: Osaka, Japan. Mainichi Hall, Umeda
December 14: Tokyo, Japan. Sugino Hall, Meguro (a section of Tokyo)
December 21: Nashville, Tennessee. The Grand Ole Opry
December 28: Nashville, Tennessee. The Grand Ole Opry

## 1975

January 4: Nashville, Tennessee. The Grand Ole Opry
January 10: Los Angeles, California. UCLA Campus
January 11: North Hollywood, California. The Palomino Club
January 18: New York City. Madison Square Garden (on program with Tanya
    Tucker and Joe Stampley)
January 25: Alabama
February 1: Nashville, Tennessee. The Grand Ole Opry
February 8: Nashville, Tennessee. The Grand Ole Opry
February 13: Tallahassee, Florida
February 14: Kissimee, Florida
February 15–16: Walker, Louisiana. Bluegrass Festival
February 21: Moultrie, Georgia
February 22: Apopka, Florida
February 23: Tampa, Florida
March 1: Nashville, Tennessee. The Grand Ole Opry
March 4: Jackson, Kentucky (benefit for the local police force)
March 5: Williamson, West Virginia
March 6: Wilmington, Delaware. Grand Opera House
March 7: Centreville, Virginia. Partners II Restaurant
March 8: Nashville, Tennessee. The Grand Ole Opry
March 13: Goldsboro, North Carolina
March 14: Raleigh, North Carolina
March 15: New Bern, North Carolina
March 22: Lafayette, Indiana (on a program with the Bluegrass Alliance)
March 29: Nashville, Tennessee. The Grand Ole Opry
March 30: Bean Blossom, Indiana. Brown County Jamboree (season opening—per-
    formance and Easter egg hunt)
April 5: Minneapolis, Minnesota
April 9: Sparta, Georgia

April 12: Nashville, Tennessee. The Grand Ole Opry
April 19: Statesville, North Carolina
April 25: Uddingston, Scotland. Greyfriars Monastery, near Glasgow
April 26: Redcar, England
April 27: Newmarket, England. The British Grand Ole Opry
April 28: Liverpool, England. Liverpool Philharmonic Hall
April 30: Birmingham, England. Birmingham Digbeth Hall
May 1: Eastbourne, England
May 2: London, England. BBC Studios
May 3: London, England
May 8: Utrecht, Holland
May 14: Tübingen, Germany
May 15: Hamburg, Germany
May 16: West Berlin, Germany
May 17: Neusüdende, Germany (near Oldenburg). Neusüdende Bluegrass and Old Time Music Festival
May 23–25: McClure, Virginia. Ralph Stanley's Fifth Annual Memorial Bluegrass Festival, the old Stanley home place, between McClure and Coeburn, Virginia
May 30: Louisville, Kentucky. Bluegrass Festival of the United States, Riverfront
May 31–June 1: Indian Springs/Hagerstown, Maryland. The Fourth Annual Indian Springs Bluegrass Festival
June 5: Somerset, New Jersey. The Spare Room
June 7–8: Carlisle, Ontario. Bluegrass Canada '75, Courtcliffe Park
June 11: Nashville, Tennessee. Grand Ole Opry House. Bluegrass Concert, Country Music Fan Fair
June 13–14: Merrimac, West Virginia. Fireman's Bluegrass Festival
June 18–22: Bean Blossom, Indiana. Bill Monroe's Ninth Annual Bluegrass Festival, Brown County Jamboree Park
June 28: Coushatta, Lousiana. Red River Valley Bluegrass Festival
July 4–5: Cosby, Tennessee. James Monroe's 5th Annual Tennessee Bluegrass Festival, Kineauvista Park, Cosby/Newport, Tennessee
July 6: Rosine/Beaver Dam, Kentucky. Hall of Fame Show with Pee Wee King and Ernest Tubb, Monroe's Bluegrass Musicland Park
July 10: Milwaukee, Wisconsin
July 12–13: Memphis, Tennessee
July 17: Nashville, Tennessee. Opryland
July 19: Nashville, Tennessee. The Grand Ole Opry
July 20: South Bend, Indiana
July 26–27: Lavonia, Georgia. Seventh Annual Georgia State Bluegrass Festival, Shoal Creek Country Music Park
August 2: Ottawa, Ohio. Fifth Annual Ohio National Bluegrass Festival, Hillbrook Recreation Area
August 3: Bean Blossom, Indiana. Brown County Jamboree
August 8–10: Jackson, Kentucky. Bill Monroe's Sixth Annual Kentucky Bluegrass Festival, Bluegrass Park (three miles west of Jackson)

August 15–17: Stumptown/Glenville, West Virginia. Ralph Stanley and Bill Monroe's Second Annual Old-Time West Virginia Bluegrass Festival, Aunt Minnie's Farm and Country Roads Park

August 22–24: Henderson/Brighton, Colorado. Bill Monroe's Third Annual Colorado Rocky Mountain Bluegrass Festival, Adams County Fairgrounds (just outside of Denver). Presented by Bill Monroe in cooperation with the Colorado Bluegrass Music Society

August 27: Anniston, Alabama

August 29–31: Rosine/Beaver Dam, Kentucky. Bill Monroe's Homecoming Bluegrass Festival

September 1: Atlanta, Georgia. Fairgrounds

September 5–7: Chatom, Alabama. Fourth Annual Alabama Dixie Bluegrass Festival, Lochwood Park. Presented by Bill Monroe and the Sullivan Family

September 11: Stanton, Kentucky. Fairgrounds

September 13: Nashville, Tennessee. The Grand Ole Opry

September 14: Bean Blossom, Indiana. Brown County Jamboree, Hall of Fame Show

September 19–21: Friendship, Indiana. Friendship Bluegrass Festival

September 27: Nashville, Tennessee. The Grand Ole Opry

September 28: Memphis, Tennessee. Going to Market

October 3–4: Lawtey, Florida. Fourth Annual Florida State Bluegrass Music Convention, Bluegrass Music Park

October 11: Richmond, Virginia. King's Dominion Amusement Park

October 12: Lenoir, North Carolina. Bluegrass Festival

October 15: Nashville, Tennessee. The Grand Ole Opry (the Opry's fiftieth birthday)

October 17–18: Dahlonega, Georgia. Gold Rush Days Bluegrass Convention

October 24–26: McKinney, Texas. Bill Monroe's fifth Annual Lone Star Bluegrass Festival, Trade's Day Park

November 2: Cocoa Beach, Florida. Bluegrass Festival

November 9: Bean Blossom, Indiana. Brown County Jamboree Park (closing of the season)

November 14–16: Montpelier, Louisiana. Bluegrass Festival, Running Water Campground

November 22: Nashville, Tennessee. The Grand Ole Opry

December 7: Tokyo, Japan. Videotaping for TV show on NHK (Japan's public broadcasting station)

December 9: Osaka, Japan

December 10: Tokyo, Japan. NTV. *11 PM* TV show—live appearance

December 11: Ueda, Nagano, Japan

December 12: Matsumoto, Japan

December 13: Nagano, Japan

December 14: Tokyo, Japan. FM Tokyo—live appearance

December 15: Tokyo, Japan. Yubinchokin Hall, Shiba (a section of Tokyo)

December 16: Yamagata, Japan

December 17: Tokyo, Japan. Nakano Sun Plaza Hall

December 18: Kyoto, Japan
December 19: Nagoya, Japan

## 1976

January 2: Little Rock, Arkansas. Teamster's Union Hall. First of a series of eight
    bluegrass-gospel shows with James Monroe and the Sullivan Family
January 3: DeRitter, Lousiana. DeRitter High School
January 4: Runnelstown, Mississippi. South Mississippi Music Hall
January 9: Ponchatoula, Louisiana. South Louisiana Hayride Building
January 10: DeVille, Louisiana. Buckeye High School
January 11: Bay St. Louis, Mississippi. Star Theater
January 16: Eufala, Alabama. Eufala Courthouse
January 17: Apopka, Florida. Apopka Memorial High School
January 24: Nashville, Tennessee. The Grand Ole Opry
February 7: Missouri
February 14: Nashville, Tennessee. The Grand Ole Opry
February 21: Virginia
February 28: Nashville, Tennessee. The Grand Ole Opry
March 6: Grand Rapids, Michigan
March 7: Madison, Wisconsin
March 13: Nashville, Tennessee. The Grand Ole Opry
March 19: Centreville, Virginia. Partners II Restaurant
March 21: Syracuse, New York. Civic Center
April 3: Nashville, Tennessee. The Grand Ole Opry
April 9: Rolla, Missouri
April 10: St. Louis, Missouri
April 15: Knoxville, Tennessee
May 1: Livingston, Texas. Polk County Fairgrounds
May 7: Hamburg, Arkansas
May 8: Meridian, Mississippi. Twenty-fourth Annual Jimmie Rodgers Festival
May 15: Lanesville, Indiana
May 16: Mason, Michigan
May 27–30: McClure, Virginia. Ralph Stanley's Sixth Annual Memorial Blue-
    grass Festival, the old Stanley home place, between McClure and Coeburn,
    Virginia
June 2: Nashville, Tennessee. Opryland
June 5–6: Indian Springs/Hagerstown, Maryland. Indian Springs Bluegrass Fes-
    tival
June 7: Nashville, Tennessee. Bluegrass Concert. The Fifth International Country
    Music Fan Fair, Municipal Auditorium
June 10: Madison, Tennessee. The New Deal (official club opening)
June 12: Williamson, West Virginia
June 16–20: Bean Blossom, Indiana. Bill Monroe's Tenth Annual Bluegrass Festival,
    Brown County Jamboree Park
June 24: Coushatta, Louisiana. Bluegrass Festival. Red River Valley Bluegrass
    Festival

June 26: Charlotte, Michigan. Stringbean Memorial Festival, Fairgrounds

July 2: Cosby, Tennessee. James Monroe's Sixth Annual Tennessee Bluegrass Festival, Kineauvista Park, Cosby/Newport, Tennessee

July 5: Philadelphia, Pennsylvania

July 9: South Bend, Indiana

July 10: Glenwood, Indiana. First Annual Lost Acres Bluegrass Festival

July 11: East Troy, Wisconsin. Alpine Valley Ski Resort

July 15: Nashville, Tennessee. Opryland

July 16: Modoc, Indiana. First Annual Tall Trees Bluegrass Festival. Tall Trees Campground

July 17: Viola, Illinois. Bluegrass Festival, Randolph's Ranch

July 24–25: Lavonia, Georgia. Eighth Annual Georgia State Bluegrass Festival, Shoal Creek Country Music Park

July 30: South Bend, Indiana. Vegetable Buddies Festival

July 31–August 1: Hillsdale, New York. Berkshire Mountains Bluegrass Festival, Merrilea Farms

August 5–8: Mine LaMotte, Missouri. Bill and James Monroe's First Annual Missouri Bluegrass Festival

August 13–15: Sanders, Kentucky. Bill Monroe's First Annual Eagle Valley Bluegrass Festival

August 20–22: Stumptown/Glenville, West Virginia. Ralph Stanley and Bill Monroe's Third Annual Old-Time West Virginia Bluegrass Festival, Aunt Minnie's Farm and Country Roads Park

August 27–29: Henderson/Brighton, Colorado. Bill Monroe's Colorado Rocky Mountain Bluegrass Festival

September 3–5: Rosine/Beaver Dam, Kentucky. Monroe's Bluegrass Musicland Park. Monroe Homecoming Festival

September 10–12: Chatom, Alabama. Fifth Annual Alabama Dixie Bluegrass Festival. Presented by Bill Monroe and the Sullivan Family

September 13: Nashville, Tennessee. Municipal Auditorium

September 18: Charlotte, North Carolina. Bluegrass Festival, Carowinds theme park

September 19: Bean Blossom, Indiana. Brown County Jamboree

## Appendix B
### Additional Information about Some of the People and Groups Mentioned

**Akeman, David ("Stringbean")**

David Akeman, known by his stage name of Stringbean, was often called Stringbeans by Bill Monroe and others who had known him for a long time. (Stringbeans was Akeman's first stage name, before it was shortened to Stringbean.) The first banjo player ever to be a member of the Blue Grass Boys, Stringbean recorded with Bill Monroe in 1945. By the 1970s he was a comedy star of television's *Hee Haw*, as well as of the Grand Ole Opry. He was said not to trust banks, and he often kept thousands of dollars in the pockets of his overalls, showing it to many people. In 1973, both he and his wife were killed by burglars in their home. Twenty years after the double murder, residents of Stringbean's old house discovered nearly twenty thousand dollars stashed behind a brick in the chimney. The money was shredded and useless, having been gnawed on by mice.

**Bailey, DeFord**

DeFord Bailey (1899–1982) was a black entertainer known as the Harmonica Wizard. Born forty miles east of Nashville, he was one of the earliest performers on the Grand Ole Opry. He joined the Opry when it was still called the WSM Barn Dance. One of the tunes he was best known for was "Pan American Blues," featuring his imitation of a fast-moving freight train. Short, and weighing less than one hundred pounds, Bailey had to fight physical disability caused by infantile paralysis. Racism was another hurdle he had to overcome. He was dismissed from the Grand Ole Opry after an apparent disagreement with George D. Hay. After that he became a shoeshine man—the only employment he could find in Nashville. Many people (including me) feel DeFord Bailey should be inducted into the Country Music Hall of Fame because of his important early contributions to the musical genre.

**Blake, Norman**

Norman Blake was born in Tennessee in 1938 and grew up in Georgia. He has been playing professionally since the age of sixteen. His style of guitar playing is relaxed and ornate, highlighted by richness of tone and beauty of melody.

Bluegrass Alliance, The

Originally formed in the late 1950s by fiddler Lonnie Peerce, the Bluegrass Alliance performed until the late 1970s. The band was re-formed in 1998 by banjoist Barry Palmer.

Carter Family, The

The Carter Family, from Virginia, left more of a mark on country music than practically anyone else. A. P. Carter collected hundreds of folk and country songs, performing them with his wife Sara and sister-in-law Maybelle. Those songs later became part of the standard repertoire of folk, country, bluegrass, and even rock performers. Maybelle's guitar playing, called "Carter picking," also set the standard for guitar players for many years afterward. Beginning in the 1920s, the Carters performed and recorded for nearly half a century. Though changes in personnel took place, the music always remained in the family. Some of the Carter Family's more famous songs include "Wabash Cannonball" and "Wildwood Flower." In 1970 they were the first group inducted into the Country Music Hall of Fame.

Cline, Curly Ray

Curly Ray Cline was born in the early 1920s in West Virginia. As a youth he was inspired by Fiddlin' Arthur Smith. In 1938 he and his brother Ezra organized the legendary Lonesome Pine Fiddlers. In 1963 he joined the Stanley Brothers. He continued to play with Ralph Stanley after Carter Stanley died. Cline retired from the music business in 1993.

Cooke, Jack

Jack Cooke played bass with Carter and Ralph Stanley in 1955. He was a Blue Grass Boy from 1956–1960, serving as lead vocalist. After performing with several other groups, Cooke returned to the Clinch Mountain Boys in 1970. Ralph Stanley often introduced him on stage as "the ex-mayor of Norton, Virginia," because Cooke served a half-term as mayor of Norton (his hometown and lifelong residence) in 1963.

Country Gentlemen, The

Formed in the late 1950s in the Washington, D. C., area, the Country Gentlemen played traditional bluegrass as well as contemporary country and music from other genres. In 1959, the most classic and memorable lineup of musicians included Charlie Waller (guitar), John Duffey (mandolin and Dobro), former Blue Grass boy Eddie Adcock (banjo), and Tom Gray (bass). The group recorded with Starday, Folkways, Mercury, and Rebel Records.

Dillards, The

The original Dillards band consisted of Missourians Doug Dillard (banjo), and Rodney Dillard (guitar). In the early 1960s they teamed up with Mitch Jayne (bass) and Dean Webb (mandolin). Signing with Elektra Records in 1962, the Dillards recorded a number of albums on that label. Doug Dillard left the band in the late 1960s and was replaced by Herb Pederson on banjo. The Dillards continued to perform and record throughout the 1970s.

## Enloe, Lyman

Lyman Enloe (1906–1997) is one of Missouri's treasures. Born in 1906 in the upper Ozarks, he was inspired to play the fiddle by his father, Elijah "Lige" Enloe and his half-brother Wade. His album, entitled *Fiddle Tunes I Recall,* is a collector's item among fans of old-time fiddle music.

## Everly, Ike

Isaac "Ike" Everly (1918–1975) came from a family of coal miners and railroad workers around Central City, Kentucky—only about thirty miles from Bill Monroe's hometown of Rosine. As a young man, Everly learned to play guitar in the local style. He was a friend of Merle Travis, and the two musicians developed their finger-picking techniques along similar lines.

Ike Everly married a local girl, Margaret Embry, in 1935, and they had their first son, Isaac Donald, in 1937. Soon afterward, the family moved to Chicago. There, in 1939, a second son, Philip, was born. Everly performed in the honky-tonks and nightclubs of Chicago until 1944, when he got a job on radio station KASL in Waterloo, Iowa. The next year, he moved his family to Shenandoah, Iowa, where he joined the staff of radio station KMA. His sons, Don and Phil, began performing on the family radio show, which later became know as *The Everly Family Show.* In 1952 the family moved their radio show to WIKY in Evansville, Indiana, and in 1953 they moved on to WROL in Knoxville, Tennessee. There, Ike and Margaret Everly tried to supplement their income by becoming a barber and a beautician, but the business didn't work out, and they had to go on welfare. Shortly afterward, in 1957, Don and Phil Everly's recording of "Bye Bye Love" reached number one on the country music charts, becoming a million seller and thereby securing the family's future.

Ike Everly came out of retirement briefly in 1970 to perform with his sons on a television special entitled *Johnny Cash Presents the Everly Brothers.*

## Flatt and Scruggs

Acknowledged as being the group that made bluegrass famous, Lester Flatt (guitar) and Earl Scruggs (banjo) were brought together by Bill Monroe in 1945 when they became fellow Blue Grass Boys. Leaving in 1948 to form their own band, the Foggy Mountain Boys, Flatt and Scruggs went on to become one of the best-known bluegrass teams in history. They parted ways in 1969, and Flatt formed the traditional-style bluegrass band Lester Flatt and the Nashville Grass, while Earl formed the progressive Earl Scruggs Review.

## Graves, Josh

Josh Graves performed as a member of Lester Flatt and Earl Scruggs's band, the Foggy Mountain Boys, from the late 1950s through 1969. He has performed with the Earl Scruggs Review, as well as with Charlie McCoy, Steve Young, J. J. Cale, and Kris Kristofferson. He is often credited with keeping the Dobro alive, as well as being a major influence in the development of modern bluegrass Dobro techniques.

## Greenbriar Boys, The

Formed in the late 1950s in New York, the Greenbriar Boys were one of the earliest urban bluegrass bands. Signed by Vanguard Records in 1962, the group consisted at that time of John Herald (guitar), Bob Yellin (banjo), and Ralph Rinzler (mandolin). They appeared on a number of albums on Vanguard. Rinzler left to become director of the folk department at the Smithsonian Institute, and was replaced on the group's final Vanguard album by Frank Wakefield (mandolin) and Jimmy Buchanan (fiddle). The Greenbriar Boys disbanded in 1967, occasionally regrouping for later reunion concerts.

## Hay, George D.

Known as the Solemn Old Judge, George D. Hay (1895–1968) began his radio-announcing career in 1924 on the WLS National Barn Dance in Chicago. A year later he moved to Nashville and went to work for WSM, announcing the WSM Barndance. He renamed it the Grand Ole Opry in 1927. George D. Hay was elected to the Country Music Hall of Fame in 1966.

## Jarrell, Tommy

Tommy Jarrell (1901–1985) was born in Surrey County, North Carolina and began playing banjo around the age of seven, and fiddle around the age of thirteen. He was a storyteller and singer with a warmhearted nature, and musicians frequently made journeys to his home to visit with and learn from him. In 1982 he was recognized by the National Endowment for the Arts as one of fifteen master folk artists in the first National Heritage Fellowships.

## Jim and Jesse

Raised in Virginia, Jim McReynolds (guitar) and Jesse McReynolds (mandolin) began playing professionally in 1949. They signed with Capitol Records in 1952 and began recording as Jim and Jesse and the Virginia Boys. They became members of the Grand Ole Opry in 1964, and have since become well-known and loved by all traditional bluegrass fans. Jim McReynolds passed away in 2002.

## Jones, Bob

Bob Jones joined the Blue Grass Boys in February 1976 after Ralph Lewis left the band. He remained in the group until May of that year. We recorded the CBC Radio Network show *Country Road* (released later on record) during the period when Bob Jones was in the band. Jones had lived in Virginia and Maryland as a child, and prior to joining Bill he was the leader of a west coast band called the Blue Ridge Mountain Boys. He left the Blue Grass Boys after five or six weeks, and Wayne Lewis, who was living in Portsmouth, Ohio, took the job of guitar player.

## Krauss, Alison

Winner of thirteen Grammy awards (collectively and individually), Alison Krauss is a true bluegrass success story. She began to play classical violin at age five, and she turned to bluegrass fiddle at age eight, winning contests and playing at festivals. She is now a major acoustic country and bluegrass singer, musician, producer, and film and television artist. Krauss was featured on three songs on the multi-platinum *O Brother, Where Art Thou?* soundtrack.

## Lewis, Wayne

Wayne Lewis, who was Bob Jones's replacement as guitar player for the Blue Grass Boys, was a full-time member of the band for over ten years. He continued to work occasionally as a Blue Grass Boy until Bill Monroe's death. He was a close friend of Bill's, and the two had a great deal of respect for each other. They often worked on the same shows together—Wayne with his band and Bill with his. On those occasions Wayne frequently joined Bill for onstage reunions.

## Macon, Dave ("Uncle Dave")

Uncle Dave Macon (1870–1952) was born David Harrison Macon, near McMinnville, Tennessee. He learned to play the banjo when he was fifteen, inspired by vaudeville and circus performers. In 1920, at the age of fifty, he became a full-time vaudeville singer and comedian. He played banjo in the "frailing" or "rapping" style, and his foot-stomping, unrestrained performances were very entertaining to audiences. He started playing on the Grand Ole Opry in 1925 (when it was still called the WSM Barn Dance) and remained with the show until his death in 1952.

## Magaha, Mack

Known as Nashville's Dancing Fiddle Man, Mack Magaha (1929–2003) performed with Dolly Parton, Porter Wagoner, and Reno and Smiley. He cowrote (with Don Reno) the song, "I Know You're Married But I Love You Still," which has been recorded by Bill Anderson and Jan Howard, Red Sovine, Reno and Smiley, Patty Loveless and Travis Tritt, Jimmy Martin, Rodney Crowell, and Bad Livers.

## Martin, Jimmy

Also known as the King of Bluegrass, Tennessean Jimmy Martin worked for Bill Monroe from 1949 through 1954. Blessed with a very strong singing voice, Jimmy is very much a traditional bluegrass singer. Along with his band, the Sunny Mountain Boys, Jimmy recorded many songs on the Decca label from 1956 through 1974. He joined Starday/Gusto Records after leaving Decca, and remained with that label for nearly ten years before forming his own label, King of Bluegrass.

## McGee, Sam and Kirk

Sam McGee (1894–1975) and Kirk McGee (1895–1983) were born and raised near Franklin, Tennessee. They both learned to play the banjo when they were children, and they later learned other instruments as well. Sam met and played with Uncle Dave Macon in 1925 and appeared with him on the Grand Ole Opry in 1926. Kirk joined them soon after that and they performed together as Uncle Dave Macon and the Fruit Jar Drinkers. Sam and Kirk also played

with Fiddlin' Arthur Smith as the Dixieliners. They both stayed with the Grand
Ole Opry until their deaths.

### Morris Brothers, The

The Morris Brothers, Wiley and Zeke, were an old-time duet from Asheville,
North Carolina. They began to perform together in the 1930s, and their roots
went back to the beginnings of bluegrass. Two of Bill Monroe's greatest banjo
players, Don Reno and Earl Scruggs, had both played with the Morris Brothers
prior to working for Bill.

### New Deal String Band, The

The New Deal String Band formed in 1967. When I first saw them in 1971,
the group included Frank Greathouse on mandolin, Leroy Savage on guitar
and lead vocals, Bob (Quail) White on bass, Buck Peacock on lead guitar, Al
McCanless on fiddle, and Bob Isenhour on banjo.

### New Grass Revival, The

The New Grass Revival was started in 1972. The band's first album was
released in 1972 on the Starday label, and the group later recorded many
albums on the Flying Fish and Sugar Hill labels. In 1986 they were signed by
EMI Records and made three more albums that launched them into music's
mainstream. Shortly after the release of their third EMI album in 1989, the
group disbanded.

### Osborne Brothers, The

The Osborne Brothers are a gifted bluegrass duo from Bill Monroe's home
state of Kentucky. Bobby (mandolin) and Sonny (banjo) joined the Grand Ole
Opry in 1964. Among their numerous country chart successes was the song
"Rocky Top," which has become one of the most famous bluegrass songs ever
recorded. Sonny became a Blue Grass Boy in 1952 at the age of fourteen. He
was the youngest musician ever to record with the band.

### Reno and Smiley

Don Reno and Red Smiley both grew up in rural North Carolina and began
playing duets together in 1950. A Blue Grass Boy in 1948, Don possessed a
highly original style that is considered by most banjoists to be very hard to
duplicate or copy. He cowrote the tune "Feuding Banjos" (later called "Duel-
ling Banjos") with Arthur "Guitar Boogie" Smith.

### Rodgers, Jimmie

Jimmie Rodgers (1897–1933) was born in Meridian, Mississippi. While still
a teenager, he worked as a brakeman on the New Orleans and Northeastern
Railroad, thus earning him the nickname the Singing Brakeman. Also known
as the Mississippi Blue Yodeler, Rodgers wrote and recorded many songs that
stand as classics today, including "T for Texas," "Waiting for a Train," and
"In the Jailhouse Now." Besides guitar, Jimmie Rodgers also played banjo and

mandolin. In 1961 he was the first person to be inducted into the Country Music Hall of Fame.

### Sauceman, Carl

Born March 6, 1922, in Green County, Tennessee, Carl Sauceman learned country songs from his mother. He also listened to Opry radio broadcasts, as well as 78 rpm recordings of the Monroe Brothers. Sauceman made many recordings on various labels, including Mercury, Capitol, Republic, and Rich-R-Tone.

### Sieker, Rolf

Rolf Sieker, a pioneering European five-string banjo stylist, now lives in Texas. He and his wife, Beatte, have made many first-rate recordings that showcase their vocal duets and original songs, along with Sieker's unique banjo talent.

### Smith, Arthur ("Fiddling" Arthur)

Called the King of the Fiddlers, Fiddlin' Arthur Smith (1898–1971) had a professional career that lasted for almost 50 years. Performing and recording with many different groups, he developed a large and loyal following among old-time fiddle lovers. His fame was enhanced in no small measure by his numerous appearances on the Grand Ole Opry.

### Spray, Delbert

Recognized by the Missouri Arts Council as a Master Fiddler, Delbert Spray (1923–2001) began learning to play fiddle at the age of six, from his father Albert Spray. In 1972, Delbert, along with his wife, Erma, organized the Kahoka Festival of Bluegrass Music, held at the Clark County Fairgrounds in Kahoka, Missouri.

### Stanley Brothers, The

The Stanley Brothers, from Virginia, began performing their style of bluegrass around 1946. Carter Stanley, who possessed a strikingly emotive voice, played guitar and sang lead. Ralph Stanley sang strong tenor and played fingerstyle-type banjo (and occasionally frailing style). With their band, the Clinch Mountain Boys, the Stanleys recorded for many different labels including Rich-R-Tone, Columbia, Mercury, Starday, and King. Carter Stanley passed away in 1966 at the age of forty-one. Ralph Stanley continues to perform to this day.

### Stuart, Joe

Stuart was one of bluegrass music's unsung heroes. A likeable fellow with the nickname Sparkplug ("Sparkplug" was a comedy role that had been played by several Blue Grass Boys, including Stuart), he was adept at all the instruments of bluegrass: banjo, fiddle, guitar, mandolin, and bass. He also had a low, resonant singing voice that was much to be admired. I got to record with him several times, and took part in numerous jam sessions with him—many of which took place in the home of our mutual friend, Kenny Baker.

Taylor, Tut
Born in Possum Trot, Georgia in 1923, Dobro player Tut Taylor has recorded with such musicians as Porter Wagoner, Glen Campbell, David Bromberg, Clarence White, and John Hartford.

Travis, Merle
Merle Travis (1917–1983) was born in Kentucky, the son of a coal miner. Learning guitar at the age of twelve, he mastered a finger style that later became known as Travis-style picking. He wrote some memorable songs, including "Sixteen Tons" and "Dark as a Dungeon."

Turner, Grant
Grant Turner (1912–1991) was widely known as the Voice of the Grand Ole Opry. He was hired as a WSM staff announcer on D-Day, June 6, 1944. Soon after that he became an Opry announcer, holding the position for nearly fifty years. He was elected to the Country Music Hall of Fame in 1981. Turner passed away on October 19, 1991, only a short time after finishing an Opry broadcast.

Vincent, Rhonda
Rhonda started playing music as a small child, as a member of her family's band, the Sally Mountain Show. Later, she switched to a contemporary country format, recording two albums on Nashville's Giant label. Eventually she returned to bluegrass and formed her present band, the Rage. I played with the Rage during 1997 and 1998.

Wakefield, Frank
An original stylist on the mandolin, Tennessean Frank Wakefield teamed up with bluegrass singer and guitarist Red Allen in 1952. After going their separate ways, they reunited in 1962 to form the famous group Red Allen and Frank Wakefield and the Kentuckians. The two performers remained partners until 1972. In 1974, Wakefield recorded an album entitled *Pistol Packin' Mama* which featured musicians Jerry Garcia, Dave Nelson, Don Reno, and Chubby Wise. Frank has an eccentric sense of humor, and he is famous for his talent of talking backwards (for example: "backing talkwards"). Lots of bluegrass fans call him "Wake Frankfield."

Watson, Arthel "Doc"
Arthel "Doc" Watson was born in North Carolina in 1923. Struck by an early childhood illness that left him blind, Doc began playing banjo at the age of ten, and guitar at the age of thirteen. Doc's distinctive style of guitar-playing and singing won him two Grammy awards—in 1974 and 1979. His flatpicking guitar method is often imitated.

# Notes

## Foreword

1. Tony Trischka and Pete Wernick, *Masters of the Five-String Banjo* (New York: Oak Publications, 1988), 13.

## Chapter 1: Remembering the Old Days

1. Trischka and Wernick, *Masters of the Five-String Banjo,* 12.
2. See the NPR 100 profile of Earl Scruggs's "Foggy Mountain Breakdown," April 1, 2000 <http://www.npr.org/templates/story/story.php?storyID=1072355>. Louise Scruggs confirmed, in an e-mail to Randy Escobedo (dated April 16, 2004), that Earl wrote "Bluegrass Breakdown," but that it was Bill Monroe rather than Scruggs who got credit for it. Escobedo added that Scruggs had earlier told him, when they talked about the tune, that he had indeed written it (e-mail dated April 17, 2004).
3. *Portrait of a Bluegrass Fiddler* (County Records 719, 1969) was recorded in 1968 and released the following year. I studied this album and several later projects by Kenny Baker. A few years after that, I was actually getting into jam sessions with him.

## Chapter 2: My First Days as a Blue Grass Boy

1. Credited to Thomas P. Westendorf, 1882. Many thanks to Tom Ewing for providing me with the lyrics, which he pieced together from recordings made by the Monroe Brothers (which were garbled) and by J. E. and Wade Mainer.

## Chapter 3: Live and Unrehearsed

1. Bill recorded "Scotland" in 1958. The twin fiddles on that recording were played by Kenny Baker and Bobby Hicks.
2. Steve Rathe, "Bill Monroe," *Pickin'*, February 1974, p. 4.
3. Recorded in 1999 on my album, *Banjoy* (Green Valley 145).

## Chapter 4: Bluegrass 101

1. According to Les Leverett, in his book, *Blue Moon of Kentucky,* (Madison, N.C.: Empire Publishing, Inc., 1996)
2. From an interview conducted at Grass Valley, California, on June 15, 2002.
3. The complete title of this tune is "Say Old Man, Can You Play the Fiddle? Yes by God, I Can Play a Little."

## Chapter 5: The Children of Bluegrass

1. In 2002 my second cousin, June Coon, wrote some very pretty lyrics to "The Chickadee Waltz":

> Each day when I wake up and look out my door
> God's love all around me I see,
> Like the birds in the treetops a-winging their way
> To the beautiful Chickadee Waltz.

> Now I know there are those unable to see
> God's grace sets us free
> Like the birds in the treetops a-winging their way
> To the beautiful Chickadee Waltz.

> I think of our loved ones who've gone on before
> And I know on that heavenly shore
> We'll all get together and listen once more
> To the beautiful Chickadee Waltz.

## Chapter 6: A Tough Act to Follow

1. Calliope members included Iowa City native Guy Drollinger on fiddle, guitar, and hammered dulcimer; Mary Lata, from Iowa City, on cello and flute; and Bill Cagley, from Waterloo, Iowa, on lead guitar.

2. Bill recorded this song in 1977 on an album entitled *Bluegrass Memories* (MCA2315).

3. Originally released on the Puritan label, those recordings are now available on the Rebel label (*The Puritan Sessions*, REB1108–CD, 1989).

4. Banjo players: it's not an *all-original* 1937 Gibson. It has a replacement neck and resonator.

5. Harvest Home at that time included Al Murphy (fiddle and mandolin), Aleta Murphy (bass), Warren Hanlin (guitar), and me on banjo.

## Chapter 7: Just Like the Old Days

1. GroundSpeed, *Charlotte's Waltz* (Elite Special 733–507, 1990), Switzerland.

2. Bill's band had two different members since the last time he had been there: Wayne Lewis, from Kentucky (guitar), and Mike Feagan, also from Kentucky (fiddle).

3. Bill composed "Blue Moon of Kentucky" in the late 1940s. The song has been recorded by many other singers including Ray Charles, Patsy Cline, and the Stanley Brothers. Carl Perkins often included it in his early live performances. Paul McCartney has performed it on stage as well.

4. Bluegrass historian Neil Rosenberg told me of a similar experience at Bean Blossom in 1994, during which Bill traveled to and from the stage area in an ambulance, but suddenly came alive when he got on stage.

5. From the liner notes of his 1972 recorded tribute to Uncle Pen, *Bill Monroe's Uncle Pen* (MCA500).

*Afterword*

1. Bill thought of 1938 as the year that marked the beginning of bluegrass music, because that was the year he first started performing without being influenced by either of his brothers, Charlie or Birch.

2. Any of the numerous writings about Bill Monroe contain information about the lean years of country music in general, and bluegrass music in particular, during the second half of the 1950s, when rock and roll dominated the airwaves.

# Suggested Listening
## and Reading

*The Music of Bill Monroe, 1936 to 1994* (MCA, MCAD411048, 1994) is a four-CD set that provides an excellent chronological sampling of Bill Monroe's work across the entire span of his career. Higher-priced, but much more inclusive, are the Bear Family boxed sets *Bluegrass, 1950–1958; Bluegrass, 1959–1969;* and *Bluegrass, 1970–1979* (Bear Family, BCD 15423, 1990; BCD 15529, 1991; and BCD 15606, 1995, respectively). *Ladies on the Steamboat* (Green Valley Records 147) is a CD reissue of my 1979 solo album, with additional tracks containing live performances with Bill Monroe and the Blue Grass Boys. It can be ordered on the Internet at www.banjoy.com or by writing to Green Valley Records, 10693 338th Ave., North English, Iowa 52316. Another Bear Family boxed set, *Far Across the Blue Water: Bill Monroe in Germany 1975 & 1989* (BCD 16624 EK, 2004) contains two live CD recordings of our shows at *Neusüdende* (May 17, 1975) as well as two live CD recordings and a DVD of Bill Monroe and the Blue Grass Boys' performance at Streekermoor, Germany (July 30, 1989). Some of Kenny Baker's finest fiddle playing can be heard on *Frost on the Pumpkin* (County 2731, 2003), along with banjo playing by me that is representative of my Blue Grass Boy years. Earl Scruggs's masterpiece, *Foggy Mountain Banjo* (County 100, 1995) is an absolute must-have for all bluegrass banjo students and fans because of its clarity and simplicity—it contains all the important basics of the most popular and influential style of banjo playing ever created.

In my opinion the definitive history of bluegrass, that no one interested in the music should be without, is Neil Rosenberg's *Bluegrass: A History* (Urbana: University of Illinois Press, 1993). A compilation of fascinating and enlightening articles about Bill Monroe can be found in Tom Ewing's book, *The Bill Monroe Reader* (Urbana: University of Illinois Press, 2000). Les Leveritt has assembled a book's worth of beautiful, captioned photos of bluegrass and country-music personalities called *Blue Moon of Kentucky* (Madison, N.C.: Empire Publishing, Inc., 1996). Carl Fleischhauer and Neil Rosenberg have put together a superb volume of photographs with insightful commentary entitled *Bluegrass Odyssey* (Urbana: University of Illinois Press, 2001).

# Index

BOB BLACK is a banjo player, singer, and songwriter. He has published articles in *Bluegrass Unlimited,* and in 2002 received the Iowa Arts Council's Traditional Artist Award. He has toured nationally and internationally for over thirty years with many different groups, including Bill Monroe and the Blue Grass Boys. A graduate of Drake University in Des Moines, Iowa, Bob Black holds a bachelor of fine arts degree in the field of graphic design. He and his wife, Kristie Black, have their own band, Banjoy.

## Music in American Life

The University of Illinois Press
is a founding member of the
Association of American University Presses.

---

Composed in 10/13 Sabon
with Sabon display
by Barbara Evans
at the University of Illinois Press
Designed by Paula Newcomb
Manufactured by Sheridan Books, Inc.

University of Illinois Press
1325 South Oak Street
Champaign, IL 61820-6903
www.press.uillinois.edu